THE CROSSING

Like *1984* for teenagers—direct, passionate, and powerful. However, in the heroine Maryam and her companions, the system that seeks to stamp them into rigid submission meets its match—asserting the ability of an individual to break free from exploitation, and to blossom into an adventurous true self. This story of courage and escape from a sinister and repressive society is only the first book in this series. . . . Roll on Book Two!

—Margaret Mahy

BLOOD OF
THE LAMB

BOOK ONE

MANDY HAGER

THE CROSSING

an imprint of **Prometheus Books**
Amherst, NY

Published 2013 by Pyr®, an imprint of Prometheus Books

Cover illustration © Larry Rostant • Cover design by Jacqueline Nasso Cooke

Inquiries should be addressed to

Pyr
59 John Glenn Drive
Amherst, New York 14228–2119
VOICE: 716–691–0133 • FAX: 716–691–0137
WWW.PYRSF.COM

17 16 15 14 13 • 5 4 3 2 1

Library of Congress Cataloging-in-Publication Data

Hager, Mandy.
    The crossing / by Mandy Hager.
        p. cm. — (Blood of the lamb ; bk. 1)
    Summary: On the post-apocalyptic island of Onewere, Maryam lives a cloistered life, chosen as a young child to fulfill religious duties and join the island's spiritual leader when she reaches puberty—a fate she tries to escape after learning the truth.
    ISBN 978-1-61614-698-6 (cloth) • ISBN 978-1-61614-699-3 (ebook)
    First published: New Zealand : Random House New Zealand, an imprint of Random House Group New York, 2009.
    [1. Fundamentalism—Fiction. 2. Religious life—Fiction. 3. Survival—Fiction. 4. Islands—Fiction. 5. Science fiction.] I. Title.
PZ7.H1229Cr 2013
[Fic]—dc23
                                                                2012031656

Printed in the United States of America

To Debbie, Nicky, and Belinda, with admiration and love

"The thing that hath been, it is that which shall be; and that which is done is that which shall be done: and there is no new thing under the sun."

CHAPTER ONE

Maryam ran through the jungle, her heart rapping against her ribs, but she dared not stop. Ruth was gaining on her, and if she caught her now all would be lost. She veered off into the lush undergrowth, the crunch of Ruth's sandals on the shell pathway loud in her ears. Ahead, a whimbrel burst from the shelter of a pandanus palm, its flight up through the dense canopy of palms and breadfruit trees haphazard as it sought the sun. *Tet-tet-tet*, it cried, the rhythm building on the percussion of Ruth's pounding steps and the pulse of blood that forced its way through Maryam's veins.

The piercing scent of the pandanus leaves crushed underfoot arrested her and she dropped to her haunches for a moment to regain her breath, closing her eyes, allowing the heady aroma to calm her down. Not far behind, Ruth was now wading through the undergrowth and Maryam imagined her—arms spread wide to sweep the leaves aside, small prickly burrs of the kakang weed clinging to her thick black hair. She was fast, Ruth, and no one yet had slipped her grasp. But there was always a first time.

Maryam drew on all her strength, ready to sprint forward once again, but a sharp pain shot through her abdomen. She stifled a cry, clutching a palm trunk as a wave of nausea rocked her. *No! Not now!* Then the pain dulled to a dragging cramp, and she gulped down deep lungfuls of the muggy air. If she didn't make a break for it now she would be caught.

No longer caring if Ruth heard, she rose and flung herself

toward the far-off opening in the trees. If she could only make it to the beach then she could race along the heat-baked sand to the safety of the mangroves by the deep lagoon. But the cramps persisted, leaching her energy.

"I can see you!" Ruth shrieked, and Maryam turned to the voice, unable to resist looking around.

Ruth was there, right by Maryam's resting place, and her teeth flashed white against her skin as her grin grew wider and more determined. Maryam tried one final reckless dash but her foot caught in the exposed roots of a beach naupaka and tripped her, sending her sprawling onto the soft sandy ground. Prone amidst the cool green understorey of the jungle, she realised there was no escape. She rolled onto her back, resigned to yielding as the village dogs did when Zakariya raised his heavy stick and yelled abuse. And there was Ruth's triumphant face, looming up above her like a hungry shark.

"Enough now. I admit defeat." There was no point denying it. She had dared to challenge Ruth and lost.

Her pursuer reached out a strong brown hand, jerking Maryam to her feet so quickly that her brain swam around inside her head. "You never should have tried," she laughed, "I always win." Her smile disappeared as she saw Maryam pale and wince. "Are you all right?"

"My stomach hurts," Maryam said.

Ruth wrapped her arm around Maryam then, her chest still heaving from the prolonged chase. "Excuses, excuses," she joked, squeezing reassuringly. "Let's get you back to Mother Elizabeth and tell her you are sick from shame!"

"I would've beaten you if I'd been well," Maryam sighed. She poked her friend in her well-covered ribs. "Beware: the Lord is granting your prayers for abundance by placing it around your waist!"

"Just because you were born a tiny anti-ma-aomata don't blame me!"

Maryam snorted. "If I *was* a fairy, you never would have caught me—no matter how intense the pain!"

They made their way back along the track, arms linked as they headed for the village compound—the only home either had known since their memories had first formed and fixed. Ruth towered above her, even though Maryam was older by a good two years, and Maryam's charcoal-bright eyes, round and dark-lashed like those of the baby seals that sometimes surfaced in the main lagoon, just added to the vulnerability that others presumed. Despite her fifteen years, her fragile frame unfailingly caused jokes among the other Blessed Sisters, who labelled her "te bebi," while Mother Elizabeth and the other House Mothers tutted and fussed, and forced extra goat's milk on her in a fruitless bid to help her grow. They worried, the Mothers, that she never would receive the Lord's blessing and take up His Call. And their worry had rubbed off on her. Each night she prayed for the Lamb to reveal to her His wondrous plan.

But now the pains were upon Maryam her hopes lifted. They all knew of this, how the Blood was heralded by pain and cramps—Te Teinako, the miraculous Calling to surrender all to the overwhelming power of the Blood of the Lamb.

By the time they reached the compound, the other Blessed Sisters already milled around the shingled borders of the maneaba, the sacred meeting house, in time for prayers. Mother Elizabeth, her long hair wrapped up into a crowning bundle on her head, glanced up at them sharply from her seat before the restless group.

"Late again?"

Ruth blushed the colour of ripe pomegranate seeds and slunk into the crowd, while Maryam crossed to Mother Elizabeth and bowed her head.

"I'm sorry, Mother," she apologised. "It was my fault. I challenged Ruth to a race and we'd nearly reached the mangroves before she caught me up."

Mother Elizabeth's face softened and she smiled, fine lines gathering at the corners of her honeycoloured eyes. "When will you learn, te bebi? Ruth has twice the length of legs as you. You were bound to lose."

"But I nearly had her," Maryam protested. "If my pains had not come upon me hard I would've won."

"Your pains?" Mother Elizabeth's gaze shot up to Maryam's face. "That's news indeed." She took Maryam by the hand and squeezed it reassuringly. "The Lord be praised."

She rose then, calling out as Maryam rushed away to take her place. "Come to my sleeping hut before bed tonight, child. We will speak some more."

With this, she ushered the first of the Blessed Sisters into the maneaba as Maryam returned to her rightful position at the rear of the group. Mother Elizabeth stooped beneath the low eaves of the colossal pandanus-thatched roof and disappeared inside, followed first by the smallest Blessed Sisters: the toddlers who arrived after last summer's Judgement, still confused and grieving at the loss of their birth parents; then came the five-year-olds; sixes; sevens. . . . One by one the girls entered until at last Maryam—the eldest—dipped beneath the low-slung eaves and bowed as she passed the pillars of white coral that held the giant roof aloft.

Inside, a brooding brown coolness shed a calming air across the Blessed Sisters, as they sat before the altar so lovingly erected by the first Apostles of the Lamb. There, a life-size figure of the crucified Lamb stared mournfully down upon them, pain bleeding from His eyes as surely as the trails of bright red blood that leaked from the terrible gashes in His body and the raw wounds at hands and feet. The golden wood had softened to a dusky tan, the knots and whorls adding to the illusion that the flesh was real. He was so life-like, in fact—His ribs and muscles so clearly defined by the master who had sculpted him—that Maryam could never quite look Him in the eye, scared of what she might discover in His ageless gaze.

The maneaba whispered with the all-pervading voices of sea, wind and trees. Between the soaring pillars the Blessed Sisters sat cross-legged in their ranks, silent as their ancestors, whose carved images peered back down at them, hollow-eyed yet all-seeing, from their resting places high up above the flimsy flaxen walls, in the darkened beams.

Finally, the other six House Mothers filed in, plus Zakariya (leaning hard upon his stick), the helper Simon and the new man James. As they took their places on either side of Mother Elizabeth, she raised her hands and Simon strummed the opening bars of their first song on an aging ukulele.

When the Bridegroom cometh will your robes be white?
Are you washed in the Blood of the Lamb?
Will your soul be ready for the mansion bright,
And be washed in the Blood of the Lamb? . . .

As they sang, the pains intruded into Maryam's consciousness even more intensely than before. She stifled a gasp, breathing through her mouth until they faded to a hot dull ache. She looked up to see Mother Elizabeth's eyes upon her. The older woman nodded ever so slightly and slid her gaze toward the door. Maryam understood and mouthed her thanks, backing out of the maneaba so slowly that none bar the kindly Blessed Mother noticed her silent retreat.

She crossed the compound to the sleeping hut she shared with Ruth, far less majestic than the maneaba although the basic building materials were the same.

Inside, she made to lie down but the cramps again gripped her, and she felt the desperate need to run. She charged for the outhouses, past the other sleeping huts and down the fig-tree-screened pathway. This was so unlike her: although petite and slow to mature, she had always been healthy. But then, on her undergarments, she saw the telltale stain of blood. So this, it seemed, was the end of her childhood. Her moment to serve had finally come.

The singing had died down by the time she made her way back to her hut. Mother Elizabeth would be reading from the Holy Book now, the little ones restless as they tried to fix on a past they were yet to understand—about an angel, and hail and fire mingling with blood, and a star that fell upon the waters as the sun and moon were devoured by the poisoned dark. Maryam remembered how confusing such lessons had been when she first came—how, although she had been taught the rudiments of English by her birth parents, the words seemed harsh and complicated, compared to the soft flowing language of her native past. It had been so hard, not understanding why she'd been wrenched from the family who had borne her, and still upset by the strange ritual of the Judgement that had sealed her fate.

When they'd drawn her blood with the sharp needle and mixed it with the blood of Father Joshua to see if it would clot or flow, she could still recall the warmth with which the Apostles had received the news that she'd been Blessed. How they'd smiled; Father Joshua himself had scooped her up to hold her high above his head as he sang his praises to the Lord. He had frightened her, this tall white man, and she'd screamed with fear—not understanding the laughter that had rippled through the gathered flock at her response. Each time she watched the Judgement now it brought this back. The fear and, most of all, the terrible pain that swept across her birth mother's face as they carried Maryam away and rowed her to this tiny atoll off the coast.

It haunted Maryam, this woman's face. A face that seemed to meld into her own now, as she studied herself in the patchy mirror back in her hut. Delicate nose, round black eyes, and lips that turned up like ripe bananas on her small, thin face. Would they tell her birth mother of her first Blood? Or was she dead, a victim of the dreadful Te Matee Iai that devoured the population of the island at an alarming rate?

Perhaps she could ask Mother Elizabeth? It was she—still a girl herself, Maryam now realised—who had been there to soothe her when Maryam had first arrived. And Mother Elizabeth was still the one she ran to in times of great uncertainty or fear. For there were nights the Lord seemed to leave her side, and the looming unknown in her future preyed upon her mind far more, it seemed, than it bothered any of the other Sisters here. While they seemed to wait upon their fate with calm acceptance—even joy—she had the burning desire to know just what really lay in store. She would find out now her Bloods had come.

The conch shell sounded for the end of prayers, and Maryam left her bed and sought out Mother Evodia for the sea sponges to stem her blood. As well, the kind hunchbacked old Mother gave her bitter-tasting plant potions to ease the pains. Then Maryam joined the other Blessed Sisters for their evening meal. Ruth sidled up beside her and squeezed her hand.

"Has the pain settled?" she asked.

"A little," Maryam replied. The uncertainty about her fate had left her pensive, and she struggled to shake off the mood. Ruth would never understand: it was all so clear to her—her life one joyful journey in her service to the Lord. "What was the Lesson?"

"The Rules of course! Number Eight." Ruth skipped on the spot, her thick hair shining in the last of the sun as she recited, *"As with the Lamb who went so willingly to slaughter, we too must sacrifice up our lives in readiness and joy."*

Maryam, too, knew the Rules backward—had heard them every day since memory began. But now, this minute in this hour of this suddenly transforming day, the words took on new meaning. *Readiness and joy.*

These words stayed with her as she collected her food and joined the other Sisters in their prayer of thanks. She was ready, sure enough—relieved, in fact, that this day had come. It quelled the nagging sense of shame she'd felt at being the oldest of the Blessed Sisters by at least two years. Never in the memory of the Mothers had a Sister taken quite so long to shed her Blood. There was worry, to be sure, that the sickness that still plagued the islands might have defiled her—not outwardly, like the stooped, disfigured villagers she saw each summer at the Judgements, but somewhere deep inside the place where children grew. And that uncertainty—humiliation—had constantly accompanied her these past two years. Even faithful Ruth, herself already budding up and showing signs of readiness, had taken now to praying nightly that her Bloods would come.

The meal, freshly caught snapper doused in mangoes with steamed swamp taro, slipped down easily enough, but Maryam hardly tasted it. Neither did she really hear the happy chatter of the other girls. Instead, Rule Six from Captain Saul, the founding father of the Apostles of the Lamb, took form and sang inside her head: *By the Blood's great power, the most humble of us may Cross to the Holy City into the Lamb's presence and live there Always.* It reassured and soothed her just to think of this. To live in the Holy City, the awe-inspiring *Star of the Sea*, would surely be a joy. There, she hoped, all fears about her future life would drop away.

Later, at Mother Elizabeth's sleeping hut, she found her mentor deep in prayer, on her knees—her hair set free from its thick plait to tumble down her back and sweep the floor. Maryam knocked on the carved doorframe and waited to be called inside.

Mother Elizabeth, looking like an angel in the spluttering lamp light, finished her prayer and rose gracefully to her feet, turning to Maryam with a welcoming smile. "Come in, Sister," she invited, taking Maryam's small brown hand. "No more can we call you our bebi, eh? Evodia tells me that your Bloods have come." She sat down on her sleeping mat and patted the space beside her. "Come, sit here."

Maryam obeyed, smelling the same rich scent of pandanus on Mother Elizabeth's skin as she had smelt in her jungle hiding place that afternoon. She must have bathed in the crushed leaves, Maryam realised, noticing the oily sheen upon the older woman's skin.

"And so, at last, you are to leave us." Mother Elizabeth's gaze swept her face. "Are you ready, child?"

Maryam nodded, not trusting her voice.

"We will summon the boat at first light, then I will come to your hut and help prepare you for the Crossing."

Again Maryam nodded, hoping Mother Elizabeth would forgive her for her lack of words. It was all so big—so sudden—and the realisation that she was to leave her home, her friends, hit hard. "I will be ready," she eventually croaked, and Mother Elizabeth responded with a warm embrace.

"Don't be sad, my dear. This should be a time of great celebration!"

"But I will miss you all," Maryam said, fighting to suppress her tears.

Mother Elizabeth sighed, holding Maryam at arm's length to read her eyes. "But Rebekah will be there, and Sarah, too—they will not have forgotten you in the two years since their Crossing. And Miriam and Abigail: surely you remember them?"

"Of course I do, but it's not the same. Ruth is like my real sister, and you . . ." She could not continue, her throat closing up in her effort not to cry.

"Come now, I will see you soon enough." A blush crept up Mother Elizabeth's neck and consumed her face. "You mustn't tell the others this, but I am—" she stopped, swallowing as if the words were choking her, "—I am, you see, newly with child, and will make the Crossing soon myself."

Despite the news that Maryam would see Mother Elizabeth again, this other admission left her deeply shocked. With child?

She had never heard of such a thing, in all the time that she'd been here. "But how?"

Mother Elizabeth rose from the sleeping mat and paced the room, more like a nervous girl than the leader of the Blessed Mothers. She spun to face Maryam, her eyes dark with dread. "I should not have told you, and you must promise me your lips are sealed."

Maryam nodded mutely, even as her mind swirled at the news.

"Go to bed now," Mother Elizabeth said. "You will need your strength for tomorrow's ceremony, take my word." With that, she swept Maryam's mass of hair away from her forehead and gently kissed her there. "Go well."

Maryam embraced her one last time, unable quite to meet those eyes, and left the hut. By now the night had grown black, with just the twinkle of the torches beside each sleeping hut to light her way. How could she sleep, with the promise of the Crossing so soon upon her? It seemed impossible. And now with this other secret to carry . . . would the Apostles of the Lamb meet Mother Elizabeth with open arms or anger? She had no idea. But she felt a surge of protectiveness toward the woman who had raised her with a kindly hand and sureness of faith.

Too full of turmoil to take to her bed, Maryam traversed the silent compound and made her way down to the shore. She passed the scrubby ground where the chickens roosted underneath the breadfruit trees, the musty scent of their droppings spicing the crisp evening air, and took the beaten path through the taro patch to avoid any encounter with the village goats. They were tame enough, but she did not want to disturb the sleeping Sisters by startling the noisy troublemakers. Above her head, a giant fruitbat glided from palm to palm on the gentle breeze. Torchlight washed its pale underbelly, glowing much as angels might in Heaven's sky.

A half moon floated high above the bay, lighting up the busy foraging of the translucent, bandy-legged tairiki crabs. She tiptoed through them, careful not to disturb their nightly hunt for food, until she stood at the water's edge with the sea lapping playfully at her toes.

And there, across the water, connected to the main island by the causeway, shone the Holy City. The sight was so familiar, she knew its outer detail as well as her own skin. The impenetrable sides, ten times higher than the tallest jungle trees, were streaked with rust where time had weathered them. The tier upon tier of little windows, some lit with such a steady light it must surely be radiating straight from the Lord. And the crowning cap that bore its name: *Star of the Sea*.

Tomorrow she would Cross. And from that time on, Maryam suspected, her life would never be the same.

CHAPTER TWO

Ruth was still awake when Maryam finally slipped back into the sleeping hut. She rose up on one elbow and peered through the gloom. "Are you all right?"

Maryam wrapped her blanket around herself and huddled up against the wall. "It's strange, you know, I've waited for this moment for so long and now it's here I feel scared."

"Why scared?" Ruth sat up too, reaching across and squeezing Maryam's arm reassuringly. "The others who have Crossed are there—they will look out for you. Besides, we are the Chosen. The Blessed Sisters. We're the lucky ones."

"But why? Just because my blood didn't clot with Father Joshua's? What proof is that?"

"The Lord's way is mysterious," Ruth replied. She shrugged and nestled back down onto her mat. "All I know, or care about, is that I've been given this gift straight from Him—and however He wishes me to serve I gladly will."

Maryam sighed, sliding down until she lay flat on her sleeping mat as well. There was no point having this conversation now, or any time again, with Ruth. She'd felt this way herself at Ruth's age. But in these last two years, despite the fact her body had refused to bloom, a creeping change had taken place in her mind.

She thought about the last two Judgements she'd attended on the main island of Onewēre, where she was born. How she'd watched the villagers with new eyes, seeing past their reverence and ritual to something more unsettling and secret. She could not name these feelings, just sensed the swirling undercurrent that made her heart beat fast and jittery, as though she faced an enemy she could not name.

She played out these feelings again now, running her mind's eye over the dancing villagers with their paint-streaked faces and stamping feet. The faraway look in the eyes of the hip-swaying women as they sang; the sagging skin of the old men, their backs stooped as they led the dance. And, then, the sharp outlines of the Apostles' serving men.

How they'd sized her up, those brash young men, as if she was a frog or fish they planned to eat. They strutted past her like mangrove herons, stretching out their necks and almost preening as they met her gaze. She'd felt undressed, despite the pure white robe each Blessed Sister wore at Judgement time. Felt as though they looked right through and saw her quaking nakedness beneath.

She knew so little of men, except old Zakariya, who tended the gardens and the animals, and poor crippled Simon, who caught the fish and helped with the daily chores. These two formed the backbone of her life here, quietly going about their business undisturbed unless a wayward Sister obstructed them or did some wrong. Then Zakariya would chastise them, furiously waving his stick at them. Simon never said a word. When first Maryam had come here she'd been scared of him—his wasted foot and lumbering limp, together with his split top lip, marking him as a victim of Te Matee Iai. Yet he was a lucky one, the plague merely disfiguring him while he was still tucked tight within his mother's womb, not stealing his life or mind. And she liked him now, the way his crooked smile would greet her shyly each time they passed; the way he stroked the animals so tenderly and met their needs.

When Brother James had arrived the previous year he'd caused a stir. A young Apostle of the Lamb, his skin was white. Up close, Maryam could see the veins lay like paths beneath, as though he lacked the strong layers of protection offered by her own brown skin. He was friendly enough, teasing all of them— especially Mother Elizabeth—until they'd blush. But, beneath the charm, Maryam sensed something else. That same unsettling rawness as the village boys.

Again she sighed, wishing sleep would come upon her so her mind would cease its restless swirl. Perhaps it was the thought of entering the Holy City and living amidst men for the first time that stirred her so? Yes, perhaps.

She could hear the steady rise and fall of Ruth's sleeping breaths and focused in on them to calm her own and try to ease the nagging pains. If only she . . . no, just follow the breaths. Day would bring the answers that this night denied. Just breathe and sleep. Breathe and sleep. The day was near.

*　*　*

The first strangled crows of the old rooster woke Maryam from her dreams of swimming, of diving down into the rainbow world of coral near the deep lagoon. The sense of freedom, of total weightlessness beneath the waves, stayed with her as she washed and dressed, dealing with her stained undergarments and the seep of blood.

She ate her morning meal in silence, as they all did—the time laid aside to contemplate the day and make their daily peace with the Lord. But this morning the fresh fruits stuck in her throat and their sweet juices churned her already fragile stomach. She pushed the plate aside and went back to her hut to wait.

Unsure what to do with herself, she collected her belongings and lay them on her blanket, ready to wrap: her few clothes, her toiletries, her Holy Book and its accompanying Rules, and the woven flax basket of shells she had collected and added to since she was young. She took down the rare albatross feather she had fixed to the rafter above her bed and added it to her meagre pile. The mirror she would leave for Ruth, unsure she would be allowed such a blatant object of vanity in the Lord's sacred home.

Mother Elizabeth appeared in the doorway. "Are you ready for your big day?" Maryam laughed nervously. "As ready as I'll ever be." She gestured toward the pile on her bed.

"I've packed."

Mother Elizabeth entered and took from the pile the white gown Maryam wore each year to observe the Judgement. "Wear this today to make your trip." She put her arm around Maryam and led her to the threshold of the little hut. "The boat will come to take you to the village in one hour's time. Brother James will accompany you to the causeway—from there, as you know, you must make the last part of the Crossing on your own. It is the custom."

"Will I still have time to say goodbye to everyone before I leave?"

"Of course! You don't think we'd let our little Sister go without a word!" Mother Elizabeth crushed her in a sudden embrace. "It will be fine, te bebi, you will see. Your Sisters in the Holy City will support you. You have been chosen for greatness—and, believe me, the Holy City is more miraculous than you ever could imagine." Her eyes lit up, as though she were seeing the vision there in front of her. "Such colours. Such height."

Now she released Maryam and grew more solemn. "Just remember, all that you will experience is the Lord's will. It is not for us to question Him. At first it will all seem strange and overwhelming, so much to learn. But if you listen and only do as you are told, all will be well. And pay heed to the Ninth Rule: *None may question the authority of the Lord's chosen representatives: the sacred Apostles of the Lamb.*" For a fleeting moment last night's dread again clouded her eyes, before she shook her head as though to clear it. "Now," she continued, in a tone that brooked no argument, "please come with me."

Maryam followed her across the compound to the bathing huts, aware of the envious gaze of the other Blessed Sisters upon her as they passed. Zakariya must have risen early, for the tub was filled with steaming water in which pandanus leaves were steeping.

"The scent will help to ease your pains," Mother Elizabeth explained. "And I have asked Mother Evodia to mix up more tonic for you to take."

The familiar scent permeated the hut, its wild, sun-drenched fullness calming the knot in Maryam's stomach as she raised her two fat plaits and lowered herself into the ancient metal tub. She took the soft coconut soap, worked it to a sweet-smelling lather and scrubbed until her skin shone sunset pink. Then, somewhat reluctantly, she stepped into the drying cloth Mother Elizabeth held out for her, and dried herself.

Mother Elizabeth shook out the long white gown and helped Maryam to slip the fine linen fabric over her head. She showed her how to pack her undergarments with the leaves of the octopus bush, to prevent any leakage of blood. Then she took Maryam's braids and gently released them from their knot, brushing out the wiry curls until they fizzed in a dark sweet-scented halo around her face. "Now, my dear, I think you're ready."

They strolled back across the compound to collect Maryam's belongings, joined by others as they passed. By the time Maryam arrived nervously down by the water to await the longboat, the whole of the community stood beside her as one family group. At first a silence settled on them as they watched the longboat cut through the calm early-morning sea and glide up onto the glistening beach. But then all reserve vanished as Maryam was swept from one loving and familiar pair of arms to another, receiving her Sisters' heartfelt blessings this final time.

The little ones began to cry, their grief releasing a memory of her own tears when Sarah and Rebekah Crossed two years before. Thirteen then, she'd been devoured by jealousy that their Bloods had come ahead of hers, when they were barely aged eleven and twelve. It marked her out as different, the one whose Call had been delayed. And earlier, like these little ones, she'd cried purely because she sensed the heightened feelings that had rippled through the group like restless seas as others Crossed.

Now old Zakariya made his way to the front of the crowd and kissed her cheek. "Go well, Sister Maryam. I'll miss your smile."

That the old man would say this—a man of so few words and little outward sentiment—caused a swelling in her chest. She bit her lip, scared now that her tears would turn to sobs and shame her. Then it was dearest Ruthie who stood before her, and Maryam's heart felt that it would snap in two.

"Remember me," Ruth whispered, slipping something smooth and round into Maryam's hot sticky hand. "I'm coming over to you, just as soon as I can call the Bloods." She threw her strong arms around Maryam's neck and hugged her close. "Goodbye, my Sister. We will race again!"

This was too much for Maryam, and she stumbled toward the longboat now to hide her ragged emotions from the crowd. Brother James held the boat steady as she raised her gown to board, but then she stopped. *Mother Elizabeth!* She ran back to her, uncaring now if she did not seem composed and, despite her size, swept Mother Elizabeth off her feet.

"I will look out for you," she whispered fiercely in the older woman's ear. "Seek me out."

Mother Elizabeth nodded, wiping tears away from her streaming eyes. "Of course, my dear. But now it's time."

At last Maryam stepped into the longboat and turned to wave. From the beach, the Sisters broke into song. *"When the Bridegroom cometh will your robes be white ? . . ."* Their voices carried across the water as the longboat slipped effortlessly through the sea, the steady rise and dip of its oars keeping time with the Sisters' parting song.

Maryam could watch no more, her eyes too flooded with tears to see. She turned toward the island, so Brother James could not observe her pain. Slowly her wits returned, and she felt Ruth's gift clutched tightly in her palm. She opened her hand to reveal a pebble of the clearest blue she'd ever seen. It was like a jewel. Like the sea had been captured and magically frozen there. She pressed the stone against her heart, not shifting now until the longboat reached Onewēre's golden shore.

* * *

A crowd of villagers met the longboat at the beach, obviously expecting her. While some sang an old native song of welcome, others merely stood and gaped as Brother James led her from the longboat to the small wooden chapel in the clearing, on the far side of the village huts.

Maryam searched each woman's features, as she always did when she stepped foot on Onewēre, for the one face she might recognise and call her own. But her memory deceived her—each woman here had something of her birth mother, yet nothing she could pick for sure. The faces spoke of work-worn lives, of hard losses, and even those about her age seemed lacking in light. She tried to read each set of eyes, always alert for fleeting recognition or some sense of ownership, but none shone back.

As always, the village struck Maryam as chaotic and noisy compared to her own small atoll home, where people and animals numbered no more than thirty combined. Here, hordes of dusty pigs and thin dogs with mangy hides and weeping sores snuffled through the clutter, while scruffy chickens ran amok amidst the eighty or so villagers who lived in this beach settlement. At last year's Judgement, when the Apostles gathered every person on the island to attend, they'd counted over five hundred souls. But few would survive into old age, Maryam knew: sickness and the unrelenting toil of raising crops on barren land took their toll, and many babies died at birth. Still, the Apostles tended to them all, praying over the sick and preparing them to meet with the Lord should their bodies grow too weak to serve.

Inside the chapel Brother James joined three other white-clad Apostles who stood waiting there, lit the candles, and motioned for Maryam to kneel as the villagers filed in behind and took their seats. He began the ceremony with a recitation of the Divine Lesson.

"The Lord is the creator of Heaven and Earth and all living things," he intoned, projecting his voice to carry right to the back row, "and His son, the Lamb, shed His Blood to save us from our mortal sins. When Lucifer, the evil one, tempted us into wrongdoing, the Lord sent forth the Tribulation to purge us all." He smiled now, the gracious bearer of good news. "But we can still be saved, my children, if we look to the Lord and the Lamb and their Apostles, and obey their Rules."

Now he placed his hand on Maryam's bowed head. A spark like flint on rock ran through her and she dipped her head even lower to disguise her blush. Unaware, he began to grill her on her understanding of the Apostles' Rules and, although she never faltered in her answers, her mind itself fled far away. This closeness to a man, it frightened her—despite the fact he'd officiated for the Blessed Sisters for the last six months. Somehow his presence today, and that of the three unknown Apostles at his side, stole all her calm. She could feel her head trembling as she bared her tongue to take the sickly sweet te rara berry from him—the symbolic gift of the Blood of the Lamb.

When the last of the villagers had also filed up to accept the gift of Blood and returned to their seats, he turned his attention directly back to her. "Will you, Sister Maryam, who are meek and lowly in heart, be gentle and unresisting as our sweet Lamb, all the time surrendering your will to the Holy Fathers who have blessed us with their presence and worked with the Lord to save us from the Tribulation's wrath?"

Maryam nodded. "I will." Shakily, she took the hand Brother James now offered her and kissed the holy symbol inscribed upon the ring of bone he wore, her lips accidentally brushing the soft pale hairs on his knuckles as she did so. Again the spark seared through her and a kind of panicked buzzing filled her ears. She dared not look around her, focusing instead on the chapel's sculpture of the Lamb, whose mournful gaze seemed to judge her ignorant and weak.

But then, thankfully, the ordeal was over and she was escorted outside by all four Apostles, as the villagers threw blood-red bougainvillea blossoms at her feet. Now she stood before the man-made causeway that led out across the water to the Holy City far beyond. The village chief, a strong-armed man adorned with a shark's teeth collar and flax skirt, dragged forth a struggling goat from amidst the bystanders and, before Maryam had time to turn away from the animal's terrified rolling eyes, he slit its throat. Brother James bent down beside the poor creature and held an ornamental gourd up to the gaping wound to catch its blood.

Maryam swallowed down rising vomit as the goat's glazed eyes accused her of its sudden death. Shakily she lowered her hand, which had shot up to her mouth, and tried to slow her breathing down to clear her head. Why hadn't Mother Elizabeth warned her of this? Then, at least, she could have prepared herself and closed her eyes.

The coppery smell clung to her nostrils as Brother James dipped his finger into the still-warm blood and smeared it out across her cheeks. She tried not to shudder when he dipped again, running his finger down her chin and staining her white gown as his finger glided earthward. Once more he dipped and smeared until, upon her chest, a crimson cross was outlined. Then he took the gourd and poured the remaining blood across the entrance to the causeway, so she would have to step through it to reach her goal. "Go now, Sister Maryam," Brother James intoned. "Go now, as our Lamb once did, to serve your Lord."

At this, he pressed her pitifully small bundle of belongings back into her arms and when she did not move he pushed her forward, propelling her bare feet through the sticky blood and up onto the bamboo slats that formed the causeway out to sea. The villagers began to sing, their voices rising and filling the sky as she took her first tentative steps. "*I taku nako im, Tei rake, ao tabeka am kainiweve ao nako n am auti . . .*"

The causeway rocked beneath her feet, and she realised that it floated on the surface of the water like an anchored boat. Ahead, the great hulk of the *Star of the Sea* beckoned her, rust streaks as starkly outlined on its vast steel body as the reeking cross of blood she wore. And now, behind, a trail of bloody footprints linked her future to her past, her only known world.

A sea breeze had risen since her journey to the island and it rocked her now, tugging at her gown and hair. She looked ahead, watching the causeway undulate like a sea snake, and tried to focus her mind on staying steady in the centre of its swaying tail. Of course, if she fell in she could always swim. But caked in blood like this she'd draw the interest of te bakoas, the sharks that prowled around the reef. They were always hungry, these heartless beasts, and had plucked the life from many an unfortunate who crossed their path. Besides, none whose Bloods were on them would dare risk a swim.

She wondered at the people who had built this causeway, desperate for help in the dark days after the Tribulation when the sky had erupted with great bursts of poisoned fire, while monster storms raged around the planet, blew up all the power sources and the other trappings of that godless age, and churned the sea. All the Sisters had been taught how flying machines fell from the sky, buildings toppled and boats were sunk, the whole world in a toxic fiery meltdown as the Lord sent forth His wrath.

Here, too, the islanders were struck down by the fires, the storms and pestilence, many blinded, most destroyed. And those few who remained were powerless against the Tribulation as they watched their crops and fish stocks die—both sea and soil blighted—and their children born with monstrous defects that passed down through generations and were present still.

Meanwhile, in the midst of this, the great *Star of the Sea* floundered in the massive waves until they hurled her, by the Lord's sweet grace, onto Onewēre's brutal reef. Nothing they could do would move her, as her bowels hemorrhaged deadly black pools of oil toward the land. But the ship refused to sink. And her surviving crew, kept alive to aid the villagers by a now forgiving Lord, shared their wealth and soothed the sick—even as their own kind died. And, when it seemed the world had ended and all hope was gone, the great and caring Captain Saul received the Word of the Lord and formed the Apostles of the Lamb, making this great city rising from the reef their holy home.

It was a wonderful story. That they, the simple people of Onewēre, would be chosen to survive and serve these great Apostles, these living mouthpieces for the Lord . . . it had always overwhelmed Maryam. And now she was to enter this great towering structure by herself.

As she approached, she could see a group of dark-skinned

figures moving above. Were her old playmates waiting there to greet her as she stepped aboard? From an opening a third of the way up a platform was lowered by massive ropes, landing at her feet just as she reached the end of the long causeway. She peered up then, way up, straight into the watchful face of a young native server. He waved and roared down at her, "Climb aboard."

And she did as she was told, clasping the side ropes as they hauled her higher and higher up the chipped and salt-encrusted sides, toward this new and wondrous home.

CHAPTER THREE

The moving platform neared the opening—momentous as the opening of the door to Heaven in the Holy Book—and Maryam turned back toward her island home. The tiny atoll, so lush and green compared to Onewēre, seemed no more than a mossy pebble inside a shallow moat of palest blue. And Onewēre itself, reaching up to the thickening dark clouds at its mountainous centre, struck her as small and vulnerable against the backdrop of unending sea.

But now the platform drew level with the opening and she could feel her pulse quicken as four strong servers secured the ropes and motioned her to step aboard. She looked around, searching for a familiar face, but none stared back. The server, a man in his middle years, offered his hand to steady her as she crossed the threshold, her bare feet registering the cold hard steel of the dirty scuffed deck.

"Welcome, Sister," the man greeted her, and led her through a steel hatch into a long narrow passageway. "I am Mark."

"Thank you," Maryam murmured, unsure of how she was to answer him. She had never felt so enclosed before, the ceiling pressing down on her as they walked through the empty corridors, their footsteps deadened by the strange worn fabric matting on the floor. The air smelt damp and musty, not unlike the bath-house after winter rains and, mixing with the cloying scent of goat's blood, it caught in her throat.

"Mother Michal sends her greetings and apologies," Brother Mark told her. "Sadly, we have had a death and she helps prepare the body for its final journey back to the Lord." He opened a door and motioned her through. "Just wait in here, and I'm sure she will be with you soon."

Maryam stepped out into an enormous space, as big as the whole compound she'd just left. Nothing could have prepared her for this glorious sight. She tiptoed over the smooth stone floor, amazed by the vein-like seams that ran through the perfectly cut squares, and at the range of patterns and shades embedded there. But it was the vast ceiling—higher by many, many times than the tallest point of the maneaba—that stole her breath. Great circles of gold, inlaid with iridescent flower shapes, shimmered like the finest mother-of-pearl. And the colours! Soft glowing golds, pale cloudy creams, blues brighter than clear skies on a sunny day, the yellow of soft sunsets, the hazy pinks and lavenders of sweetest dawn. The only other place she'd ever seen anything remotely like this was the one small coloured window in the chapel by the bay. This, indeed, was made by the Lord. It had to be.

A wide sweeping stairway, bordered by solid ropes the silver of fish scales and framed by two tall palm trees, led to a circular raised platform from which other steps and walkways bloomed. High above, Maryam could see people moving in and out of doorways, yet this expansive floor where she stood right now was empty, save for her. The desire to climb that magical stairway grew too strong to resist, and she slipped up the cool stone steps until she stood at the very heart of the circular platform and looked up. High above, amidst the patterns and swirl of the domed ceiling, she saw herself reflected back in countless fractured copies. Her face, still streaked with blood, looked unfamiliar, nervous and very small. Perhaps this was how the Lamb saw her as He looked down?

A woman's voice shocked her back down to earth. "Ah, Sister Maryam. I'm sorry I was so delayed."

The speaker stood beside a tower of glass, its surface etched with intricate designs worked through in gold. Tall and imposing, in clothes both oddly shaped and bright, the woman had long pale hair that Maryam marvelled at—the colour of beach sand, straight and fine. Everything about her was as different from Maryam as night from day. The Apostles of the Lamb were white-skinned, like the Lamb; those from Onewēre, like Maryam, were brown.

The woman walked toward her now, her smile stopping at her strange blue eyes, the colour not unlike Ruth's pebble, which Maryam still clutched tightly in her sweaty palm. The dress this woman wore was patterned with bright splashes of colour, and hugged the full curves of her body in a shameless way. Up closer, Maryam saw too that she had coloured her pale skin with some substance to make her cheeks and lips blush red. Now she gestured to the ceiling. "Is it not a wondrous sight?"

Maryam nodded, her gaze once again sweeping the vaulted dome. "I was told the Lord's place was beautiful, but I never could have imagined this." She swept her arm around to encompass it.

The woman was less intimidating now she stood close. Her eyes looked tired, with dark shadows deepening her eye sockets. "I'm Mother Michal. Welcome." She bent forward and kissed Maryam on the forehead, her lips brushing the very place Brother James had first anointed with blood. She smelled of flowers, fresh and clean. "We call this place the atrium. Come, and I will show you around."

She led Maryam back down the steps, through the empty

stone foyer to a door on the far side of the enormous room. "This," she said, opening the door, "is where we all take our meals."

She stood aside to let Maryam pass, and they entered another cavernous room. The ceiling low, this room was meagrely lit by two walls of windows that once must have looked out to sea but now were crazed and caked with spray. The floor was covered with the same strange matting as the corridors, tinted blue with swirling green foliage and exotic orange flowers woven into a pattern that repeated all around the room. Maryam bent down, running her hand across the surface to try to see how it was made. The fabric felt like the pelt of some unknown creature—smooth and soft. Around the other internal walls dark wood paneling, cracked and peeling, framed enormous paintings from a foreign world. She was drawn, through the maze of matching chairs and tables, to one mural that depicted a grand building made of rough-hewn stone. At the building's entrance—an enormous arch-shaped wooden door—a group of white-skinned men, clad in richly coloured garments, sat astride magnificent four-legged beasts. "Where is this?" she asked.

"This once was ancient England. Now it's gone." Mother Michal pointed to another of the murals. A great city of stone sat amidst murky water, where curved-bowed boats were pushed along with poles held fast by laughing men. "This place was destroyed as well." Another showed a busy street, more like the villages Maryam knew, where black-skinned women, barely dressed, displayed their wares. "And this."

"So this is what the world looked like before the Tribulation?"

"Long ago." Mother Michal's eyes met Maryam's. "Just thank the Lord we live here now. All that world has been destroyed."

There was so much, Maryam realised, she didn't know. Of course she had been taught about the evils of the world before the Tribulation—how Lucifer got his grip upon the minds of those who lived back in those far-off times. But of the world itself, its shape, its size, the makeup of the people who once lived there, she knew little more than whispered scraps.

"Come and see where we prepare and cook the meals," Mother Michal now said. They crossed the dining room and entered through a swinging door. This room, again vast, could not have been more different from the last. Its surfaces were forged from metal, dull silver as smooth as water on a windless day. Here, at last, many men and women worked together, preparing food.

Despite a desperate desire to see someone she knew, Maryam shrank back behind Mother Michal, suddenly very conscious of her bloodied face and gown. She felt strangely sullied, even though she knew the mark of her Crossing should make her proud. But no one else here dressed as she. The Apostles of the Lamb, she knew, all wore pure white, while the garments the male servers wore she'd seen before each Judgement time— black trousers and white shirts beneath black sleeveless fitted vests. And the women in this room wore similar outfits: mid-length black skirts with clean white shirts. She wondered if these were the clothes she, too, would wear from this day on: she longed to fit in again, to feel part of a community. But now she focused back on what she saw, trying to imprint each new sensation and discovery on her mind.

Along one wall, steaming vessels sat atop what Maryam guessed were fireless cookers. She had seen two or three of these on Onewēre in the past, old discarded remnants from far-distant times, but had never seen one work before. What gave them heat?

Mother Michal noticed her puzzled frown. "We generate the energy we need to run the stoves and lights partly from windmills," she explained. "The first of our great Apostles knew the workings of such things and harnessed the Lord's endless breath to keep the Holy City running after all the old systems collapsed."

"Windmills?" Maryam questioned. "What are they?"

Mother Michal laughed, as did the three servers close enough to hear. "I'll show you presently," she promised, lifting the lid of a large cooking pot to sniff the steam.

"Chicken soup," a girl explained, her back to Maryam. She took a ladle and turned, shyly passing it over for Maryam to taste.

Maryam blew onto the hot soup and sipped the rich broth hungrily. "Thank you," she responded once the broth was gone. "It's delicious."

The girl retrieved the empty ladle, watching Maryam intently. "Welcome, Sister Maryam," she murmured. "Do you remember me?"

It was the girl's smile that chimed in Maryam's memory. "Rebekah!" She reached forward, eagerly embracing her old playmate. But, even as joy rose in her heart at finding a Sister she knew here, shock dampened it. This was not the stocky laughing Rebekah of her childhood, but one much more serious and painfully thin despite what Maryam realised was the swelling of pregnancy. Their eyes met, Rebekah's unexpectedly welling up with tears.

"You will be seeing more of Rebekah later on," Mother Michal cut in now. "She sleeps across the hall from you." She smiled at Rebekah and dismissed her. "Off you go."

Rebekah turned away again as if slapped, and moved down the long kitchen where basket-loads of mangoes were now being chopped. Although brown-skinned, to Maryam's eyes she looked quite pale and her bones protruded sharply underneath her skin. There were food shortages enough on land, that much Maryam knew. But, with all the villages contributing food for the Apostles, and such a miraculous way to cook it in the Holy City, how were such signs of hunger possible here?

She quickly checked the faces of the other dozen or so female servers in the room. Four looked familiar, though quite old— probably in their late twenties—and two of these were large with child. Another, closer in age to Maryam and Rebekah, moved sluggishly as she scrubbed the mud off taro at a distant bench. Her hair hung lank, and she did not raise her eyes like all the others in the room. Maryam stared. Could that be Sarah?

She had no time to find out more. Three young men, each tattooed around the neck like the people from Aneaba, on Onewē re's southern coast, stepped into her line of sight and stared at her unashamedly as they piled more muddy taro on the bench. Their tattoos, winding around each sinewy neck like a black-skinned mangrove eel, held her gaze. Something about them niggled at her, familiar yet unplaceable, like the tune of a song that echoed in her memory but refused to deliver up the words. She reluctantly turned her eyes away, unsettled by the curious smiles that tugged their lips. No matter, Maryam comforted herself: she would seek out Sarah and Rebekah again the first chance she could.

"Before I take you to your room, first come and see above deck." Mother Michal directed her back and they climbed three flights of stairs, up to a glasslined walkway that ran right around the edges of the atrium.

Several other doorways led off this, and Mother Michal pointed to a double set of doors signposted "Theatre." "This is where we hold our services—you're to return here for this afternoon's funeral, then we'll celebrate your Crossing while we're in one group."

Maryam longed to peek inside this sacred space, but Mother Michal proceeded to a large metal door that bore the sign "Deck 4 and Pool." They stepped out into fresh sea air, colder now as the storm promised by the dark clouds swept the bay. Here, three perfectly circular gardens were protected by an open-sided roof, held aloft by metal beams. Wave forms decorated the low protective walls and Maryam ran her hand across them, fascinated to know how they were produced.

"Tiles," Mother Michal explained. "You'll see them on many of the surfaces—they have withstood the passing of time well."

"How are they made?" Maryam asked. The tiles felt smooth under her fingers and she marvelled at the time it must have taken to place each one.

"Wet earth called clay is formed into these shapes then baked until dry. Their colours are created by painting on a coat of glaze that's made from minerals before they're fired." Mother Michal pointed to another wall, where a creature, half woman with a fish's tale, was displayed. "They call these smaller tiles mosaics—the art goes back to ancient times."

"Those early people must have had some good in them," Maryam mused, "to have created such intricate works."

Mother Michal shook her head sadly. "So much talent, and yet they allowed Lucifer to control their souls and waste their creative gifts on trivial and sinful ways."

She pointed now to the vegetable patches, where several more male servers watered healthy green plants and rooted out any errant weeds. "These gardens were once artificial pools filled with fresh water, for the passengers to swim."

Maryam laughed, her arm sweeping toward the sea. "They swam in tiny rock pools when they could have had the oceans? How bizarre!"

The older woman looked at her sharply. "You're a clever one, Sister Maryam. I see your mind grasps such ironies fast." She gestured, then, to four large columns towering above the deck. Atop each column whirling arms spun in the chilly wind like the seed pods from the kikonang tree Maryam had played with when she was small. "These, my dear, are the windmills that provide our power for heat and light."

"*These* make the lights that we see shining from the shore at night?" Maryam had always presumed their source miraculous, like the walled city in the Holy Book, sent down from Heaven with no need for light from sun or moon.

"Indeed they do," Mother Michal laughed. "But please don't ask me exactly how—these things are better explained by others far more skilled than me!"

Maryam stared up at the four great columns with the circling arms. That they could provide both light and means to cook without an open fire was astonishing indeed. "They look simple enough, so why haven't the villagers on Onewēre built windmills too?"

The smile dropped from Mother Michal's face. "The Lord saves His gifts for those who are the most deserving."

She turned on her heel and disappeared back through the doorway, leaving a puzzled Maryam to run behind. What had she said that had angered Mother Michal? Would the villagers not praise the Lord for such a gift?

Mother Michal did not relent in her pace: Maryam was marched down stairways and winding corridors with such speed she doubted she would remember how to find her way once on her own. She wondered where everyone was—surely Mother Elizabeth had told her that at least four hundred lived aboard?

Eventually she found herself escorted back down the dark low-ceilinged corridors, each lined with identical numbered doors. At Room 312 Mother Michal paused. She took a jangling chain from her pocket and slid a key into the lock.

The door took some opening, but then it gave. Inside, Maryam found a bed unlike her sleeping mat—it stood off the ground, covered in a shiny fabric mildewed with age. One bed; one room for her alone. This surprised and unsettled her. Always she had shared her sleeping hut with someone else—for many years this had been Ruth. The thought of Ruth, so unreachable now, pricked her eyes with sudden tears. But she blinked them back, determined she would not be seen crying. Besides, had Mother Michal not said that Rebekah would be sleeping nearby?

There were two cupboards in the room, all her own. And on the bed a neatly folded pile of clothes—all black and white, just like the clothes of other women servers she had seen. As well, a folded towel and face cloth lay upon a small cabinet beside the bed.

"Do not change your clothes or wash as yet," Mother Michal instructed. "We must still formally welcome you—things are just a little out of kilter with this sudden death." She handed Maryam the towel and cloth. "But I'll show you where to toilet while you wait."

As she made for one of the cupboard doors Maryam thought she must have been mistaken, but the door opened into another small room. Completely tiled, it contained several fixtures and fittings she did not recognise, besides a bath. A large bucket with a lid sat on the smooth floor, as did another filled with water.

"The bathrooms do not work as once they did," her guide explained. "The power that we generate is not enough to service these." She pointed to the water bucket. "Each morning you can collect warm water to wash with from the service room on Level Two. Rebekah will show you where. We have a way of taking out the salt from sea water so there is never any shortage, and your body wastes are emptied once a day into the tanks down there—Father Ahazaih has worked miracles and can convert this into the fuel that runs the desalination units and heats our water." She pointed to the bathtub, which was stained with green. "Your waste water will still flow away, however, so bathe in there."

Maryam nodded, too scared now to voice her racing thoughts. The ability to turn sea water to fresh was just as great a miracle as water to wine. And waste to fuel? If only they knew of this on Onewēre, where the winter nights grew cold and often stole the lives of sick and old in their sleep. "Thank you, Mother Michal," she said instead. "What am I to do next?"

"Just wait," Mother Michal replied. "I will send Rebekah down with some food before the time is reached." She made for the door, turning at the last moment to meet Maryam's eye. "An enquiring mind is good, Sister Maryam, but you will find your life here much more pleasant if you silently accept your role. The Rules will guide you—just heed their words." With this she left.

Maryam sat down on the bed, impressed by its softness, and closed her eyes—thinking about Rebekah's pregnant belly, and the other pregnant women she had seen. Mother Evodia had told all the Blessed Sisters, once they reached a certain age, how babies were made—but Maryam had never considered it for herself before. She had never realised that Blessed Sisters might lie with men . . . yet somehow Mother Elizabeth had. And now Rebekah . . . and many more again, it seemed.

Opening her eyes again, she stared down at Ruth's parting gift, glowing blue in the hazy light that sneaked in through the grimy window. What would Ruth be doing now? Playing with the little ones inside the maneaba until the storm had passed? She longed to be back there, in that place where everything felt safe and known. Here, nothing did.

Her stomach rumbled, and she realised she was really hungry for the first time since her Bloods had come. And the pains had receded, thanks to Mother Evodia's herbal brew. She returned to the bathroom, took a cup and dipped it into the container of water. It tasted flat, not like the sweet stream water of her home. There was so much that was new to her; so much she had yet to learn.

She lay down on the bed, trying to ignore the rumbling of her stomach and the dull ache in her chest that promised tears. The next thing she knew, someone was knocking at her door. She must have dozed.

Rebekah entered, offering a steaming bowl of soup and still-warm bread. "I'm sorry, but you'll have to eat this quickly," she said, passing Maryam the food. "I must take you to the meeting place very soon."

Gratefully Maryam began to eat. She motioned for Rebekah to sit beside her on the bed and they smiled at each other shyly. "So," she started, through a mouthful of bread, "how is it here?"

"There are many things I did not understand at first,"

Rebekah said, "but the Lord has helped me see the light." Her lips clamped together and her hand rested on her stomach as if guarding it.

All the things Maryam longed to ask died in her throat. She felt as though a wall had somehow slipped between them. "A baby," she said at last, not sure what else she could say.

"Yes." Rebekah patted the bulge. "I still have four more months to go."

"You have a husband, then?"

Rebekah flushed and her gaze dropped down to her hands, which now twisted a loose thread from her skirt. "I am a bride of the Lamb." Her chin lifted at this and, again, she met Maryam's eyes. "Once you've been here for a while you'll understand."

There was a smugness in her voice that rankled. She was two years Maryam's junior, yet she made Maryam feel so young and ignorant. Maybe she was embarrassed, or just shy?

Maryam took Rebekah's hand and squeezed it. "I'm very glad to have you here." Her other hand hovered near Rebekah's belly and she felt a great urge to touch the skin that housed the tiny life. "May I?" she asked and, at Rebekah's nod, gently lowered her hand. She was surprised by the hardness of the bulge, like goat skin stretched over a drum. Then, to her amazement, the baby kicked. "I felt that!" she laughed and the wall between them just as quickly disappeared. "Do you want a girl or a boy?"

The smile that had sprung to Rebekah's lips dropped again. "Just healthy," she mumbled. "My first baby did not grow more than three months inside. The second died just two days old."

Rebekah's pain was obvious and Maryam's heart went out to her. But the calculation in her head burst out into words before she could dam it back down. "This is your third?" Surely she was still only fourteen?

Rebekah sighed, drawing herself back off the bed. "There is still much for you to learn. But, for now, we'd better move." She picked out a set of server's clothes from the pile of clothing on the bed and handed it to Maryam. "Bring these. You'll need them soon."

Maryam rose and followed her toward the door. At its entrance, Rebekah spun around and embraced Maryam urgently. "Welcome, dear Sister Maryam. I'm glad you're here."

CHAPTER FOUR

As Maryam followed Rebekah along the claustrophobic corridors a conch shell sounded, several times. It was as though the ship erupted, people now streaming from doorways at every turn. Many wore the black and white of servers, yet a number of the white-skinned group wore a strange mix of clothing—a wild blend of patterns, colours, shapes, and styles. They jostled the two girls, some glancing curiously at Maryam as they hastened past.

"We must hurry," Rebekah urged her. "The funeral is to begin."

"Who has died?" Maryam asked.

"Father Jonah." Rebekah now hooked her arm through Maryam's and led her up the atrium stairs. "He was birth brother to Father Joshua—once one of the inner circle and a well-liked man."

"How did he die?" Her question drew piercing stares from those around. Lips thinned to disapproval. Eyebrows rose.

Rebekah pulled Maryam to the side of the rising tide of people, leaning in close to her ear. "We do not question the Lord's methods or actions. It was his time." Then the great surge swept them along the glass walkway and in through a wide set of doors, Rebekah clutching Maryam's hand and tugging her through the masses as if she was blind.

Maryam struggled to take in their surroundings: row upon row of seating rippling up and out from the central space, a large raised platform fringed by richly textured blood-red drapes. At its heart a candle-lit altar stood beneath a huge figure of the Lamb—one even more lifelike and awe-inspiring than the burnished wooden sculpture in the maneaba at Maryam's old home.

To each side of the altar hung an enormous painting. One showed the wretched people of Onewēre fleeing from great fireballs flung straight from Heaven, the sea boiling and the forests seething, many people struck down or blinded, huts incinerating as tormented souls were trapped inside. It was a terrifying vision, at odds with the serene depiction on the other side. There, a smiling white-skinned Lord bent down to bless the place on the platform where a single chair—elaborately carved and glittering with gold and jewels—stood beneath His holy hand.

But it was the body lying on a flower-strewn mat at the foot of the altar that most captured Maryam's attention. A white-skinned man in his middle years, clad head to foot in white with golden trim, his cheeks and eyes had sunk into deep dark hollows formed by the surrounding bones. She wondered again what had killed him, since the Apostles were protected from the plague that stole so many of her own kind. Whatever the reason, there was no denying his breath had fled—it was as if the Lord had reached inside this man and blown out the fragile flicker of life. He was a vessel, empty now and grown cold.

Even as Rebekah hauled Maryam down the aisle toward the central platform, the seats around them began to fill. As many people as the entire population of Onewēre, it seemed to Maryam, all of them cramming into this great space—the air alive with their muted whispers and the tread of feet. The white-clad Apostles and their families filled the seats down at the front and, apart from their strange array of clothing, Maryam found them hard to tell apart. Their features all seemed so washed out—as bone might look bleached by the sun. Then, in the seats toward the back, the servers took their places, men and women separated on either side.

Rebekah led Maryam up onto the stage, pushing her firmly toward the mass of curtains at the side. "Wait behind these until you are called upon," she whispered. "You can watch the service from back here." She squeezed her friend's hand one last time. "Do not be shamed by what is to befall you—it is the custom, and all of us have passed through this." With this she fled back up the rows of seats and took her place with the other women servers on the right.

Do not be shamed? What on earth could Rebekah mean? Maryam had no further chance to ponder this, however, as an older male server entered from the opposite side of the stage and sat at a strange polished object made from wood. It stood upon four legs, the main body almost leaf shaped, and some kind of lid stood open to reveal a mass of long ropes, or strings. He raised his hands and the huge congregation hushed. Then, in what could only be a miracle, he lowered his hands to the black and white teeth of this instrument and music began to pour from it as his fingers moved. Wonderful music, like nothing Maryam had ever heard before. And now the crowd started singing, their voices filling the space and reverberating with a richness that consumed her with the glory of the Lord.

Amazing grace! How sweet the sound
that saved a wretch like me.
I once was lost, but now am found,
was blind, but now I see . . .

As the song continued, twelve Apostles approached the stage. They stood on each side of the stepped walkway, framing it, as Father Joshua emerged from the crowd and made his way toward the altar. His uniform was almost glowing, such was its whiteness, and the gold that decorated his shoulders, cuffs and chest glinted under the flicker of the candles as he moved. He bowed to the great image of the Lamb and bent to kiss the forehead of the deceased man. Then he crossed to the bejewelled chair—an inexplicable golden light raining down upon him as he took his seat. The light radiated around his head as if from the loving hand of the Lord.

Maryam's heart pounded in her chest and all her formless fears and worries swept away as Father Joshua began to lead the cycle of prayers. Gathered around him now, the Apostles lit additional candles and te ribano incense, spreading the familiar pungent scent out into the praying crowd.

There was no denying it: the songs, scriptures, and ritual seemed a fitting way to send a soul back to the Lord's care. Father Joshua's voice filled every corner of the enormous room, almost echoing as he spoke with warmth of his lost brother and the contributions he had made. Maryam studied the faces of those who sat below the stage—the families of the white-skinned Apostles whose ancestors had created this sanctuary from the stricken world. She'd expected men and women, but it never had occurred to her that younger people would be part of the inner circle, too. She counted nearly thirty, from infants to a handful of young men near her own age.

"Let us hear from Jonah's widow, Mother Deborah," Father Joshua now declared. A young man helped a crying woman up the steps and comforted her as she struggled to compose herself.

He was perhaps a little older than Maryam, she decided, and had the frail look of one who fought Te Matee Iai. Would he be protected from its consequences, as the older Apostles were? She hoped so. No one deserved to die in such an awful way.

"Jonah was a good man," the woman began. "He loved the Lord with all his heart and believed that each of us had a duty to uphold His laws. He respected everyone and everything—convinced that the Lord made us all equally worthy of His love."

Mother Deborah then broke into sobs and the young man wrapped his arm around her, murmuring something in her ear. She drew herself together, directing her next words to Father Joshua. "All of us, dearest Joshua. Bar none."

A buzz rippled through the congregation. Father Joshua, drawing his lips into a tight line, sliced Mother Deborah with his gaze. It was over so quickly Maryam questioned whether she had really felt it, this sudden chill.

But the atmosphere had changed, the Apostles seeming to straighten and grow more rigid with Mother Deborah's every word. "Jonah welcomed his journey back to the Lord, bowing to His will with grace. While we who loved him begged him to defer it—" Again she faltered, "—he chose his path. I pray that the Lord will celebrate his sacrifice and spare, now, Joseph, our only son." No longer able to speak, she threw herself across her husband's body and wept. Joseph—the young man was so like her, he must be her son—fought back tears.

Leaning forward, Maryam tried to understand what she was seeing. Mother Deborah's tears washed lines down the dead man's strangely shiny skin, and Maryam realised his face was coated with some kind of substance that her tears disturbed. Beneath the sheen, was that the ghost of the blotches that Te

Matee Iai stamped on the faces of all who knocked at death's dark door? She had seen it again and again, as beloved Sisters succumbed to the Lord's call. But the Lord protected the Apostles from this fate: what she thought she saw could not be true.

She had no further chance to study him, as one of the Apostles now stepped forward and placed a shroud across the dead man's face. At this, Mother Deborah let out a great cry, her agony driving straight into Maryam's heart—such pain echoing the gnawing ache she still carried from the loss of her birth mother long ago.

From her sheltered vantage point, she studied Joseph's face as he squatted to coax his mother back toward her empty seat. His eyes were the most brilliant blue—the colour of Ruth's pebble—but ringed with dark bruises of sleeplessness and pain, standing starkly out against his golden hair and ghostly pallor.

The two were descending the steps when Joseph swayed and seemed about to keel over. Another young man in the front row sped forward and supported him, virtually dragging both mother and son back to their seats. This boy, taller than Joseph and slightly darker, bore an uncanny resemblance to Father Joshua. Maryam saw his jaw twitch and clench, as though he bit back words he longed to say. There was a coldness in his eyes, a coldness that she did not like, despite his obvious concern for Joseph.

Father Joshua rose from his throne and crossed to kneel before his brother. The twelve Apostles led the congregation: *"To everything there is a season . . ."*

As the beautiful recitation finished, Father Joshua swept the air with incense and began the final rites. Although Maryam had never seen such an elaborate funeral before, she recognised the words he now spoke. *"Ashes to ashes, dust to dust . . ."*

The Apostles circled Father Jonah's shrouded body and each took hold of the mat on which he rested, lifting him so he lay suspended, slung between them.

They slowly made their way down the steps, bearing him past the rows of silent mourners until they disappeared out through the doors.

"We will cremate Father Jonah's body presently," Father Joshua announced. "But first, we are blessed with a new servant to our flock." He peered out into the congregation. "I know this is an unusual coupling of ceremonies, but the Lord has told me we should purify her now, since we are already gathered here." With this, he looked in Maryam's direction.

She hesitated, unsure what was expected of her, still clutching the pile of clothes. Should she lay them down and go to him?

"Come," he now ordered, and she stumbled from behind the curtains, aware that every eye now tracked her progress as she made her way to Father Joshua's side. "Lay the clothing down," he said, and she did as she was told.

She felt so vulnerable in her plain linen gown, the bloody cross now dried and dark upon her chest. Father Joshua stepped up behind her, taking her by the shoulders to position her right before the figure of the Lamb. "Kneel," he said.

Her face heating and her stomach turning over, she knelt.

"Sister Maryam, we welcome you to the Holy City, and call on you to obey the Lord's every whim. Each of us must carry out His plans with humility and grace." He rested a hand upon her shoulder and she struggled not to tremble beneath his grip. "Will you, Sister Maryam, meek and lowly in heart . . ."

The words were almost the same as Brother James had spoken

in the chapel that morning: ". . . be gentle and unresisting as our sweet Lamb, all the time surrendering your will to we Holy Fathers who have blessed you with our presence and worked with the Lord to save you from the Tribulation's wrath?"

She nodded, not daring to raise her focus from the floor. "I will."

"Amen," the crowd responded. Behind her, Father Joshua seemed to shift away, and she heard the pouring of liquid. He returned, passed a silver cup to her, and whispered hot breathy words into her ear. "Drink this right down, and don't stop until it's all gone."

She raised the gleaming silver cup to her lips. The liquid inside smelt bitter and burned her throat as she forced it down. Once swallowed, it smouldered deep inside her gut.

The congregation broke into the familiar song. "*When the Bridegroom cometh will your robes be white? . . .*" But Maryam's head started to fog, and she found it hard to follow the words. Something was not right. Something . . .

"Arise," Father Joshua now said, and she wobbled as she tried to stand. The drink! Whatever it was made from, it muddied her thinking and stole her natural sense of balance. "Are you ready, Sister Maryam, to live out your fate?"

"I am," she croaked, forcing her assent out through a thick sea fog. She risked glancing upward, trying to pick Rebekah's comforting face out in the crowd. But the faces swam before her and she could not focus as far back as the servers' seats. Instead, she found herself staring straight into the stark blue eyes of Joseph. Quickly, she looked away.

"As the Lord has gifted you this glorious new life, we strip away the memories of your past." Father Joshua hooked both his hands into the collar of her gown and, before she could react, tore the garment right down her back and flung it off into the crowd. She stood naked, apart from her underwear, and her arms instinctively rose to hide her breasts. "Lower your arms," Father Joshua hissed, and she fought back sobs as she obeyed.

"Amen! Amen!" The crowd erupted. Maryam hunched before them, ashamed, closing her eyes as their applause built and swelled inside her head. How could Father Joshua treat her so? She longed to run, to flee the hot humiliation that swept over her in dizzy waves.

Just as she thought she could stand the disgrace no longer, someone—a woman, from her gentleness—came and dressed her once again. Maryam steadfastly refused to open her eyes until the strange new clothing, the black and white uniform she had brought, was in place. Then her gaze fell straight on the smirking face of the young man in the front row, the one who had helped Joseph.

"Now, Sister Maryam, recite the Rules," Father Joshua ordered.

Maryam struggled against the befuddling effects of the drink. The Rules? She knew them back to front, did she not? But the words would not form clearly in her mind. The congregation hushed, and panic gripped her throat. *"Rule One: There is but one thing . . ."* What thing? What? How could she forget this now?

She cast her gaze about, desperate for Rebekah's help, but still she could not locate her and still her brain refused to yield the sacred words.

". . . in the world," someone in the rows below her prompted, and she looked straight into the sapphire eyes of Joseph—*"that can cleanse us of our sins,"* he mouthed.

She had it now, suddenly remembering what came next. *"And that is the power of the Blood of the Lamb."* She swallowed. *"Rule Two: By the sacred power of His Blood . . ."*

The words flowed from her now, even as the fog closed in. She fought to reach the end of the recitation, stumbling over easy words she should have known. The urge to sleep—to escape—seeped into every part of her body and, by the final Rule, her lips felt swollen and could barely move.

She struggled to remain upright as Father Joshua led a prayer. Then, it seemed, the trial was over. "We will now proceed to the upper deck," he said, taking her firmly by the arm, down the stairs, between the rows of the clapping congregation and out through the doors.

Outside, he turned to her. "You are small," he said. "I hope you can fulfil your task." He bent down until they met eye to eye. "Wherever you go and whatever you're doing, Sister Maryam, remember that the Lord watches you. And that I, as his chosen vessel, see and know all."

"Yes Father," Maryam responded dully, unable to hold his gaze. Waves of sickness rolled through her and she closed her mouth, scared the roiling drink inside would soon erupt.

But now the first of the congregation burst through the doors, and Father Joshua guided her along the walkway to the open deck. Outside the wind had lessened and it smelt so good to be up in the clean sea air.

Against the railing four strong servers quietly stood beside Father Jonah's body, now on a pyre of wood aboard a raft. The deck filled with onlookers, and through them Joseph edged his grieving mother. She bent down and kissed her husband one last time, her mouth lingering upon his shrouded forehead.

Very gently, Joseph drew her away and they held each other in a tight embrace.

Father Joshua prayed once more, nodded his head, and the servers clipped back the railing, maneuvering the raft over to the edge. They lifted it until it hung in mid air, high above the restless sea.

Joseph stepped forward to receive a burning torch from another of the waiting servers, before stumbling toward the raft. Maryam, through her haze, wanted to cry out to him—tell him he did not need to be the one to start the fire—but Mother Deborah began to weep again and this enlivened him, as though he hurried now to ease her pain. He pushed the burning torch into the pyre and it caught immediately—the wind feeding the flames' hunger as they leapt from kindling to wood, wood to flesh. The servers carefully lowered the raft down the side of the great *Star of the Sea* and, when it reached the waves below, released the burning body to the sea.

Again the crowd began to sing, but Maryam could not follow the words. Her head now pounded with a fury that shot tears into her eyes and she struggled to hold them open. The singing and the crush of people amplified around her and she sensed that she was losing grip. She cast about, desperate for someone who might ease her plight. But now she was falling . . .

CHAPTER FIVE

Deep red pulsing pain clamped her brain. She had no idea where she was or what had befallen her—and try as she might, she could not move. Even her eyelids refused to break their seal and she lay trapped somewhere, blind and prone. Then, slowly, the funeral and the welcoming ritual came back to her. She groaned, the sound enormous in the void around her.

She heard the scrape of a chair. The rustle of clothes. And sensed someone leaning over her as the light before her eyelids dulled. "It's all right, Sister Maryam, nothing to fear." The voice was male, breathy as the wind through palm fronds.

She tried to speak, to question him, but her mouth, like her eyelids, ignored the urgent messages shouted in her brain. Where was she, and who was this person? Fear rose in her: she was helpless and alone with a strange man.

A warm hand patted her arm. "I'm Hushai, Sister Maryam. Please do not be afraid." She heard him move away from her, then the sound of pouring water. He returned, placing a warm cloth over her eyes and gently wiping there. She felt her eyes ease beneath the warmth. Slowly she blinked them open, but the light seared like hot charcoals in her already pounding head. She cried out, an animal sound bereft of words, and an age-wrecked Island face suddenly hovered in her line of sight— unfocused through the stream of her tears.

"Try to sip a little of this water, it will help." He held a cup to Maryam's lips, gently lifting her head a little so she could swallow.

The water eased the burning in her throat enough for her to whisper, "What happened?"

Hushai patted her arm again. "The sacred anga kerea toddy you drank from the chalice—it has powerful charms."

So it *was* the drink. Maryam blinked and tried to focus on the man who spoke. He was quite the oldest person she had seen, the lines upon his face as marked and rugged as the bands of weed that tiered the beach after a storm. And his eyes, which seemed to look down on her so kindly, were as milky as those of a long dead fish. Could he even see her?

It was as if he read her mind. "The good Lord long ago removed my sight. But He has not left me blind, oh no—He gifts me with the power to sense what others see." Again he offered her the cup, and this time the water flowed more freely down her throat.

While her head was tilted up to drink she looked around her. She was in some new place—a small white enclosure with rows of glass-doored cupboards and well stocked shelves.

"This is our hospital," Hushai said.

"Hos-pi-tal? What is that?"

He chuckled. "Sorry, little Sister. I forgot that there is much you do not know. This is the place for healing, where those who need it are cared for and eased." He laid her head back down tenderly and wiped a small dribble of water from her chin. Something like a sudden sea squall rippled out across his ancient face. "It is potent stuff you drank. Not good. Refuse it whenever possible—or do not drink the full amount."

"But Father Joshua . . ." She bit back the other words. Questioning the great Apostle's reasons for plying the drink was foolishness. Had he not warned her that he, along with the

Lord, knew and saw all? Besides, she did not know this Hushai. The best response, she guessed, was silence.

She sighed, her head so full of questions and confusion that it throbbed all the more. The old man laid the cooled cloth across her forehead. "This should help to dull the pain."

Again she felt as though he read her thoughts, and she tried to block the dangerous doubts and questions from her mind. He smiled down at her, taking each of her hands into his own. The gesture was so kindly done she did not shy away from his touch.

He leaned in toward her, until he was so close she could hear his breath. "There is something in you, Sister, that shines past the haze that blinds me. Look into my eyes and just relax— show me what is in your heart."

She stared up, unsure what it was he wanted from her. But she felt compelled, her heart speeding. The old man's eyes looked as though a cloud had crossed the sun; a strange light still seemed to emit some warmth. How terrible, she thought, to lose the gift of sight. To never see the sun set coral pink against a glassy sea, or the bright bursts of colour when the flowers bloomed in the jungle. How achingly sad, never to look upon the faces of those you love.

Hushai squeezed her hands, smiling down. "What a heart," he murmured. "There is indeed a greatness there. I see a strength: a mind both questioning and true. You have a task that none but you can carry out. This is your destiny, which you must serve."

She smiled despite her pain. The old man said nothing that she did not know. "Then I have met my destiny, for have I not promised to serve the Lamb's Apostles this very day?"

Outside the door footsteps approached. Hushai quickly ducked down, until his mouth was crushed against her ear.

"That is not of what I speak," he whispered. "There are other—"

"Ah, I see you have regained yourself." The voice belonged to a woman.

Hushai rose quickly, turning toward her. "Holy Mother! Sister Maryam has just roused."

The woman was tall and middle-aged, her dark hair swept back from her face. She was clothed in the white uniform of the Apostles, the starkness of the fabric draining her face of colour while straight dark eyebrows stood out like horizon lines above narrow brown eyes. She crossed to Maryam and looked down upon her with an assessing eye.

"How do you feel, child?"

"As though my head has burst," Maryam replied.

"Indeed." The stranger patted Maryam's arm with a cool hand. "You must be very sensitive—you have already slept one full night."

One full night? Surely she had just arrived?

Turning to Hushai, the woman said, "Prepare the draught."

Hushai's blind eyes scanned over Maryam, his mouth set hard as though he fought to hold back words. He bowed his head, shuffling from the room. "As you wish."

Now the woman's gaze returned to Maryam. "I am Mother Lilith—the physician here. I must check your health to ascertain how best you'll serve."

Maryam nodded vaguely, unsure what Mother Lilith meant. "I have my Bloods," she offered, wondering if there was a need to prove her claim.

Mother Lilith crossed to the benches below the cupboards and washed her hands in a bowl of water. "You would not be here if there was any doubt of that, my dear. Now I must check that everything inside you is in place." She started to lay strange-looking instruments out on the bench.

Hushai returned, bearing a cup. He crossed to Maryam, positioning himself so his body blocked her from Mother Lilith's line of sight. "Drink this all up," he instructed loudly, supporting her raised head with one hand as he drew the cup toward her lips.

The smell repelled her—the same bitter scent as the drink that had landed her here. She did not want to swallow it, felt the bile rise in her throat just at the thought.

"Take only a little," Hushai whispered, so softly that she barely heard. She swallowed the first mouthful, gagging as it burned her throat. It tasted stronger, this draught, than the one she had downed from the silver cup. How much more time would she lose once it worked its powerful charm? Another day?

As Hushai guided the cup back toward her lips, he seemed to misjudge his aim, spilling at least half of it down the side of her pillow. Then he offered her the last mouthful, virtually just mouthing the words that tickled at her ear. "This much alone will help ease your pain." While Mother Lilith's back was still turned, he flipped the pillow over, hiding any evidence of the spilt draught.

Maryam struggled to swallow the last mouthful, feeling every drop as it scorched a path down to her stomach. The effects were almost immediate—the same dizzying desire to sleep; the same sickening creep of fog that slowed her brain.

Hushai patted her arm. "I will attend you later, little

Sister," he said for the benefit of Mother Lilith. Then he bent
down close. "Be strong."

With that, the old man left Maryam alone in the room with
Mother Lilith, who approached her now, carrying a strange
metal device. "I must give you an internal examination," she
explained. "You will not recall it when you wake."

The words came to Maryam through an increasing haze,
which dampened down her rising panic as Mother Lilith
reached up beneath her skirt and removed her undergarments.
She pushed Maryam's legs back, so her knees were bent, and
removed the sponge that stemmed her blood. Why was she
doing this? It was terrible—humiliating—and Maryam longed
to cry out, to rise up from the bed and run. But the draught was
hitting her hard now, and she felt the limb-numbing concoc-
tion deaden her, as though it was detaching her body from her
will to move.

Maryam struggled to keep her eyes open, to see what was
happening as Mother Lilith took the glinting metal device and
started to push it into her most secret place. The pain! It shot
through her and she cried out. How could Mother Lilith do
this evil thing? Then the physician pushed the cold hard object
again, as though forcing through a barrier, and the pain grew
too intense for Maryam to bear. It overcame her, spiralling her
down into a place of nothing, as dark as death.

*　　*　　*

Voices roused her, pressing through the layers of her dulled
consciousness like the cries of sea birds carried from far out
at sea. She tried to move. A cruel dull ache, starting down

between her legs and radiating up into her abdomen, caught at her breath and brought back scattered memories of what had taken place. She did not want to recall it; could not understand why Mother Lilith would do such a disgusting thing. She felt so ashamed; sure that the Lord would look down on her now and know immediately that she was dirty and defiled.

She tried to block this from her mind, concentrating as hard as possible on the low rumble of voices until she could hear past the pulsing hammer in her head. Mother Lilith was arguing with someone, in frantic whisperings outside the slightly open door.

". . . do predict problems and there could be more I cannot see."

"That's perfect then," a male voice replied. She knew that voice. Had heard it recently. Hushai? No, too vigorous and strong. "Start her with the boy as soon as we can separate him from Deborah . . ."

"She's so small, Joshua. There are others who—"

"No matter," he snapped. Father Joshua? Yes, it had to be his voice. "The best way forward is to use the subject who will least be missed."

"But the boy is—"

"Our nephew, Lilith. My brother's son. And I will not lose another when we have the means to save him." His voice calmed a little now, losing its edge. "Besides, we have our status to maintain."

What were they talking about? If only her head would clear of the draught so she could think. His brother's son? Could that be the kind boy Joseph, who had helped her with the Rules?

"I cannot guarantee she'll have the volume to complete the job."

Father Joshua's voice dropped to an icy hiss. "Take it all, if you must. Do you really think I care?"

Mother Lilith laughed at this. "No, my dear. I've known you far too long ever to think that of you!"

There was more, but the strain of trying to listen was taking its toll. Whatever was in that awful toddy it had the most peculiar effects. It stole her ability to concentrate, to hold clear thoughts together in her mind. She gave up now, letting the talk blend back into the background as her misery overflowed. Fat hot tears rolled from her eyes and pooled together in her ears and she let them fall, her arms too leaden to move and her will all gone. Was the Lord punishing her? Testing her faith? This was not the Holy City she and all the other Blessed Sisters longed to reach. Had she not prayed hard enough? Had the Lord looked inside her soul and seen the tiny specks of doubt?

She must have dozed off again, for when she next grew conscious all hint of daylight had gone. Hushai, lit by a single candle, sat in an upright chair beside her bed, his old fingers stroking bone-carved beads as he mouthed prayers.

"Hushai?"

The old man stopped, turning toward her with a sad smile. "Ah, little Sister, you awaken at last." He stood and crossed to her, placing his papery hand upon her forehead. "I am so sorry for your pain."

He helped her raise a cup of water to her mouth, and the sweet coolness worked its magic on her throat. A question pressed her lips and before she could contain it, Maryam whispered, "Why did she do that? Have I sinned?"

Hushai shook his head. "Never believe this is your fault," he replied urgently. "You must be strong, my little one. You must keep your wits."

"How will I—"

Hushai broke in, holding his finger to his lips. "Quiet now, I hear them come. There is little time, so remember this: The tairiki crab sees best at night, when others' minds are dulled by sleep. Build a shell around yourself for protection like the crab, and use the night's long dark to hunt."

Maryam now, too, could hear footsteps, but she did not understand his words and tried to speak. "But I—"

"Shhh. Hold this message close inside yourself, but know I'm here." He could say no more, as the door was thrust open and Mother Michal entered.

"Ah good, I see you are awake." She smiled as though there was nothing wrong, and held her hand out to Maryam. "Come, I'll take you back now to your room."

Maryam tried to rise, her head dizzy and her limbs half dead. Mother Michal pulled her upright, seemingly oblivious to Maryam's discomfort. A sharp pain shot through Maryam's abdomen and she bit back a cry. Shame heated her cheeks as she saw the stain of blood upon the bed where she had lain, yet Mother Michal seemed not to mind. "I have asked Rebekah to bring a light supper to your room, then I'm sure you'll want to rest." She smiled brightly, turning to Hushai. "Change the linen, Hushai, then you may go."

She led Maryam toward the door, supporting her feeble steps by grasping one arm. Maryam turned back to Hushai. "Thank you," she said. "I will not forget."

"Forget what?" Mother Michal questioned, as they entered a long dark corridor.

"Kindness," Maryam muttered, not daring to meet her eye.

True to Mother Michal's word, Rebekah awaited her back in her room. She had placed a plate with bread, goat's cheese and a ripe mango on the table next to Maryam's bed. "I wasn't sure how much you'd eat," she said. "I can always go and fetch you more."

Maryam shook her head. "Thank you but I couldn't eat." The walking had disturbed her pain, and all she longed for was to lie back down and escape in sleep.

Mother Michal beckoned Rebekah to the door. "Leave her now. The Lord wishes her to meditate in silence, until she's called upon to serve the Lamb." She pushed Rebekah out and leaned back in to address Maryam. "You speak to no one now, Sister. Your mind must be emptied and your heart pure."

Maryam just looked at her, hysterical laughter threatening to erupt. After everything she'd gone through since she left her home—was that really yesterday?—and now she could not even speak? She threw herself down on the bed and reached for the albatross feather she had brought with her to this new home. She held it to her nose and drew in the pungent oily scent of it, closing her eyes and trying to take herself back to the atoll where she had so freely roamed. If only she had wings to fly, like the albatross, she would be back there in her sleeping hut this very night—snuggling in right next to Ruth and releasing her tears. Nothing was as she'd imagined it.

She rose gingerly, relieved that Mother Michal had left her, and laid her meagre pile of belongings in the drawers. She picked up her Holy Book, letting it fall open at a random page, one of the Psalms, and whispered the words, trying to find comfort in them. *"The Lord hear thee in the day of trouble . . . Send thee help from the sanctuary, and—"*

There was a gentle knock, the door slipped open and Rebekah rushed across the room. She collected Maryam up into her arms, her ripe belly pressing against Maryam's tender frame.

"I cannot stay. But one day I promise, Sister Maryam, we will talk." She noticed the Holy Book lying open on the bed. "It is good to see you use the Lord's words to comfort you." She drew back, staring wide-eyed into Maryam's face. "Remember Rule Eight: *As with the Lamb who went so willingly to slaughter, we must sacrifice up our lives in readiness and joy.*" She gave Maryam one final squeeze, then fled the room as quickly as she had entered.

Maryam retreated to the bathroom, using most of the remaining water to wash away all signs of shame. She felt bruised inside, but the thing that hurt most was her heavy and unhappy heart. Whatever she had thought that she would find here, it was not so. Nothing made sense. Nothing was as it should be.

She tried to sleep, to block the dark thoughts from her mind. But the night rolled on over her, and her mind would not still. It was so quiet: no sleeping breath of Ruth. No barking dog nor nagging goat. No constant whisper of the sea.

When she could bear it no longer, sometime in the thick of night, she crept stiffly from her bed. She tracked the long corridors back to the atrium, careful not to be found out. The great space shone in the slivers of moonlight that fell inside, so beautiful and still, at odds with the turmoil inside her heart. Her hand trailing on the smooth silver handrail, she climbed the stairs and slipped outside.

Oh, the sweet sweet smell of the sea rushed down into her lungs and soothed her as it lapped the ship's vast sides with its gentle song. The sky was clear; a million stars looked down on her from Heaven. She needed this; needed to remind herself of the Lord's magnificence and reach. He had a plan for all, mapped out as intricately as the stars that led the ancestors on their great voyage. She had to put aside her pain and fears and trust that He would reward her service and bring her joy. She would believe in this—*had* to believe in this—otherwise all hope was lost.

She leaned against the railing and closed her eyes, letting the night breeze brush over her. Perhaps Mother Michal was right, that silence now could still her mind. She would use the time for rest and prayer. She had believed—had trusted the Lord would eventually reward her faith. And now that He was testing her, was tempting her to lose that faith, she must stand firm.

"Well, surprise, surprise." The voice, mocking and low, nearly burst her from her skin. A figure stepped forward through the gloom, smoke issuing from his nose as he cast his tobacco tikareti over the side.

Maryam made to run, but he stepped forward and clamped a cold hand around her arm. "What have we here?"

She looked directly at him then, recognising the hard-eyed boy who'd helped Joseph back to his seat. She tried to shake his hand away, but he only held on tighter.

"Lazarus," he introduced himself and, as she watched, his tongue emerged and swept a lazy circle round his lips. "Sister Maryam, I presume?"

She dared not answer, mindful of Mother Michal's instruction. But she nodded, ducking her head to escape his stare. He laughed, tugging her so suddenly she stumbled up against his chest. His arm wrapped around her like a sea snake and, although she struggled, he merely smiled and held her tight. His body was hard and unforgiving, and he smelt of smoke. With his other hand he pinched her chin between his forefinger and thumb and raised her head to study her. "Nice," he purred.

Before she could duck away, he crushed his mouth against

hers—his tongue forcing through her shocked lips and delving deep. She wanted to gag, wanted more than anything to break away. She fought beneath his vice-like grip but he was taller and more strongly built, and backed her against the handrail until she leaned precariously out over the sea.

Then, just as suddenly, he pulled away. She ran at him, slapped him so hard on his smirking face that he reeled back, the sound an explosion in the sleeping night. Something mean crossed his face. Holy Father, what had she done? She ran for it then, just reaching the doorway, relieved that he did not pursue her, when his parting words stabbed through her like a sharpened spear.

"Are you a bleeder or a breeder?"

She stumbled, wounded and confused by this. What, in all Heaven, could he mean?

CHAPTER SIX

Sleep eluded her, as Maryam struggled to make sense of Lazarus's words. She was a bleeder, she supposed, in that her Bloods had finally come. But breeder?

She thought of Rebekah, ripe with her third child, and the other pregnant women she had seen. Was this how she was destined to serve? As breeding stock, like the female goats put to the billy to increase their flock? And Mother Elizabeth, was she subject to this, too?

What frightened her was not the thought of bearing a child, although she knew virtually nothing of this. It was the process to conceive the child that scared her so. If only she could speak to Mother Elizabeth now—to tease out some sense from everything that had passed these last two terrible days. It seemed impossible that she had looked upon her journey here as the start of something fine and good. But now, regardless of whether the Lord was testing her or not, she feared the approaching dawn.

When, finally, her brain had tied itself into such tired knots her thoughts lost sense, she drifted into fitful sleep. Strange disjointed dreams chased her down dark corridors and, when Rebekah knocked on her door bearing breakfast, Maryam had to force her way out through the maze to wake.

"Make sure you drink every drop," Rebekah instructed her, as she laid a tray beside the bed.

Maryam took up the offered cup, recognising the caustic smell of the anga kerea toddy before she even saw it. Anga kerea. What did it mean? The language of her childhood hid deep beneath the overlay of English words she had since learnt. Then it came to her—*sacrificial*. So why must she drink this yet again? Had she not gone through the sacrificial rites already? She looked up at Rebekah, not daring to speak, but trying to transmit her worry through her eyes.

Rebekah giggled. "I know it tastes horrible, but you get used to it after a while—even start to want it. And as you get more used to it, it will not send you off to sleep, just make the day pass easier." She stood there, hands on hips, waiting for Maryam to down the drink. "Anyway, it's not as strong today, now that you've been tested."

"Tested? What do you—"

Rebekah held up her hand, silencing her. "Please, Maryam, do not speak. Mother Michal is close by and if she hears you we will both be punished."

Maryam bit back her frustration. If she could not even speak to another Blessed Sister, then how was she ever to understand the workings of this strange new place? They seemed so unfair, these so-called tests, and she was terrified that she would fail—that the Lord would see inside her heart to her resistance and send her straight to burn in Hell. She raised the cup to her lips and drank a quarter of the toddy down, trying to hold back the wave of nervous nausea that swept her. Rebekah nodded, encouraging Maryam to drink it all, and she took the rest in one mouthful—holding it unswallowed while Rebekah made to leave.

"I will return shortly," Rebekah assured her, "to show you where to fetch the water for your bath." As the light from the corridor caught Rebekah side on, Maryam registered an unusual tinge of yellow in the whites of her eyes.

Alone again, Maryam spat the toddy straight back into the cup. Her mouth felt numb, tingling from the drink's magic. She crossed into the bathroom and poured the residue down the drain hole of the bath. May the Lord forgive her: she could not stand to drink it all. It was bad enough to go from humiliation to humiliation, without also losing the ability to think things through. The mirror reflected her worried face back to her. Dark smudges of sleeplessness framed her eyes and, there, where her eyeballs should be white they, too, were muddied by a yellow hue. Was it just the diffused light, or had something else turned them so?

"Sister Maryam?" Mother Michal called.

Maryam dashed back to her bed, placing the empty cup beside her just as Mother Michal entered the room. "Ah good, I see Rebekah has been here."

Mother Michal patted Maryam's shoulder, a kindly gesture that almost brought tears swelling in Maryam's eyes. "I have asked Rebekah to show you where to fetch your water and then you can join the others in the kitchen to help prepare our meals."

Maryam nodded, unsure if she was allowed to respond. It seemed not: Mother Michal checked the cup was empty and reiterated that complete silence now would aid her journey toward the Lord, then left. The toddy made Maryam a little dizzy, despite the small amount she had consumed. She dragged on her clothes, eating the breakfast of fresh fruit and nuts hungrily as she did so. The thought of joining the others in a normal task was reassuring. Maybe the trials they'd put her through were over. Please, she prayed, let this be so.

When Rebekah returned, she led Maryam down through a maze of corridors, reminiscent of her scattered dreams the night before. There were many more people about today, black-clothed servers rushing silently from job to job. The girls made their way down to the very bowels of the great ship, where huge steel vats, tarnished with age, filled the cool dark space. It was noisy here, as the motors powered by the waste converted the salt water into fresh. Maryam longed to take the controlling server aside and deluge him with questions as to how it worked. But she dared not speak, conscious of the eyes of the Apostles upon her. They seemed to be everywhere, supervising the servers at their tasks.

Once they had delivered the fresh water to her room, Maryam followed Rebekah up to the kitchens, cheered by the rumble of warm chatter that greeted them as they entered. "Come and I'll introduce you," Rebekah offered, and she started reeling off servers' names so fast that Maryam could not keep up. But what she did register, with each new face, was the same strange yellowing of the eyes.

"And you remember Sarah," Rebekah now said, pulling a reluctant girl from her place slumped by a sink.

So this washed-out girl *was* Sarah, who had played with her when she was young. She wouldn't meet Maryam's eye, squirming like a bonubonu worm brought to light. Her face was a sickly grey, dry skin patching both her cheeks. And her lips, as pale as driftwood, were split and cracked. Her hair, which Maryam remembered as strong ropy curls, hung limp and unkempt, and her hands trembled as she took Maryam's offered hand and shook it with the limpness of a slaughtered chicken's claw.

Maryam swallowed a gasp, as Sarah's extended arm revealed a weeping wound at the crook of her thin elbow. The surrounding skin looked bruised and fragile. Just for a second Sarah's eyes met Maryam's then slipped away. But the pain in them, the deep resigned misery, struck Maryam. Sarah was gravely ill, she was convinced of it.

But she had no time to dwell on this, as Rebekah led her on to meet Miriam and Abigail, both of whom she vaguely remembered as older Sisters from her youth. Pregnant bellies bursting from their uniforms, the young women greeted Maryam kindly, although there was a disconnected vagueness to their speech. Was this the result of the toddy, Maryam wondered? Server after server fitted this description, as she met each of the twenty or so in the room. And yet they appeared quite happy, apart from Sarah, and nattered comfortably together as they worked. She longed to join them, to enter into their cheerful conversations, but one of the Apostles—a large woman in her later years— watched from her vantage point, an armchair placed strategically in the middle of the vast kitchen space.

"Who have we here?" this woman asked, as Rebekah led Maryam forward.

"Mother Jael, this is Sister Maryam."

Mother Jael looked Maryam over, her head to one side. "Ah, yes. Show her where the dishes are washed and stacked," she told Rebekah. "She looks as though she's careful. Is that right, girl?"

Maryam nodded, skimming her eyes over Mother Jael's wide soft face. She had never seen anyone quite so fat before, skin dragged down by the weight of undulating rolls that wobbled, independent of her, as she moved. So much food, to grow this big. The Lord surely must provide richly for His own.

The work was tedious yet soothing and Maryam found herself relaxing for the first time since her Crossing. To have something practical to do, to focus on, helped subdue the anxiety that still swirled inside her head. Meanwhile, all about her, the servers worked in calm harmony, some breaking into song as they performed their tasks.

When the stack of breakfast dishes was finally cleared, the male server Brother Mark, who Maryam had met when first she Crossed, approached. "Mother Jael suggests you help us with the toddy," he announced, smiling. "Please come with me."

She followed him to the far end of the kitchen, where several other servers ground huge piles of nuts and herbs into fine yellow paste. "This forms the basis of our toddy," Brother Mark said. "We mix it with the sap of the coconut blossom spike for sweetness and leave it to ferment overnight." He handed her a large rounded stone. "Use this to grind the paste."

He set her up next to the youngest of the servers there, a boy in his early teens who shot her a shy smile. "This is Brother Ethan. He will show you the right mix of herbs."

Maryam turned to the boy, whose face flushed red at her attention. His hands, like those of the other servers around him, were stained yellow by the paste. He cleared his throat. "These," he said finally, showing the same vague sense of disconnection as Miriam and Abigail, "are sida leaves and flowers. We use about twenty of the leaves for each brew and four of the flowers." He showed her the small serrated leaves—soft to the touch—and the glossy yellow flowers, then picked up a handful of kamani nuts. "The oil from these is very strong—we only use two each time." Finally he pointed out the kurap fruit, and the leaves of nambugura and te ren shrubs. "Once you've ground each of these separately, mix them together into the final paste."

He showed her how to use the stone, placing his palm

across its back and rocking it in a steady motion over the nuts upon the bench. It looked so easy, yet when she tried the nuts shot off across the room, flying into dark corners she had to scrabble to retrieve them from. Around her, the stifled laughter of the servers made her blush. She tried again, more determined, watching how the others placed the whole weight of their bodies above the stone. She stood on tiptoe, trying to press down through her shoulders and arms, not just her hand. Slowly the movement came to her. Soon she was consumed by the tangy scent the paste gave off and her hands, too, were stained with yellow. As she worked, she followed the other activity around her, amazed by the quantity of toddy being made. There were many, many large pots of it—each one heated over the fireless stove until it boiled, then strained through cloth to cool and ferment in huge clay pots. So this was how the sacrificial toddy was made. It all made sense: the yellow staining on the hands; the yellow eyes. No one could make contact with this brew and be left unmarked.

What amazed her more than anything was how frequently the servers dipped into the fermenting brew and tasted it, just to check the mix was right. They obviously liked the stuff, their smiles and laughter increasing as the morning hurried on.

By the time Mother Jael called a halt for lunch, Maryam's arms ached from the effort. She scrubbed her hands to clear the stain, following Rebekah as the servers carried platters of the prepared food into the near-full dining room.

Once the Apostles and their families had been served, the others were allowed to sit. The babble stopped, as Father Joshua rose from his chair at the very centre of the room and raised his hand.

"Let us thank the Lord for our food." He led the blessing, his eyes sweeping the faces of those gathered while he recited the words. As his gaze fell on Maryam it stopped, boring into her with such intensity she felt her brain would burst. She tried to hold his stare but failed. Why did this man frighten her so? Was he not the Lamb's special chosen one? Mother Lilith sat next to him, and the way she leaned up close to him made Maryam wonder if she was his wife. Hushai had called her Holy Mother, she recalled.

She searched the room for Joseph. Lazarus was there, bending over a young server with a condescending smile that made the poor girl shrink and blush. And Joseph's mother, Deborah, pale and silent at the table where Father Joshua now sat. But there was no sign of the boy himself, and disappointment bruised Maryam's heart. He had shown such kindness at her plight.

Now the room surrendered to the clattering of cutlery on plates and relaxed talk, and Maryam quickly dug into her own food. The green plantain curry tasted wonderful, even better than the milder version Mother Evodia was so famous for back home. There was something about the gentle pervading heat of the food, together with the ordinary happy human noises of the room, which swept away Maryam's unease. This was how she'd dreamed it, full-bellied and happy in a room of such dimension and exotic decoration that she knew she'd Crossed over to the Lord's sacred house. Perhaps all that seemed to have befallen her since her arrival was a strange delusion caused by the drink? Maybe she had dreamed it all.

Even her imposed silence bothered her less, allowing her to meld into the group without the need for constant questioning or awkwardness. Mother Michal must have known this, and

Maryam was grateful now for the older woman's common sense. There was so much she did not yet fully understand—she had to trust that the Apostles knew what was best. After all, had they not picked her out as special when she was a tiny child? Why bother to raise her on the atoll, protected from the ravages of the Tribulation that still lingered on Onewēre, if they did not have her best interests at heart?

At the end of the meal, she helped the other kitchen servers clear the dishes from the room. Feeling the prickle of someone's gaze upon her, she turned to find Lazarus smirking at her from the doorway. He rubbed the place upon his cheek where she had slapped him, wagging an admonishing finger as he grinned. But there was nothing truly friendly in the smile and she turned away, refusing to respond. He was a tease, that was all. His words meant nothing: they were designed to scare a newcomer and make her doubt. But she was stronger than he thought—she would not allow his childish games to stir her now she'd survived the tests and been accepted to the flock.

Those tests had surely stripped her of vanity and pride and it occurred to her that, now the Apostles were convinced of her conviction, they would leave her be. Besides, with this beautiful and miraculous Holy City to serve in, how could she have ever doubted the Lamb's love?

*　*　*

Over the next three weeks Maryam settled in to her new life in the Holy City, waking each morning to collect the water for her bath before going about her kitchen chores amidst the chatter of the group. During the day her required silence didn't bother her, as the other servers seemed content merely with her smile. But she yearned for the closeness she'd once had with Ruth, missing their easy conversations. Rebekah could not fill this gap, refusing to communicate anything other than the task at hand. And so each night, as Maryam lay in bed and reflected back over the day, her mind would fill to overflowing with the host of thoughts and questions she'd been unable to express aloud.

She tried, each night, to take the soothing words of the Holy Book and make them real, but always her nagging doubts would crowd them out and leave her with a sense of unease—why had she been Chosen and what was her role? It was tempting, when her mind refused to still, to succumb to the anga kerea toddy and slip into a numbing sleep. But she fought it, paying heed to Hushai's warning and, instead, she'd often sneak up to the outer decks to take in the salty fresh sea air. This was foolish, she knew, and she made sure her late-night ramblings went unobserved.

One long hot afternoon, as she helped scrub taros and scale fish for the evening meal, she found the heat pressing down upon her—her eyes longing to droop shut and her hands fumbling in their menial jobs. She was struggling to lift a heavy water container when Mother Michal approached.

"Sister Maryam? I thought you'd like to know that Sister Ruth and Mother Elizabeth are to join us tomorrow—Ruth's bloods have come."

This news was like a gift straight from the Lord.

At last! Her dear friend and Mother Elizabeth, too! She clapped her hands, wishing she could let out an unholy yell. *Now* her life here would be happy and complete.

Mother Michal helped wrestle the huge container onto the

bench. "I'd like you to come with me now." She smiled at Maryam and winked. "I'm sure you will not mind if I drag you away!"

Maryam returned the smile, happy the tension she had sensed initially between them had now been erased. In fact, everyone seemed so much warmer now.

She waved goodbye to Rebekah and the others and followed Mother Michal out. Today she was relieved of chores, and then tomorrow she'd see Ruth! But as they traversed the endless corridors, Maryam began to ponder just what this imminent arrival would really mean. She'd have to get to Ruth before she, too, was thrown into the dreadful testing unaware.

Then she recognised where Mother Michal was leading her—back toward the hospital. Try as she might, she could not stem a sudden fear. What if Mother Lilith had found something wrong with her insides at the time of the examination? What if she was really sick? She longed to ask Mother Michal what lay in store, yet dared not break the rule of silence. Instead, she prayed frantically inside her head. *Merciful Lord, He who knows and sees all, please protect your little Sister . . .*

The words soothed her. When they reached the hospital corridor, Mother Michal turned. "The Lord has spoken to Father Joshua and told him how you're best to serve." She reached over and patted Maryam on the arm. "You are indeed lucky, child. The Lord has given you the power to heal."

To heal? If only she could ask what this meant, but Mother Michal led her now into a small stark room. All that it contained was a strange bed, elevated near the low ceiling, with one small chair and table at its side.

"Sit," Mother Michal gestured. "I will tell Mother Lilith you are here."

Perhaps, Maryam thought, she was to be trained in the ways of herbs and medicines by Mother Lilith, as Mother Evodia had been many years before? What a joy that would be, to bring an end to others' suffering and pain. This would make the tests worth it and must mean, surely, she had passed.

It was Hushai, not Mother Lilith, who now entered the room. "Ah, little Sister. I have feared that one day I would find you here."

"Feared?" Maryam whispered. There was no other way to communicate with him, as he could not see her face, and the urge to know of what he spoke was great.

The old man shuffled over to her, a cup in his hand. "I have nursed others who have been before you, and I fear the outcome is not good."

Panic broke over Maryam like a sudden wave. "Please, you must tell me all you know."

Hushai stood perfectly still, as though listening, before he spoke again. "We have little time. I have been instructed to give you this draught. It is strong enough to make you sleep. It is up to you to decide whether you will take it."

"What do you mean?"

"I cannot see, little one. But I know you have a questing heart. If you are brave enough . . ." he reached out, brushing her face with his long fingers, ". . . and I do believe you are, then you might discover what is going on here by feigning sleep and observing for yourself."

"But why do you fear that it is bad?"

The old man sighed. "Other Sisters have come before you to this room, and all eventually die."

"Die?" Had not Mother Michal said that she was destined to heal?

"You must decide, for soon they'll come. But I have reached an age where I can no longer sit silently by. I want to face the Lord with a clear conscience when I meet Him." He held the cup out to her, so close that she could smell the anga kerea paste. "It is your choice, Maryam. I will not blame you if you choose to hide in sleep."

She took the cup from him, shaking so badly that the liquid splashed on her hand, and started to sip the toddy, feeling how it burnt inside her mouth. No! Whatever the Lord now held in store for her, she would go forward with open eyes. She passed the cup back. "Take the drink. I will feign sleep." She could hardly say the words.

Hushai drank the toddy down in one. "My body is more used to this than you. Besides, I am an old man prone to drop-ping off—no one will guess." He pointed to the raised bed. "Climb up there and close your eyes. Whatever happens, do not let them know you hear." He drew her to him, gently embracing her. "My room is down the hall from here—Room five-five-two. Tonight, when all is silent, see if you can come to me and we will talk." This he whispered rapidly: voices now echoed from the corridor outside.

Maryam trembled as she climbed up. "I am frightened, Hushai," she whispered back. "I'm not brave."

The old man reached up and cupped her face. "There is more inside you than you know. Be still, child. I will wait nearby."

As the door handle turned, Maryam lay down quickly on the bed and closed her eyes. She tried to still her breathing, which was jagged now from real fear.

"Thank you, Hushai. You may leave now," she heard Mother Lilith say.

Maryam heard him shuffle from the room. Heard someone move toward her, then her wrist was grasped.

"Her pulse is running very fast," Mother Michal's voice seemed to boom.

"Probably chasing boys in her drunken dreams! You know how these native girls behave," Mother Lilith laughed. "Bring the trolley over here, beside the bed." Metallic rattling filled the air as something was wheeled across the room.

Maryam faked a sleepy sigh, turning her head toward the wall to hide the tears that leaked from her eyes. She had to concentrate not to give herself away. Why was the Lord doing this? Was her sin of doubting really so great that she must die?

Now Mother Lilith's voice cut through her frantic thoughts.

"Everything is ready now. Bring in the boy."

CHAPTER SEVEN

It was hard, concealing the fact that she could hear every little sound. One of the Mothers still remained, and Maryam could hear her preparing something on the trolley next to the raised bed. She focused on breathing, struggling to keep each breath smooth despite the hammering of her heart.

"Now, my dear," Mother Lilith muttered, "the work begins."

With this, Maryam felt Mother Lilith take her arm and stretch it down from the bed to dangle unprotected there. She fought the desire to snatch it back as Mother Lilith wiped the crook of her elbow with something cold and wet. Next, she felt a band being placed around her arm, pulled tight and then tighter still, to form a painful stranglehold around her bicep. She could feel her blood straining up against the fabric of the band, as Mother Lilith took her hand and pumped it into a firm fist. Then, before Maryam could prepare herself further, something sharp pricked through the fragile skin of her inner elbow. She startled as something burrowed into her pulsing, pressurised arm.

Mother Lilith laughed to herself, patting Maryam's fisted hand. "Sorry, little cherub—not even the toddy can completely numb you to such a jab!" Now she worked the object in deeper, as Maryam fought to keep control.

Rule One: There is but one thing in the world... She continued with her silent recitation as she felt the band release, her arm heating as blood flowed gratefully back down toward her tingling fingers. Mother Lilith now fastened whatever she'd inserted there in place, humming indistinctly.

"Here he is," Mother Michal's voice announced, and something else was wheeled into the room. Maryam longed to open her eyes, to find out what was going on, but didn't dare. She had no idea what they might do if they discovered she was still conscious.

"He is fully drugged?" Mother Lilith asked.

"Indeed. I made him drink the strongest brew—we should have at least two hours before he stirs."

"And Deborah?"

"Joshua has taken her to Onewēre overnight."

"Right then. The cannula is all in place here, so let's waste no time to hook him up."

Maryam's arm ached and her shoulder threatened to cramp in its awkward position. She listened to the undecipherable sounds, fearing what would happen next.

"Okay, it's in," Mother Lilith now said, and Maryam felt pressure as whatever was fixed to her arm was moved and stretched. "Easy does it—don't connect the other end until I've drawn more through."

Maryam heard a sucking noise, and then a faint tinkle as liquid flowed into a dish.

"It seems a little thick," Mother Michal commented. "Are you sure she had the proper doses of toddy to thin down her blood?"

"She wouldn't be passively lying here if not," Mother Lilith replied. "But I do agree with you, it's definitely slow. I told Joshua the girl was risky—late bloods, undersized and a womb that will never birth a child . . . we may as well get the most out of her while we can. I don't think she will last too long."

To hear herself so described, as if she were nothing more than the still-twitching organs of a sacrificial goat inspected for a reading by the village chief, left Maryam unnerved. *Never birth a child?* How strange that hearing this should hurt so much.

"Okay now, let's join them up." Mother Lilith's voice was tense with concentration as Maryam felt more tugging on the device—the cannula—inside her arm. It didn't exactly hurt now, just throbbed dully in time to her fast-beating heart.

"There, it's in." Mother Lilith's voice relaxed. "Given that her flow is slow, I'd say we leave it in for an hour."

"A whole hour?" Mother Michal asked. "Surely that will take too much."

"Joshua's orders were explicit. He wants the boy saved, despite the foolishness of both his parents. If the girl does not last the distance, others must be sacrificed to take her place."

"I don't know who. We've had so many losses lately and that stupid girl Sarah is no longer suitable. She has the look of death upon her—I don't think she'll last the night. And nearly all the others are with child."

Sarah might not last the night? Maryam just managed to stifle a gasp. So she was right: Sarah was very sick indeed. As she pictured Sarah's weeping wound, Maryam's stomach did a frightened lurch. That wound, the place from which it radiated, was identical in position to the cannula inside her own arm.

"Perhaps we will have to consider using the male servers— I've never understood why Joshua's so adamant to spare them," Mother Michal said.

Mother Lilith laughed. "The girls are so much easier to manage. The last thing we can afford is an uprising among the men." Her voice grew more distant: perhaps she had moved somewhere across the room. "This should go smoothly enough now. I'll go and check the other patients if you don't mind waiting here?"

"That's fine," Mother Michal replied. "I've brought the Holy Book to read."

Maryam heard Mother Lilith leave the room and the turning of pages as Mother Michal settled down to read. She waited for what seemed an age, daring not to move or to alert Mother Michal to her conscious state. Then, when she could contain herself no longer, she slowly—silently—moved her head to face the room.

She cracked open her eyes a fraction, focusing first on the plain white wall opposite. Then she peered down at her aching arm. At the crook of her elbow, the needle-like cannula disappeared into her skin. From its other end a clear tube extended, and through it she could see her own blood flowing from her arm. She carefully tracked the tube, alert to any movement from Mother Michal. There appeared to be some kind of regulator that controlled the direction of the flow, and further down a strange bulb-like attachment and then more tube. Her blood gleamed crimson and it scared her to see this precious substance drawn from her body in such a steady flow.

Then the hairs on the back of her neck sprang up as she saw the boy Joseph lying there as still as death, her blood pouring into his veins through a needle in his arm. And worse, from his other prone arm, his own blood flowed away into a bowl. What were they doing, pumping her precious life blood into him? Surely *this* was not the gift of healing Father Joshua had consigned her to? How could this be part of the Lord's loving plan?

Mother Michal stirred and Maryam quickly closed her

eyes. She heard a door opening and a new voice spoke. "Mother Michal, Mother Lilith asked if you could leave for a moment and come with me. Three more patients have arrived and we're short of hands."

"Of course," Mother Michal responded, and the chair scraped as she rose.

Maryam waited for the sound of retreating footsteps before she risked opening her eyes again. Indeed the room was empty now, except for Joseph and her. She leaned out from the raised bed to study his sleeping face. The deep purple bruises of sickness under each eye were stark against his pasty skin. And the first angry whorls of Te Matee Iai mottled the boy's long neck. This realisation staggered her—had not the Lord granted the Apostles reprieve from this? Yet she knew the signs. Had seen others submit to its grasp. Like Joseph's father . . . perhaps she *had* seen the fatal signs on Father Jonah after all.

Joseph mumbled in his toddy-induced sleep, lines of worry creasing his brow. He was handsome, Maryam conceded—not in the broad glowing way of native boys, but his nose was thin and straight and his lips, though pale, were full and soft. And, beneath the long pale eyelashes she knew his eyes were striking blue. Such a waste to see his life hang in the balance like this, and yet . . . surely they would not save him at her expense?

Fear pressed in. It seemed to be true, from the words of the two Mothers, and the proof that pumped her blood away. He was the son of an Apostle, after all. For all she knew he was already old enough to be made one of their leaders. Yet had not the Holy Book said that all would be equal under the Lord's gaze? None of this made any sense. It scared her, tied as she was to the circulation of another, to think that the sacrifice of the

Rules was not some vague term for humility and commitment, but real death. One thing she was sure of: she was not yet ready for her life to end.

She turned her attention to the cannula in her arm. What would be the dangers of tearing it out? Would she be able to stem the flow of blood—to heal the wound? And where could she run once it was out? There was nowhere to escape to: the Apostles swarmed the ship and even on land their control stretched from one end of the island to the other. Besides, would her removal of the cannula doom the kind-spirited boy to die? There was so much to think through; so much she still did not understand. But she did not need the Rules or the Holy Book to tell her what was right or wrong. *This* was wrong. The callousness in Mother Lilith's voice and Mother Michal's blind acceptance of what went on.

She had no further chance to study her situation open-eyed. Footsteps sounded again and Maryam lay back, willing her breath to slow, as Mother Michal approached the beds, a sigh escaping her. "Don't give up, young man," she cooed to the unconscious Joseph. "With luck we'll have you strong and healthy once again."

Such concern made Maryam want to scream. Where were these same words for her? She longed to see Mother Elizabeth, sure she could offer comfort and advice. And Ruth, her little Sister, somehow she must save her from this life—and likely death.

The room grew stiflingly quiet, as Mother Michal settled back in with her Holy Book. Maryam fought to focus, to plan. But the more blood was stolen from her, the more she grew light-headed and struggled to think. She felt as though all life, all hope, was draining from her. Her head grew dizzier, her heart-rate stampeding. And it grew cold, so cold, despite the sweat that broke out on her skin. She began to shiver, hearing from a great distance as Mother Michal quickly rose to check on her. But then her world diffused to black.

* * *

She was back in her own small room, she realised. Beyond, the ship lay silent, and she guessed it was now late at night.

She tried to stand, dizziness nearly driving her back to the bed. But she supported herself along the wall, making her way through to the bathroom to relieve her burning thirst. The water tasted stale and flat.

Her legs had turned to jellyfish, it seemed, and she slid down the smooth wall tiles, landing with a bump upon the cold stone floor. How was she to escape this nightmare? She had to speak to someone, anyone who could answer the questions and fears that seared her mind. Then old Hushai's words came back to her—*come to me and we will talk*—and she determined, now, to seek him out. He alone had seemed concerned about what took place there in that terrible room. He would know what to do next.

The light-headedness swept over her as she stood once more. Only by edging her way along the walls, stopping every few steps, did she reach her bedroom door. It was locked: she was an animal trapped inside a cage. She rattled the cursed door handle, willing someone—anyone—to aid her plight. Perhaps if she could wake Rebekah. . . . She summoned up her strength and called as loudly as she dared. "Sister Rebekah, are you awake?"

Somewhere in the bowels of the great ship something knocked and clanked, but from the door across the corridor no sound emerged.

"Rebekah! Please!" Desperation sharpened her voice and like a fish spear it pierced the wooden door, crossed the empty corridor and somehow found its way to Rebekah's ear.

"What? What?"

Hearing Rebekah's sleepy voice, Maryam risked calling once more. "Help, Rebekah!" Her heart beat wildly inside her chest: others might wake. But she could not stay caged up in here, that much she knew. Sinking down beside the doorframe, she heard Rebekah emerge and try the door handle.

"It's locked!" Rebekah whispered through the keyhole. "What is wrong?"

"I need help," Maryam whispered back, her apprehension rising at the thought of others being roused. "Please. Get me out."

"I'll find Mother Michal—"

"No!" Maryam rose to her knees. "Please, it's you I need. Just get the key."

"I don't know where it's kept. I don't—" Rebekah's voice trailed off.

"Rebekah, listen to me." Maryam ran her eyes around the doorframe, desperate for an idea. The door hinges were cut neatly into the frame and, unless the door was open, could not be reached. Come on, come on, there *had* to be something. Then her gaze returned to the lock. Maybe some kind of tool—a bone hairpin, a knife, a fork . . . "Do you have anything long and thin inside your room? A hairpin or a knife perhaps?"

"Knife?" Rebekah giggled. "No."

Maryam wanted to shriek at her. Wake up! Instead she bit back her frustration and kept her voice low. "Anything else?"

"Um . . . um . . ." Rebekah seemed to be muttering to herself.

"What did you say?"

"Mother Michal will be angry if I let you out." Her voice sounded slurred and strange. "I cannot help you, Maryam; go back to bed."

"You don't understand, I—"

Rebekah cut back in, her disinterest slicing through the void. "Take some more of the toddy, Maryam, so you can sleep. I left some by your bedside when I collected mine." With that, she returned to her own bedroom and closed the door.

So that was it—the toddy kept them tame and dosed up to the point of helplessness. Maryam felt a rage building inside her. She hauled herself upward, grabbing for the offending door handle. She closed her eyes, breathing deeply against the dizziness. She had to do this; had to find something to free the lock. But what? There was nothing in this room except the few mementos she had brought. Her clothes, the stone from Ruth, the albatross feather . . . that was it! She stumbled over to the bedside table and opened the drawer.

The central spine of the feather was thick and strong, and she flexed it in her fingers to assess its worth. Maybe it would work . . . it *had* to work. She returned to the door and inserted the shaft into the lock. Jiggled it. Spun it around. But it merely passed through to the other side, not catching on the mechanism that could set her free. It needed to be hooked and curved. She drew it back toward her, angling the feather so the shaft bent in toward the lock. Pushed it hard, feeling the shaft resist as it twisted into the narrow opening. Now, again, she jiggled it, and could feel the resistance as it slid around within the space. Metal shifted inside the workings of the lock but nothing seemed to make it work.

Just as she was about to give up, the lock clicked. She breathed out her relief and tentatively opened the door. She crept out of the room, listening for a hint of noise, but nothing stirred. Rebekah, obviously, had fallen straight back into her drugged sleep.

The effort of unlocking the door had sapped Maryam's strength, and she had to force herself along the corridor, where the snores of others combined to form a rumbling harmony. She worked her way back to the dreaded hospital wing, relying on the handrails for support.

The atrium stairwell in sight, she heard laughter from an upper floor. She slunk back into the shadows, head thudding. The great atrium dome rippled and swam in the reflections off the water, refracted through the banks of windows from the distant sea below. It might have been beautiful at other times, but now it just reminded Maryam of how far away she was from land. She doubted she could walk the length of the causeway, even if it were not guarded as she suspected. The vapid moon now lit her way and she mustered up her energy for a dash to the stairs.

The effort nearly finished her, and she sagged down inside the stairwell to regain some semblance of strength, gasping like a fish beached in the sun. Perhaps it was too late already to seek Hushai's help?

Precious minutes fled, then she struggled on. Somewhere above her, late-night conversation trickled through the warm still air, but she could neither decipher the words nor identify who spoke. She wove down to the lower deck, clinging to the shadows as she edged along the narrow corridor. Which number had he said? Five-five-what? It would not come to her and the proximity of the blood-letting room pushed all logic from her mind. Would Joseph still be in there? Had his life been saved? It mattered badly to her now—he shared her blood. But would he even know of this? From what she could recall of the Mothers' conversation, she reckoned not.

She could not resist the room. So slowly that no one could have detected it, she cracked open the door. The trolley that he'd lain upon remained inside, and no one was in the room besides an unmoving figure upon the bed. She crept in, drawn to it despite her fear, and there he lay. Even in the scrap of light from the high window she could see that the whorls upon Joseph's neck seemed somewhat faded and his brow was now smooth. But he lay there so silent, she could not tell if he breathed. Gently, like a night moth resting on a leaf, she laid her hand upon his chest. Yes, it rose and fell. For this she felt ridiculously pleased. To have forfeited her blood to him, then have him die, would have been terrible.

She was impelled to draw his fine blond hair away from his eyes, and her fingers brushed his pale skin. His eyes shot open.

"Holy—" Maryam bit back her shock, terrified she might alert someone to her presence. His eyes remained fixed on her.

"You!" he mouthed, his voice constricted in his throat. His blue eyes bound her there. He tried to shift upon the bed but could not move. "Will you release the straps?" he begged in a whisper that, to Maryam, seemed to boom out like a conch shell call.

"Straps?" Tentatively she raised the sheet, mortified to see that all he wore was a ragged pair of shorts. But she tried to put this from her mind as she noticed how his arms and legs were strapped in place. He, too, was trapped.

Embarrassment burning her face, she fumbled with the restraints, trying to avoid any further contact with his skin. As the final strap fell away he tried to rise. She knew, by the way his eyes were unfocused, that he, too, was dizzy and disoriented. She offered him her hand, carefully helping him up. As she did so, the sleeve of her plain nightgown rolled back to reveal the bandage on her arm.

Joseph's eyes locked on this. "What did they do to you?" he gasped, and the mystification in his voice confirmed that he had no idea what had really taken place.

Somewhere close by a door slammed shut and Maryam jumped. "I have to go," she whispered urgently. "If I am caught . . ." She let the consequences go unspoken, unsure where his loyalties lay.

"But, Sister Maryam—" He reached out for her but she was too fast for him, even in her weakened state.

She plunged back into the dark corridor, desperately trying to dredge Hushai's room number up from her mind. Five-five-zero? Five-five-one? Five-five-two? Five-five-three? It was no use: she would have to try a door.

With her heart beating so hard its sound must surely penetrate the sleeping night, she drew a breath and took a chance, carefully opening the one door whose number seemed to ring some tiny bell inside her head.

CHAPTER EIGHT

It was so quiet, at first she thought the room was empty. But as she leaned against the door, her heart still knocking wildly against her ribs, her eyes adjusted to the gloom and she saw that someone lay upon the bed. It was impossible to tell if it was Hushai, unless she risked a closer look. But what if she had chosen the wrong room and now accidentally roused someone else? What would they do?

She stilled herself, listening past her own jagged breathing to catch the pattern of the other's breath. It was so shallow, so weak, she had to strain to hear it at all. Despite her fear, she edged nearer, willing her eyes to pick up clues. Long tangled hair straggled out across the pillow: the sleeper here was Sister Sarah.

Sarah's eyelids fluttered, as though she see-sawed between wakefulness and sleep. Her forehead was slicked with sweat and her face, despite her naturally brown skin, was hauntingly pale. As Maryam watched, it contorted in a spasm and Sarah moaned.

Maryam could not resist the urge to reach out for her hand to comfort her. "It's all right, Sarah. I am here."

The other girl's eyes slowly blinked open. "Maryam?" Her voice was little more than a painful wheeze.

"Shall I fetch you something?"

"No! Please, do not call the Mothers in." She shuddered, trying and failing to wriggle up the bed a little. Maryam reached behind to support Sarah's bony spine as she propped her up against the pillows. Mother Michal was right. Death perched on Sarah's shoulder like a greedy frigate bird waiting to steal another's catch.

Sarah watched Maryam as if drinking her in, her gaze dropping to the bandage on Maryam's arm. "Oh no," she groaned. "They have bled you, too."

Despite Sarah's obvious exhaustion, Maryam was desperate to discover more. "You must tell me what you know."

Sarah closed her eyes. When, finally, she spoke, her words came out in a rush. "We're nothing more than slaves to them—they suck our blood to preserve their lives."

"But why should the Apostles need our blood? They have shelter, food, water to drink. And are we not told the Lord has blessed them with freedom from the plague—"

"It isn't true," Sarah cut in, struggling for breath. "They've lied to us, Maryam. They are no more resistant to Te Matee Iai then you or me. It's *our* blood that sustains them."

"I don't understand. Why, then, would the Lord let them do this to us? It is wrong."

Sarah's thin laugh reduced to a retching cough. She closed her eyes, as though willing up the strength to continue. When she did, anger forced the words from her. "We're merely stupid animals in their eyes. Most they pluck at puberty and force to lie with male servers to increase their stock of useful blood. Others, like you and me, they just bleed dry."

So Maryam's fears were confirmed, though the lessons of her childhood were hard to set aside: "But we are the Chosen—the Blessed Sisters . . ." Even though Sarah's words backed up all her private fears, to hear them said aloud made it all the more impossible to comprehend.

"Think back to the Judgements, Maryam. What was Father

Joshua testing us for? Choosing us for? Our special blood. We have some magic that makes it safe to share our blood." Her hand, no more substantial than bleached fingers of sea fan coral, reached out and raked down Maryam's arm. "That is why they bring us here. The men to serve, to run the ship and breed more bloodstock, while the women merely breed or bleed."

Like the words Lazarus used. *Are you a breeder or a bleeder?* Now she understood. And her luck, it seemed, was against her—deemed too small and possibly deformed to birth a child, she was doomed to bleed.

"I am going to die soon, Maryam," Sarah said, her head sinking back on the pillow.

"No!" her friend whispered urgently.

Sarah's cold fingers wrapped around Maryam's hand. "It is too late for me. I want to go." She sighed. "But you, Maryam, should flee. Don't let them do this to you too."

Maryam swept this impossibility aside and asked, instead, the burning question. "How is it that our blood protects them? I have seen our own Sisters die—we're not immune."

Sarah bit her lip, trying to slow her ragged breathing. "Not immune. No. But the plague robs them of something important in their blood. They use ours to replace theirs."

There was a gasp from the doorway. Maryam jumped to her feet, to fight or flee if necessary. But the sudden movement churned her brain, and she staggered, her eyes locked on Joseph's face.

"That's what they did? Gave me your blood?"

"Get out," Maryam hissed. "Your presence puts us both at risk."

She tried to push him from the room but he raised his

hands, holding his ground. "I never knew," he whispered. "You have to believe me."

Behind them Sarah coughed and great spasms wracked her whole body. Maryam turned back to the bed. "What can I do to help you, Sarah?"

Her friend struggled to breathe. Sweat now poured from her, drenching the pillow and trickling down her brows like tears. "Please," she begged. "Just help me get up to the deck, to open air."

Maryam hesitated. What would the Apostles do, if they were found wandering the ship?

"I will take you," Joseph's voice broke through her indecision. He stepped closer, steadier now upon his feet.

Sarah made to rise, but clearly both Maryam and Joseph would be needed. "I will help," Maryam said.

One either side of Sarah, they supported her as she tentatively tried to stand. Up close she smelt stale and sickeningly sweet, as though her body had already begun its final journey back to earth. Although she was as light as a small child, they laboured to hold her upright, and Maryam felt the drain upon her own strength as she helped Sarah shuffle toward the door.

At the door Joseph stepped forward to check that their way was clear. The corridor was still in darkness, and nothing stirred. "This will be hard," he murmured to Maryam. "The stairs will be our biggest challenge if we want to get her to the forward deck."

"Are you sure that's safe?" Maryam asked. This was crazy, all three escaping from their personal prisons with no guarantee of remaining free. But she could understand Sarah's need, having lived beneath these low ceilings—with no sky, no stars, no breeze to whisper of the sea's vast wealth.

"No," Joseph snapped. "Do you have a better plan?" Between them, Sarah's breaths transformed to straining grunts and Maryam sensed that they had little time to reach the air.

"No need to bite," she batted back at him. "I'm just not sure she'll make it up."

Their eyes met across Sarah's pale face and Maryam, though flinching from his glare, raised her chin defiantly.

"What in the name of the Lamb is going on? Who is there?" The voice behind them jolted Maryam and Joseph so they nearly lost their grip on Sarah.

As Joseph battled to raise her again, Maryam swung around, ready to take the consequences. There in the gloom of the corridor stood Hushai, and Maryam was so relieved she nearly wept.

"Hushai! It's Maryam. I have Sister Sarah here . . ."

"And I am Joseph, Jonah's boy."

The old man walked toward them, still ruffled from sleep. "What are you doing, child?" His hands spread before him and reached out for Sarah's drooping head. One hand lit upon her forehead, before sliding gently down her neck to rest at the place where her pulse beat swift and shallow, like the fast-winged fluttering of a small witata honeyeater as it fed. Whatever he discovered there did not please him, his wrinkled face folding into a frown. "This girl needs to be in bed. Are you both mad?"

"Please, Hushai, it is Sarah's wish to breathe fresh air." *Last wish*, Maryam tried to project to him. She feared they would not reach their goal before Sarah's fragile life snuffed out.

For long seconds Hushai's fogged eyes just stared at them, his head tipped to one side as though he listened for some secret message. Then he sighed, his whole body sagging. "You will never reach the upper deck without detection. Follow me; I'll guide you to a safe place closer to here." He quickly turned, not waiting for their response.

Maryam met Joseph's eye, and he nodded. Together, they supported Sarah down the increasingly dark corridor. Hushai, in the lead, had the advantage here, somehow able to negotiate the twists and turns of the ship's maze-like layout without the need for working eyes. Maryam and Joseph struggled to keep up.

Sarah's legs dragged like anchor stones, weighing her down toward the depths. Only willpower and the fear of discovery enabled Maryam to continue buttressing her. Maryam's jaw ached from gritting her teeth and her muscles cramped from need of rest. All the while a hard knot of knowledge formed deep inside her—one day soon the dying Sister might be her.

Finally Hushai stopped before a metal door. He spun the rusted wheel that held it shut and then heaved it open, the rush of fresh air coming as welcome relief. They lifted Sarah across the raised threshold, out onto a long open deck. Maryam recognised the space, a wide slot that ran below the window line halfway up the ship's great hull.

"Once the lifeboats were housed here," Hushai explained. "After the Tribulation many of the passengers took the boats and tried to return home. It is thought that all were lost in the wild storms that spat from the sky—only the shattered debris of the boats ever returned." He removed the fraying jacket he wore and spread it on the deck beside the wall. "Lay Sister Sarah down over here."

They lowered her as gently as they could, but Sarah still cried out as she sank toward the cold hard deck. Maryam huddled down beside her, so Sarah could lean against her to view the sea. A crescent moon hung above the highest peak of Onewēre, its soft light painting silver highlights on the rippled sea. Although not cold, the breeze brought the crisp salty freshness of the sea air in to them, to overlay the dank tang of rotting steel. It nipped around them, tingling skin grown stale from the confines of the ship. But Sarah shivered now, unable to control the spasms as her limbs began their slow dance with death.

Hushai bent down and again checked her vital signs, shaking his head at what he found. "I must go and check the other patients—it is time. But then I will return and you two must go before the morning comes."

"There are others?" Maryam felt compelled to ask. How many more were shut in claustrophobic rooms, waiting for the end to come?

"Many, child. Some fight Te Matee Iai—the fallout of the Tribulation—while others succumb to the usual illnesses and injuries of any group. And then there are the Blessed, who suffer from the Lord's secret plan."

"What do you mean?" Joseph's voice was taut.

Hushai held out a hand to halt more questions. "There is much to learn if you seek it, Brother Joseph. But now is not the best of times. I will return as quickly as I can." He left, carefully sealing the door behind him.

Sarah groaned, driving all other problems from Maryam's mind. If there was nothing she could do to save Sarah or ease her pain, then at least she could make her last moments less frightening and alone. She wrapped her arms around Sarah's frail shoulders, trying to transfer some of her own body heat to her.

Sarah's eyes were fixed on the stars that looked down from the endless sky. "What do you think will happen to me when

I die?" she whispered, her voice barely more than a prolonged sigh.

"The Lord will welcome you to Heaven," Maryam replied, trying to keep her voice free of doubt.

Sarah turned her tired eyes to Maryam. "There is no God."

Maryam's mouth dropped open in surprise. Never had she heard such sacrilegious words. What really shocked her was the tiny voice inside her head that chortled in dangerous revolt. And the realisation that if the Lord indeed did live through the Apostles, then He was complicit in their acts.

But she must block these thoughts: He would know, would hear her doubt and condemn her to the fires of Hell.

She glanced at Joseph, now settled on Sarah's other side. How would the privileged son of an Apostle react to this?

"Whatever befalls you, Sister Sarah," he softly said, "it will be better and kinder than what you have experienced here."

Maryam met the sadness in his eyes and nodded her thanks.

Joseph gently took Sarah's hand in his. Looking up at the stars he said, "My father once told me of your ancestors' creation myth, before the first missionaries arrived here with the word of the Lord. He told me Nareau the Creator ordered Na Atibu, who was stone, to lie with Nei Teakea, the Emptiness, and bear a son—Nareau the Wise. Together, then, they worked to give light to the newly separated world. But it was not an easy task for Nareau the Wise—he had to slay his father, who was filled with light. Then he plucked out his father's right eye and threw it up toward the east, to form the sun. The left eye he cast up into the western sky to make the moon, in order to reflect the sun's great light. And, finally, the ribs he scattered in the sky, where they splintered into minute particles to form the stars."

"I like that," Sarah murmured. "Perhaps I, too, will become a star." Tears streamed down her cheeks as a spasm shuddered through her body. She turned her head to Maryam. "Watch for me, Maryam. When you look up to the stars for help, I will be there."

Her eyes drooped shut, her breath coming in ever more shallow bursts. She reached out with her free hand, urging Maryam to take the fragile fingers in her own. "I am so sorry I didn't warn you," she said. "It was—" Whatever she had meant to say was swept away by another painful spasm.

Maryam didn't know what to say. Should she try to recall the passages Father Joshua had recited at the funeral for Jonah? Or the lessons Mother Elizabeth had taught inside the maneaba? Something soothing and appropriate to light the way? *To everything there is a season, and a time to every purpose under Heaven* . . . But the words simply did not fit. There was no season, no purpose, to Sarah's death.

She glanced at Joseph, wondering how he could sit there so calmly when his people had been party to this crime.

His eyes were closed, she saw, and his head slumped back against the wall. He sniffed quietly, then sniffed again, and she realised with amazement that he was crying. The memory of his grief at his father's death came back to her. Whatever part his family played in this wicked plan, it was obvious he had a heart, one that was hurting as much as hers—maybe more. And despite her blood pumping through his veins, he had the curse of Te Matee Iai upon him. She turned from him—willing the ball of anger in her chest to roll away.

Behind them, the wheel mechanism on the door started to turn and, before they could react, Hushai's soothing voice called through. "It is just me, Sister Maryam. Do not fear."

He stepped onto the deck, balancing an armload of blankets and a drinking cup. Without a word, Hushai, Maryam and Joseph worked together to cushion Sarah more comfortably and wrap her warmly. Then, Hushai crouched down beside her and raised the cup to Sarah's lips. "Drink this, little Sister. It will help."

Maryam could smell the toddy as Sarah tried to drink. She retched on it, barely able to swallow even the smallest sips.

Maryam could not contain the repulsion she felt for the numbing toddy. "Is it wise to give her that?" she asked, hating all the implications of its use.

"It will do her no more harm, little one. All we can do for Sister Sarah now is ease her way."

When Sarah had drunk all she could, her breathing grew less forced and the tight lines of pain upon her face began to smooth.

Now Hushai turned to Maryam. "You must go before your disappearance is discovered." He looked over at Joseph. "You as well. I will stay with Sister Sarah until her time."

The thought that she was now to walk away, leaving Sarah to her death, hit Maryam hard. Suddenly her birth mother's face came to mind: the warm honey of her eyes, the mouth that cried Maryam's real name as she was taken . . . She leaned down to Sarah and kissed her tenderly upon each cheek. "Do you remember your birth parents, Sarah? Do you still know the name they gave to you when you were born?"

Sarah's eyes did not open and her head shook slightly as though trying to find the words. Then, as Maryam feared she would not have the strength to answer, her words came out in a drowsy hush. "Tekeaa . . . My mother was from the village of Aneaba, in the south." Her eyes fluttered open for a second, meeting Maryam's. "The same as yours."

Maryam blinked. Her family came from Aneaba? She never knew. But the opportunity for further questioning was gone—that time was past. Maryam pressed her cheek against Sarah's, whispering into her ear. "Goodbye, Tekeaa. I will find your family somehow, and tell them of your goodness and strength." With one final embrace, she pushed herself upright, fighting the vertigo inside her head.

She longed now to put this dreadful scene behind her, but she must thank Hushai first. She leaned over to the old man, kissing his craggy cheek. "Hushai. You've been so very kind."

He reached up and cupped her face in his dry long-fingered hand. "You, too, must rest now, little one. Your life force is very weak." He squeezed her chin between thumb and forefinger. "If ever you should need someone and I am not able to assist you, go to Mark. You can trust him with your life."

She nodded, tears sliding down her cheeks as the dam inside her throat was breached. Stepping in through the metal door, she leaned against the cold damp walls of the corridor. She was so tired.

Then Hushai stood in the doorway, with Joseph close behind. "One more thing, Sister. You learnt the secret of the room?"

Maryam nodded, taking one of his hands and placing it over the needle site upon her arm. "They steal blood. They suck it right out of our veins and pump it straight back into theirs." It was impossible to keep the bitterness from her voice, and she dared not look past him to Joseph's face. "Our blood is what saves them from Te Matee Iai."

The old man sighed. "So, it is truly as I feared."

He left her then, returning to Sarah's side. But Joseph

stepped across the doorway and stood before Maryam. His face was white as coral sand, the disgust in his eyes clouding the blue. "So my recovery was the final insult that has brought about Sister Sarah's death?"

Maryam stared at him, confused as to what he meant. Then it struck her. He did not know the blood was hers. He thought that Sarah was the donor, that the responsibility for her death was his. What a weight for him to bear. But right now she could not deal with his guilt as well. She walked away, desperate to reach her bed.

"Sister Maryam. Wait!" He followed her, dragging at her arm. "Tell me. I must know the truth."

She shook away his hand and faced him squarely. Would he *really* want to know? "No, Brother Joseph. The blood they stole to give to you was not from her." She saw the faint spark of relief light his eyes and raised her arm, baring the incriminating bandage. "The blood they stole came straight from me."

The look of horror in his eyes helped a little to warm her heart. At least he did not take for granted that her life was worth less than his. "I'm so, so sorry," he mumbled. "I had no conscious part in this."

"Please," she said, "go to your room and try to hide the fact that you have been released. I need to rest and neither of us can risk being found like this." She did not wait for him to respond, just charged down the corridor as fast as her exhausted body would allow.

Joseph pursued her, his footsteps loud in the silence of the night. "Maryam, wait!" His voice reached out tendrils of need that tugged at her. "Will you at least meet with me tomorrow so we can talk?"

"All right," she snapped. "All right. But you must find a way to come to me."

With that she turned away again. She had to leave now, had to get back to her room, before she drowned in the grief she felt at watching Sarah as she died.

CHAPTER NINE

Maryam woke to the sound of a key turning in her bedroom door, which she had carefully relocked on her return the night before. But no one came, and she closed her eyes again, tiredness pressing down on her like heavy air before a storm.

She knew, without being told, that Sarah's life had ended—yet the tears she cried last night had purged her of the worst of the pain and left her calm. Today, Ruth and Mother Elizabeth would come. Somehow she must speak with them, no matter how costly the price.

Her mind played touch-tag with the information Sarah had gifted her, the name of the village from which she came. It made sense to her in retrospect, how she had felt an almost physical reaction to the tattoos of the servers from Aneaba, as though somewhere in her earliest memories she had known them. But it disturbed her to know this fact, drawing all the longing and uncertainty back to her mind. Was her birth mother still alive and living there, believing that her daughter was better off in the care of the Apostles? That she was Blessed?

"Morning!" Rebekah pushed open the door and carried in a breakfast tray. She smiled brightly, registering no hint of what had taken place between the two the night before. "Mangoes and pawpaw for breakfast, then Mother Michal wants you back at work in the kitchens to help with lunch." She slid the tray onto the bedside table and pointed at the brimming cup of toddy. "Remember to drink it all—it'll help the day pass easier." She made to leave, managing to avoid Maryam's gaze.

"Rebekah, wait!" There was no way she would defer to Mother Michal's instructions to be silent now. There was too much at stake; too much that she had to know. Maryam swung her legs out of bed, swaying a little as she sat upright. Despite her sleep, she still felt drained and very weak. "Did you know that Sarah died?"

The girl's eyes clouded, a gust of pain stirring her face. But seconds later it was replaced by what looked like a well practised smile. "*Rule Seven*," she chanted. "*Like the Lamb who suffered for us, we too must suffer in silence and pledge our obedience to the Lord and his Apostles of the Lamb.*"

Maryam gaped at Rebekah, astounded by her lack of grief. "That's it? You hear your friend has died and you smile?"

Her scorn dealt the desired blow: Rebekah reeled, her compliant façade slipping just long enough to reveal her fear. "We must not speak of this," she whispered urgently. "Punishment for lack of obedience is most severe—and Mother Michal has especially warned me not to speak with you." She checked over her shoulder, as if she expected Mother Michal to pounce right then, and crept in close to Maryam's side. "There is only one way to survive this, Maryam—and that's to close your eyes and ears and do precisely as you're told. Believe me, there's no other choice." She shuddered, viscerally underlining the dread behind her words.

"But don't you—"

Rebekah cut through Maryam's question with an angry stroke of her arm. "Don't. We will not speak of this again." She took a deep breath, pasting the smile back on her face. "See you in the kitchen soon."

Maryam stared after Rebekah's retreating back, considering

the barrier she had placed between them. There was no denying
Rebekah's fear—and no point at all in trying to shake her from
the web of compliance she'd spun around herself to survive. But
she did not blame Rebekah, she realised with surprise. Each of
them must find a way to be safe—it was just she didn't understand how Rebekah could manage to block the outrage, doubt,
and disillusion from her mind. If only it was that easy. . . . Then
Maryam recalled the yellow-staining toddy. It seemed most had
chosen submission to its stupefying effects, rather than living
with any clear-eyed view of life aboard *Star of the Sea*. And it
made good sense not to rock the boat, even if the boat was
nothing but a rotten wreck. It was safer, no doubt of that, and
helped to dull reality that could not be changed. In a way she
was jealous, wishing she could block the rising tide of indignation from her mind as easily as others here.

For now, though, it was all that she could manage to dress
herself and take the empty water bucket down to the noisy
service deck. Her head still fought off dizzying fatigue as she
filled the bucket with fresh water and hauled it back upstairs.
Four times she had to stop for breath, her heart beating so stri-
dently it seemed to bruise her chest. But at the foot of the final
run of stairs she felt the weight drop away, as someone lifted
the burden from her failing grasp. She turned, meeting Brother
Mark's shy smile.

"Let me help you, little Sister," the big man offered, the
bucket handle a mere thread in his hands.

"Thank you," Maryam responded, resisting the desire to
cry. This random act of kindness almost undid her, twisting the
cold hands of loneliness and isolation tight around her throat.
She followed him, unable to keep up with his long loping

gait. He seemed to know which room was hers, striding down the low musty corridor and setting the bucket down carefully outside her door.

"Thank you," she murmured again. "That's very kind."

He shrugged, acknowledging her words, but his face revealed a wistful sadness. "I have a message for you, Sister, from our friend Hushai. Sister Sarah is released."

Maryam nodded, allowing his words to settle on her. Whatever evils Sarah had suffered in this so-called Holy City, at least now she was free of fear, her spirit up there with the stars. "I thought as much."

She laid her small hand on Brother Mark's arm, remembering the risk Hushai had taken to help her ease poor Sarah's way. "And Hushai? My—his—actions have not brought him harm?"

Brother Mark's lips grew tight and thin and she worried she had said too much. There was no one she could really trust, until she finally made contact with Mother Elizabeth and Ruth.

"His actions have been noted and his rations cut," he said.

"But that's so—so wrong!" The words flew out before Maryam could restrain them. She felt heat flood her face. What if Brother Mark reported her? Or Mother Michal overheard?

The big man's yellow-tinged eyes searched out her own and held them, transmitting his silent agreement. He stooped down and whispered into her ear. "Be very careful, little Sister, what you say."

With a quick check over his shoulder to make sure they were unobserved he took her hand, cupping it inside his own great paw. "Hushai was right about you. You have the strength of our ancestors in your soul." He squeezed her hand, drawing her gaze back to his worried eyes. "Promise me this one thing: let no man crush that strength, no matter how hard they might try."

How easily he said the words. But did she really have the choice?

*   *   *

After she had washed and dressed, Maryam made her way up to the kitchen to begin her chores. She kept a wary eye out for Joseph, wondering what she would say to him if he appeared. He seemed so genuine, so deeply shocked by what he saw. Yet he had lived inside *Star of the Sea* for his whole life, had he not? Surely he had some notion of what was taking place on board? Was he truly blind to it, or was he merely playing games?

The kitchen was already buzzing with activity and Mother Jael assigned her to toddy-making for the day. Brother Mark led the team; she was comforted to have him working near to her, and cheered by the way he rallied his group of servers and led them in a rousing chant. But not even this was enough to feed her energy, and it was only a matter of minutes before the heavy grinding stone took its toll. She was sure she could actually feel the lack of blood inside her veins, as though her vitality had been sucked away. Each time she had to raise the stone, to bear it down onto the nuts to shatter them, it weakened her, until she could barely raise the stone above the bench.

Brother Mark observed her wiping cold sweat off her forehead. "Enough of this today, I think," he told her, taking the millstone from her and passing it on to Brother Ethan. "Take over Sister Maryam's work, would you, Brother? I need her to help me with the stocktake down below."

Maryam smiled gratefully and they descended the service stairs to a cellar far below. There was no magical lighting in this cold space, created down beneath the water line to keep the food and drink from rotting in the heat. Brother Mark took a lantern from the wall and lit it with a strike of flint. Warm yellow light flared shadows out across the walls before it settled to a constant glow. After the dead stale air inside the stairway, the smell in here was a surprise—sweet, like the pungent fragrance of ripe fruit. "Wait here a moment, Sister," Brother Mark told her. "I require another lantern to complete our job."

While he filled a second lantern with its precious fuel, Maryam peered around the room, unprepared for the row after row of neatly formed shelves stacked high with goods. She wandered between the rows, studying their contents with growing awe. Toddy enough to stupefy every person on the island was stored there in huge clear containers. She tapped the side of one, wondering if it was made of glass such as she had seen upstairs, but it sounded dull beneath her fingers and was much more pliant than she'd have guessed. Whatever it was made from, it came from the time before the Tribulation, of that she was sure.

Another row revealed a huge store of te kabubu powder. Made from the ripe fruit of the pandanus, it was a true famine food—able to be stored in its powder form for around two years. Maryam had learned the art of making it with all the other Blessed Sisters: the slicing, steaming, mashing, moulding, kneading, drying, baking, grinding process that transformed the fruit into this nourishing food. Every village had a store of te kabubu, not just for its ceremonial value when mixed with water and then drunk, but for its nourishing qualities that could sustain a man on it alone for many weeks. Once, her ancestors had used it to endure their long sea-voyages; now, she guessed, it lay here as a back-up food in times of stress.

As Brother Mark lit the second lamp she was able to see further. Loaded baskets of taro, breadfruit, coconuts, and many fruits lined the shelves—the source, she realised, of the sweet scents. Never had she seen such abundance in one space before. If she needed proof that the Lord supported his Apostles, this was it. No one could maintain such wealth of food without His will.

Brother Mark showed her how to count and record all the stores. Beside each heading on her page was a tally of each item as it came and went. At any given time, she figured, the Apostles knew exactly how much food lay within this room. There was a certain power in this knowledge, she could see. While Onewēre's people lived from hand to mouth—fishing and farming as best they could, and praying for success each day—the Apostles' food stock was secure.

Once she'd mastered the recording process, Brother Mark left her to complete the work. It was just what she needed, something demanding enough to engage her brain and stop the swill of questions there, yet light enough not to tire her as the grinding had. She worked into a kind of daze, surprised when the conch shell bellowed out, announcing lunch.

As she walked toward the dining room, Maryam's excitement grew. Her friends must have arrived by now and she was desperate to see them both. And, sure enough, when she entered the room there was Mother Elizabeth at the top table and a quick scan of the servers' tables revealed Ruth. She wore the blood-smeared Judgement gown and bore the dark stains of goat's blood upon her cheeks. Maryam ran across to her, tears welling in her eyes as Ruth met her with a rapturous smile.

"I told you I would be here soon!" Her skin shone with health and happiness, and she tucked an arm around Maryam's waist and drew her down onto the empty chair beside her. "Tell me everything you know! Is it as wonderful as we had dreamed?"

Maryam found she could not speak. This was not the time or place to answer Ruth truthfully, and yet she didn't want to lie. "There's much to tell you," she murmured guiltily, suddenly aware of several sets of eyes upon her. Heat flamed up her face and she avoided the eyes of Mother Michal, who was watching her with great intensity and whispering behind her hand to Mother Lilith. She knew Lazarus's eyes were on her, too, had felt his intense stare the moment she'd entered the room. But she saw no sign of Hushai nor, strangely, of either Joseph or his mother in this hungry flock.

She slipped her hand under the table and grasped Ruth's, squeezing it reassuringly. "Wait," she whispered, hardly daring move her lips. She could feel Ruth's confused stare but could do nothing to explain.

Now Father Joshua rose from his seat to lead them in their daily prayers before they ate. Maryam waited for him to mention Sarah's death, keen to find some simple solace in his prayer. But not a mention of the girl was made. It was as though she'd never been; as if her life counted for so little that it passed away without a word.

Anger rose in her as Father Joshua turned his attention to Ruth and greeted her as if she were a long-lost friend. Ruth glowed and turned in her chair to wave at all the diners in a cheerful greeting of her own. Friendly laughter bubbled up around her, and the warmth continued as Father Joshua welcomed Mother Elizabeth back to the fold. Mother Elizabeth caught Maryam's eye and winked at her with simple joy. And then Father Joshua announced that Ruth would undergo the ritual welcome that afternoon. *So soon?* If she did not warn Ruth right away, there'd be no chance.

Only when the servers started passing out the food did the general babble rise to a volume Maryam felt would screen her words. Making as though she was talking of the food to Ruth as she served her, Maryam whispered, "Listen to me closely, and do not look at me or speak."

She could feel Ruth stiffen beside her as she passed a dish of mashed taro along the row. "Things here are not exactly as they seem. Do not drink the toddy if you can avoid it, and be prepared—the welcome ritual is designed to shame you and you'll be laid bare."

Despite her warning, Ruth turned to her at this—her eyes wide with surprise and disbelief. "I've done nothing to be ashamed of in the eyes of the Lord."

"Look away," Maryam hissed. But already it was far too late. From the corner of her vision she could see Mother Michal rise and walk toward them.

"You look tired, Sister Maryam. I hope your duties are not too much for you?" Her words dripped concern, yet Maryam could read the warning in her cold blue eyes.

"Thank you, Mother. I am fine." She bowed her head, and began to eat with all the enthusiasm she could muster.

Mother Michal continued to stand before them, her head to one side as she considered Maryam. "Still, I do not want to wear you out. Take your meal to your room and rest there until Mother Lilith can check you."

Maryam could not contain herself. "But Ruth and Mother Elizabeth—I wanted to spend time with them."

The older woman's eyes narrowed and a nerve twitched along the line of her jaw. "I'm sure they will forgive you if you're too unwell."

"Of course you must rest if you are ill," Ruth broke in kindly. "I thought you looked a little pale." She leaned over and kissed Maryam's cheek. "Don't worry, I will see you soon!"

Maryam had no choice now but to take her plate of food and leave. Anger and frustration boiled up inside her as she made her way out past the lunching servers and went to her room. Ruth was to undergo that humiliating ritual and she would not even be there to support her. It was so unfair.

* * *

She was glad of the rest despite herself. They would be preparing Ruth for her ritual now, and there was nothing she could do but ensure that she was there to comfort her once it was over.

Meanwhile, Sarah's dying face kept invading her thoughts, and she was burdened by her pledge to tell Sarah's family of her death. How was she to do this now? It seemed that every place she went, one of the Apostles watched. But she had promised Sarah—Tekeaa—and nothing would prevent her from keeping her word. Besides, if in fact they shared the same birthplace, then she was going to find her own birth mother, and that was that. She tried to dredge up her own birth name, whispered by her lost mother and etched somewhere inside her brain. It was buried deep, and she purposefully relaxed her mind to allow the invisible fingers of inquiry to rifle through the many fragments that were layered there.

Once, the very sound of her name had brought her comfort,

she was sure. But now it eluded her, as distant from her as the sense of excitement and anticipation that she'd experienced, and saw now in Ruthie's dear face, when her Bloods first came. How foolish she had been then, only weeks ago. She felt as if that girl was gone; that the person in her body now was as different to foolish "te bebi" as the coconut moth to the caterpillar from which it was formed.

She picked up the precious stone Ruth had given her, and held it tightly in her palm until her body heat had warmed it through. Then she held it to the dingy light that leaked in through her one window, and stared into its bright blue mass. Although it was smooth to her fingers, fine streaks of darker blue rippled from its centre, like the fine whorls of lines that marked her fingertips and thumbs. She stared at it and stared some more, willing it to release secrets that might set her free. *Nanona*. The name just popped into her mind, and she recognised it—moved toward it with a sense of joy. This was the name her mother had whispered at her birth. Nanona. The word meant "love."

A playful knocking on her door roused her from her trance-like state. The door cracked open and Mother Elizabeth appeared in the widening gap. "Te bebi! I could not wait to see you one moment more!"

Maryam sprang from her bed, ignoring the dizziness as she rose too fast. She threw herself into Mother Elizabeth's open arms and buried her face into the scented plait of hair. Just the smell of her was calming, so familiar and secure.

Mother Elizabeth returned the embrace then eased her back, to study her. "You look a little tired, dear. Michal tells me that your energy is rather low."

This absurd twisting of truth made Maryam almost want to laugh. Instead, she pulled Mother Elizabeth right into the room and firmly closed the door behind her. Perhaps now she could unburden her load. But first she had to sound the older woman out. "I am so glad to see you here," she began. "Things have been . . . worrying."

Mother Elizabeth raised an eyebrow. "Worrying? How is this possible in the Lord's most beautiful and sacred place?"

There was such genuine surprise in Mother Elizabeth's face that Maryam was sure, now, she did not know the truth about the blood-taking. She would take the risk and trust her, just as she had always done. "Please . . ." Maryam sat down on her bed again and indicated for Mother Elizabeth to join her there. "I know this will sound crazy, but things are not as we believed, Mother . . ."

The story came out in one long rush, Maryam daring not to pause for breath in case this chance was interrupted. Tears filled her eyes and she fought back sobs as she told of her humiliation, her increasing fear, and of the horrors of the blood-letting. Mother Elizabeth said nothing, just sat there with her eyes wide and a hand clasped tightly to her breast. She seemed to understand that Maryam needed, more than anything, to speak of what she'd endured.

When, finally, Sarah's woeful death was told and Maryam's words had all run dry, Mother Elizabeth shook her head as though confused and drew a breath. "But Maryam, my dear, you knew that you were Blessed to serve. The Lord works in His own mysterious way, and who are we to question this?"

Maryam's mouth dropped open and her breath stopped fast. Mother Elizabeth sanctioned it? This couldn't be true. She gulped down air, trying to clear her mind to think. "You knew? All this time you raised us to believe that we were Blessed and special in the sight of the Lord and still you knew?" She felt that she was choking, that she'd stepped into a pool of quicksand and was sinking fast.

Mother Elizabeth took her hand and rubbed it reassuringly. "You're viewing this so strangely that I cannot comprehend your thoughts. What could be a greater calling than to keep the Lord's living messengers alive and well?"

Maryam tugged her hand from Mother Elizabeth's warm grasp and backed away, until the wall braced her spine. "Sarah died, Mother. And I am next. Rebekah has been forced with child. And Miriam and Abigail. Every one of us who you have raised is treated worse than Zakariya treats our goats!" Anger was upon her now. This woman, who she'd loved as truly as her own mother, must have known the nature of their peril from the moment they'd been wrenched from their families as little girls, but did not care.

Mother Elizabeth's face reddened, and she drew her arms together across her chest. "How can you accuse me of misleading you? That really hurts. I taught you girls the Rules—their meanings are quite clear to all." She patted the space beside her on the bed. "Please, come and sit back down. Have I not always treated you with love and respect for the joyful sacrifice that the Lord, in his Choosing, blesses you to make?"

"I do not want to die," Maryam squeaked, the words sticking in her throat like the stonefish's poisoned barbs. She sank to the floor, tears dripping between her knees.

Mother Elizabeth squatted down beside her. "But, te bebi, don't you see? You *are* the lucky ones. The Lord is calling you to

Heaven, to sit with Him at His table and reap the rewards." She gave a tinkling little laugh. "I'm almost jealous of your luck. I must wait till I am old."

Maryam closed her eyes to shut out Mother Elizabeth's beseeching face. There were no more words to express the sense of betrayal that gripped her. Her tears flowed on, forming a damp stain upon the bedroom floor. She wrapped her arms around her knees and dropped her head, exhaustion sweeping her like a silent squall.

She felt Mother Elizabeth's tentative hand upon her arm but did not respond. Finally, she heard her rise and cross the room to the door.

"We will talk of this again when you are calm," Mother Elizabeth said to her. "Perhaps Father Joshua can give you the spiritual guidance that you need."

"No!" Panic seized Maryam. She swallowed hard, forcing one of Rebekah's compliant smiles onto her face. "Please do not worry him with my foolish fears. I'm sure you're right."

Mother Elizabeth studied her then shrugged. "As you wish." She stepped from the room, closing the door behind her—leaving Maryam to shudder at the thought of just what form Father Joshua's "guidance" would no doubt take. One thing she could guarantee, it would not release her from the fate of bleeder.

It seemed she did not move for hours. She felt so dead inside: everything she believed in had been ripped away. There was no one here who could rescue her from this; no one who even seemed to care. Except her dear friend Ruth, but right now she was caught up in her own dark fate. And kind old Hushai, she conceded. And Brother Mark.

That was it! She would seek Mark out and ask his help. He had been the first to greet her as she boarded, so surely he could help her to escape the ship. If she could only get to Aneaba, fulfil her promise to Sarah, and perhaps find family of her own. . . . She had to try.

CHAPTER TEN

Maryam was eventually summoned back down to the storeroom by Mother Jael. So far from Ruth's welcome ceremony, she could only imagine Ruth's humiliation as the afternoon dragged on. She tried to distract herself by focusing on the stocktake, but helplessness enveloped her.

Around her the bones of the ship creaked and clanged, and the occasional distant bang echoed through to her—the only tangible proof that life continued above. She felt so utterly alone, as though already she had died and gone to Hell.

Mother Elizabeth's betrayal stabbed like a fish hook in her heart and her sole consolation was the promise of the food-packed shelves. As she counted container after container of te kabubu powder her escape plan began to hatch and breathe, and take on a more solid shape.

Careful not to spill any of the precious powder, she opened one of the containers and scooped a small amount of it into an empty bowl. Then she shook the original, redistributing the powder until its surface once again appeared untouched. She moved on to the next container and the next, repeating the process again and again until her bowl was brimming with te kabubu which, mixed with water, might not taste wonderful but would give her strength to make her break. If she was to reach Aneaba she'd need food to maintain her through the long hard walk, and te kabubu was so light she could carry it without much strain.

She was just emptying the powder into a cloth bag she

could strap around her waist, when the clamour of footsteps broke through the silence. The ceremony must have ended now. Maryam prayed that the toddy had sent Ruth to sleep. Then, at least for a few hours more, she'd have some peace.

But the footsteps kept on coming: others were traipsing down her stairs. It did not sound like Brother Mark, rather two voices—one male and one female—trickled down the stairwell and grew louder still. Unsure who was coming or why, Maryam crept to the furthest corner of the storeroom and crouched low.

"I told you it would be empty," someone gloated. "Now, come over here and have a drink."

A girlish giggle followed and Maryam heard one of the containers of toddy being slid from the shelves and a scraping sound as someone unscrewed the metal lid.

"Here, my angel. Drink this down." There was arrogance in the man's voice, as though he expected to be obeyed. And then it struck Maryam—the voice belonged to Lazarus.

She felt compelled to watch now, feeling she was safer with him in her sights. She crept slowly around the shelves until she could see the two beside the opened toddy, their faces yellow in the lantern's glow. Lazarus had his arm wrapped tightly around the woman's waist—a server in her late twenties whose features bore the wide flat look of those from Onewēre's eastern shores. It was obvious she was already full of toddy; her limbs were limp and unresisting as he fondled her and slowly started to unbutton her white shirt. Then, with one hand he took a great handful of her hair and pulled her head back hard until her mouth dragged open from the strain. With the other hand he poured more toddy down her throat. She spluttered and choked, but most of it she swallowed down in painful gulps.

"That's right, sweetheart. Uncle Laz will help you sleep." He clamped his arm back around her waist, supporting her as the effects of the extra toddy hit her like a heavy weight. She tried to speak, but already she was well past forming any words. Instead she merely whimpered as he lowered her roughly to the ground and started now, in earnest, to strip off her clothes. He was going to force himself upon the woman and perhaps worse, Maryam feared, as she watched him remove his belt and tie it roughly around the woman's neck.

Before she could stop herself, Maryam leapt from her hiding place into the light. "Stop that, now!"

He startled, swinging around to source her voice. "You!" There was fury in his eyes, but then he smiled. "Are you offering an alternative?" So confident, so completely unthreatened, he deserted the unconscious woman and circled Maryam like a cruising shark, the smirk that stretched his lips like that of the bakoas that ruled the reef.

Maryam clenched her fists, willing herself to stand her ground. Any sign of weakness from her and this shark would soon attack. "I think, Brother Lazarus, you should take your belt and quickly leave." It was impossible to keep the wobble from her voice, but she met his gaze and held it firm.

Lazarus grinned. "I must admit you sure have pluck for such a scrawny little hen. A word from me to my father, girl, and he could make life very grim."

"You think it's not already grim?" she snapped. There was something in his confidence that goaded her. Why, oh why could she not just hold her foolish tongue?

"Grim? Now, now," he clucked. "Don't you know the Lord has Chosen you? Others on the island would give anything to stay here with us." There was mockery in his voice, as though he knew the story was an ugly lie. "My father runs a busy ship. If you're unhappy I can help." He raised a pale eyebrow and slowly winked.

"Your father?"

"Come on. Surely you know I'm the son of Joshua and Lilith?" He inched closer, until they stood almost toe to toe. "So if you're thinking of refusing me, I'd think again."

How could she not have known this? His likeness to Father Joshua was plain to see—and the relationship made him even more dangerous. Behind him the young woman groaned, lolling onto her side and vomiting in one fluid burst. The stench rose sharply, drowning out the sweet aroma of the fruit.

"Oh, spare me," Lazarus barked. "You skinny ones can never hold your drink." He turned to the poor woman, rolling her with his foot until her face lay in the stinking mess.

"Leave her," Maryam hissed, crouching down next to the woman and dragging her face free of the muck. The acid smell of the vomit was so overpowering up close, Maryam's eyes watered.

"Is that an acceptance then?" There was grim humour in his voice. He squatted down beside her, and ran his hand along the strip of skin revealed between her shirt and skirt.

His touch burned a path of fire across her back. She leapt away from him, grabbing her bag of powder and making quickly for the stairs. Behind her, he laughed. "You can run, little Maryam, but you cannot hide. The Lord does not give up on his Sisters quite so easily."

She did not wait to hear the rest of his blasphemy, but simply forced herself to keep moving despite the lingering exhaustion in her legs. She burst through the doors into the kitchen, just as Brother Mark walked in.

"What is wrong?"

In between her ragged breaths, all she could get out was "Lazarus." It was enough.

* * *

The smell of vomit still hung in the air, despite Maryam's efforts to wash it away. Brother Mark had seen Lazarus off and carried the unconscious woman to her room.

When he returned to the storeroom, Maryam risked sharing her plans. "If you could just lower me down the side, I'll make my way from there on foot."

Brother Mark shook his head. "When they catch you—and they will—your punishment will be very harsh."

Maryam nodded. "Yes, I know." She swallowed hard. "But I have no choice. I promised Sarah I would go." She met his gaze, reassured by the kindness there. "I think that I was born there too."

"If you're hoping to find family there, then there are things you ought to know. You have lived in peace upon the atoll, but Onewēre is quite different."

"But I've been there for the Judgements. It doesn't seem so dissimilar."

Brother Mark laughed bitterly. "Then you have witnessed the control the Apostles hold over us all. Behind their backs some among our people may resent them, but they'll do nothing to anger our Lord."

"What am I to do, then? Does te kimoa lie down peacefully

inside a snare once he is caught?" She shuddered, picturing the slow death of a struggling rat as the flaxen noose tightened around its neck. "No, he fights until his life has gone."

He frowned, the lines rippling out across his forehead like a disturbed sea. "You understand the villagers will likely beat you and return you if you're caught? Their fear of the Lord sending forth another Tribulation will outweigh any tie of blood."

Maryam shrugged. "What other choices do I have?"

The question remained unanswered, both knowing there was none to give. Eventually Brother Mark sighed. "All right. Meet me on the lifeboat deck, where Sister Sarah passed away, tonight when everyone is asleep. I will get you to the causeway, but I cannot risk more than that."

"That much is fine. From there I'll make my own way home." Excitement and fear competed inside her, and she tried to dampen both emotions down so they did not overwhelm her now. This was her chance—perhaps her only chance—to take control and she felt compelled to risk it, no matter what the possible cost.

* * *

To Maryam's great frustration she was sent back to her room by Mother Michal. She had no chance to ask anyone how Ruth had fared, and it boiled away inside her that she could not help. It was as if Mother Michal sensed the depth of her rebellion and was taking no chances. The one consolation was that she could preserve her fragile energy for the night's escape.

Now she lay fully clothed beneath the blanket on her bed. It was at least two hours since she'd heard the last clatters of activity beyond her door, and the night outside her window was silent and black. Finally she decided it was safe to move and slipped out of bed to tie the bag of te kabubu around her waist. There was nothing left to plan—she had unlocked the door earlier, once she was sure that Mother Michal had finished her rounds.

Ears straining to pick up any suspicious sound, Maryam slowly opened the door and peered outside.

Nothing. She was about to leave, when an overwhelming urge drew her back in to retrieve Ruth's pebble. She pressed the cool stone into her palm and held it tight, as if it were some precious part of Ruth.

Her journey through the sleeping boat was hindered by the lack of moonlight. Twice Maryam missed a step and had to cling to the handrail to halt her fall. Metal surfaces gleamed dully in the suffocating gloom like the flashing underbelly of a stingray in the sea's dark depths, and the long narrow corridors seemed to elongate in length and yet reduce in height—the walls and ceilings pressing in on her as if they longed to trap her there and hold her fast. Toddy-drunk snores leaked under doors, and through the layers of rusting hull she heard the restless heaving of the swell against the reef. Before she'd come to this cursed place, she'd loved to wander in the night amidst the busy nocturnal creatures who shared her home. Yet the only creature keeping pace with her inside this sleeping city now was fear.

When she reached the lower hospital level she slowed and began to check the numbers on the doors. Brother Mark had reminded her of Hushai's room number and she did not want to go ashore without speaking to him first. She felt guilty at his punishment for helping Sarah and, besides, he was bound to know how Ruthie had fared.

She located his door and tapped upon it lightly with one fingernail, just enough to call him if he did not sleep. He must have been waiting, for he was there even before her hand had dropped back to her side. He lifted his head, his nostrils flaring as he breathed her scent. "Sister Maryam?"

"Yes, Hushai." She waited as he ran his fingers down her face. "I'm sorry that I caused you trouble over Sarah," she whispered and she fumbled with the bag around her waist. She had split the powder into two separate lots and now pressed the larger portion into his hand. "I have some te kabubu powder to share with you. Brother Mark told me they cut back your food."

"Thank you child, that is very thoughtful." He tucked the bag deep in his pocket. "Mark has told me of your plan. I know I cannot stop you but at least pay heed to what I say."

He pulled her into his room and gently shut the door. "Before the Tribulation, when our ancestors lived on Onewēre peacefully, they used to sail between the islands. When the Tribulation was sent down there followed many years of violent and lethal storms. Many tried to leave Onewēre but few returned. And those who did talked of a world where disease and pestilence and bitter battles waged destruction, and ungodly forces razed the land."

He sighed, tears rising in his unseeing eyes as though he spoke of pains inflicted recently. "As time went by and the Apostles spread their Holy light, some still attempted to resist the Lord's Chosen ones and tried to flee. To my knowledge none succeeded, and the Apostles, in their wisdom, sought out all the sailing crafts and destroyed them to prevent more deaths, and keep His people close at hand. To this day, as you well know, no one is allowed to raise a sail. To do so is strictly forbidden."

"How do you know all this?" Maryam asked. The tales Mother Elizabeth had recounted to them as they grew up warned only of a gaping void, outside the safety of the reef, that plunged all disbelievers straight to Hell. Never had she heard even the faintest whisper that there might be some who tried to leave—or somewhere they could try to go. And, truth be told, until now, it had not entered her mind that it was even possible. They were the only ones the Lord had spared from the Tribulation and that was that.

"It is a strange thing, little one. They seem to think that because I cannot see with my blind eyes I also cannot hear or think. Much has been revealed within my presence over the years, but I've kept their confidences to myself—till now."

"Why now?"

"More and more I'm called on to mop up evidence of practices I do not like. I did not know the exact details of the blood-letting—although, Lord forgive me, I had my suspicions—but I have known too many of your Sisters pass as Sarah did, or die in the act of childbirth, or just disappear. When I was young there were many who lived long, happy lives here serving the Lord. Today there is a plague far more deadly than Te Matee Iai sweeping our shores."

His words tolled out harshly in the darkened room and Maryam shuddered. "But how does what you tell me help? There is no place for me to run so I am doomed: is that what you're trying to say?"

The old man chuckled and patted her arm. "What I'm trying to say is that you should question everything—just as you are doing now. Even our ancestors were not exempt from craving power; it is a weakness that whispers in the minds of all men. I want you to remember that where there is one deception there may well be others."

"But why then—"

"Please, enough of talking now. There is no time. Mark is waiting and before you go, I have someone down the corridor you'll want to see."

Maryam's heart skipped a beat. "Please tell me it is Sister Ruth."

He smiled, his teeth glowing white through the gloom. "She sleeps from the toddy, but will rouse a little if you speak." He reopened the door and guided her back down the corridor, to the room where she had first been examined weeks ago.

Inside, Ruth lay unmoving on the bed. A candle flickered on the bench and lit her blood-smeared face. Maryam rushed over and wrapped her arms around the familiar sleeping form. "Has she had the internal examination yet?" she asked Hushai.

"Yes," he answered, taking a wash cloth from a bowl and handing it to Maryam to wipe the goat's blood from Ruth's face. "I have not had a chance to wash her down. Do it now, but make it quick."

As Maryam began to wipe away the dry blood Ruth coughed and stirred. She opened her eyes and sent Maryam a groggy smile. "Hello."

"Dearest Ruth, are you all right?" Maryam struggled with her own raw memories of the crimes that took place in this room. How she'd ached for the Mothers to show simple care. She collected Ruth up in her arms and hugged her carefully, aware that she would be tender and bruised, and nearly breaking down herself when Ruth started to sob quietly into the nape of her neck. "It's okay, Ruthie, it's good to cry." For the first time since she could remember, the gap between their ages seemed immense and all that she had learnt and experienced made her feel jaded.

But Ruth surprised her, taking in a deep shuddering breath and swallowing her sobs back down. "It's all right, Maryam. I will be fine." She drew back and rested her head on the pillow, her lovely black hair fanning out like seaweed around her.

"The ceremony," Maryam said. "How did you survive?"

Ruth's fledgling smile fell away. "I admit that I was shamed. But you had warned me so I knew it was part of the ritual and not something that I had done. That helped." Her eyelids fluttered as she fought the aftereffects of the toddy. "But I could not refuse the drink and it knocked me out."

Maryam drew in a breath, wondering how to frame the next question. "Did they—do you—remember an . . . examination . . . in this room?"

Ruth looked puzzled. "No." Her brows knitted together as she tried to dredge up memories. "I remember drinking the toddy Father Joshua gave me . . . then the next thing I remember I was here, and a Mother who I didn't know was sitting near." She smiled. "She seemed very friendly—told me I was picked out for a special Blessing." Her face lit up like the sun. "Can you imagine it, Maryam? I am to be married to the Lamb!"

Maryam's heart sank. So Ruth's body was to be possessed by those whose only motivation was to breed more stock. She leaned in close, now whispering frantically as precious seconds ticked by. "It is not as they have told you, Ruth. There is much here that is plainly wrong."

"That's ridiculous. This is the Holy City."

"I can't explain it all to you right now. There's little time. I'm going ashore tonight, and I want you to come with me so you'll be safe."

Ruth started to laugh, but when she realised Maryam was serious her laughter died. "But why, Maryam? What you are suggesting is totally mad."

From the doorway, Hushai called softly. "Come, little Sister, it is time to go."

Maryam swung toward him, desperation lighting her eyes. "But I cannot leave her here. They have marked her as ready to breed."

"Breed?" Ruth broke in. "What talk is this?"

Hushai entered and gently took Maryam's arm. He lowered his head and spoke quietly, for her ears alone. "This one is very sweet and pure. You will not shift her from her faith."

"But I cannot just desert her."

"If they take more blood and then you die, you have not helped her either. Go now, and I'll watch over her."

"But—"

"Say your goodbyes. There is one more who you have to see."

"One more?"

Hushai sighed. "Say your goodbyes."

Maryam could read as little in his face as he could see from sight alone. This was not as she had planned. To leave Ruth here—that really hurt. But she understood there was no choice. Careful not to hurt her further, Maryam clasped her close. "I will come back for you, Ruthie. Wait for me and don't despair." She kissed her friend on each cheek and forced herself to pull away. "In the meantime you can trust Hushai and Brother Mark."

Ruth did not answer; she just watched her leave with such a look of puzzlement and hurt that Maryam wished she hadn't even tried to explain. Ruth could see no evil in others' hearts, because she had none in her own.

Once outside, Hushai guided her to another door. "This one asked to speak with you and would not rest until I promised to make it so."

Maryam's stomach flipped. Had Hushai and Mark tricked her and arranged an ambush beyond the door? She looked into the old man's face and, despite the fact his eyes were blind, he seemed to be studying her just as intensely. But there was nothing in his face that seemed deceitful or unkind. Then it struck her. "Joseph?" Hushai nodded. "Then let me leave. I have nothing more to say to him. If he was so desperate to speak with me, he had all day."

"That he did not, child. In fact, I administered toddy and insisted that he sleep. His health is extremely frail, and he sat up all night with Sister Sarah, only agreeing to leave her side when she had passed."

This struck Maryam like a slap. He had stayed? She felt shame flaring up her cheeks. Without another word she cracked open the door. The room was dark, but she could see a body curled up on a narrow bed. "Brother Joseph?"

He roused with a sharp intake of breath, lunging up and swinging his feet straight to the floor. But the movement dizzied him, and he clutched the mattress for support. "Sorry, I was fast asleep."

Maryam inched forward, until she could make out the features of his face. "Thank you for staying with Sarah." A knot formed in her throat, picturing their silent vigil on the deck as the sun rose on Sarah's last day.

Even in the dimness of the room he looked almost transparently pale. "I'm sorry we didn't speak today. Please tell me everything you know."

"I'm sorry, too. But I cannot stay and talk now. I have to go."

"Tomorrow then?"

She shrugged, reluctant to trust him with her plan. "I have to go." She quickly backed out of the room and turned to Hushai outside the door. "Thank you, Hushai, for all your help."

Hushai took her hand in his. "Travel safely, my little one. I am sure Sister Sarah's journey back to the Lord will be aided by the knowledge that her family grieves her loss."

Maryam hugged him, part of her wanting to stay close to his comforting presence, but the night was calling her now. She made her way to the outside deck, where the door was wedged open to ease her escape. Outside, the air was crisp and fresh and carried up the fishy smell of kelp upon the shifting breeze. Brother Mark stood silhouetted against the night sky, his gaze directed at the outline of Onewēre's rugged mountains, dark as they were against the backdrop of sparkling stars.

"I am sorry to be late," she said, as he turned to acknowledge her. "I am ready now."

He took the end of a long heavy rope, its girth as wide as her forearm, and tied a loop. "I will wait for you to return this time tomorrow night—and if not then, I will wait the next night too," he told her. "I only pray you can evade capture until that time."

Maryam reached out and took the offered loop, finally revealing the secret that she had kindled throughout the day and that burned now like a fiery torch inside her heart. "If I find my family I will not come back."

Brother Mark snorted as he helped her pull the loop over her head and settle it under her arms. "You think they will protect you?"

"They are my family. They will not want to see me die."

"You are sadly mistaken, Sister. The people of this island will not disobey Father Joshua. You are foolish not to see this risk."

"I will help her," Joseph's voice cut in. He stepped across the threshold and approached. He turned to Maryam and smiled. "I'll come with you."

"No!" If the villagers were likely to be suspicious of another brown-skinned girl, how would they react to an Apostle's son? "I go alone." She walked to the edge of the deck and faced Brother Mark. "Lower me now."

Brother Mark showed her how to hold the rope so it would not cut into her chest and braced himself to take her weight as she backed up toward the gap between the handrails and leaned right out over the precipice.

For a moment, hanging there with the causeway far below, she doubted she could do it. Her heart pounded so loudly in her ears she could no longer hear the sea. But then, with Sarah's face in her mind, she launched herself backward with her legs and dropped.

She seemed to freefall at first and panicked until she felt the jerking tension that reassured her Brother Mark had finally controlled the rope. She bounced her feet down the hull, close to the powdery rust that flowered there, and dared not think about the void until, quite suddenly, the causeway rose under her feet.

As quickly as possible now, fearing someone would see her from the ship, she untangled herself from the rope and stepped away. Instantly the rope started trailing back up the hull as Brother Mark reeled it back in. And then she was running, the chilly night air searing her lungs as her slippered feet thudded toward land.

Halfway she was forced to stop and fight for breath. Not to be able to run further, when weeks ago she and Ruth had raced nearly the full circumference of the atoll, hit her hard. She would have to pace herself more carefully, if she was to reach Aneaba before light.

She twisted around to look toward the ship. Something was not right. The rope had descended again, and someone was detaching from it and heading her way. Her breath quickened again and she prepared to flee. Had they detected her already? Had someone betrayed her?

But no. She saw the figure clearly now. Joseph hobbled along the causeway, making straight for her.

CHAPTER ELEVEN

With nothing to conceal her on the causeway, Maryam turned her back on Joseph and jogged the rest of the distance to the shore. What did he think he was doing, doubling her chances of being detected and guaranteed to slow her down? She had to bite back the urge to yell at him to go away: all this would achieve was to carry her predicament upon the breeze to others' ears. But he was gutsy and stubborn, she acknowledged, and once she reached dry land she felt obliged to slip into the shadow of a coconut palm to wait for him to catch her up.

She closed her eyes, revelling in the pleasure of the familiar warm coral sand under her feet and the island air at midnight. The sooty aroma of the night's cooking fires underpinned the tangy mix of sea and kelp, and she was enveloped in the musky fragrance of hibiscus flowers that grew nearby. She drank in the scents, longing for her old life upon the atoll. Everything had seemed so simple then, with her route laid out for her and no real cause for fear.

Instead, all she had discovered was betrayal—and right now it seemed that the biggest traitor of them all was the Lord Himself. She had gifted Him her life, had laid her trust in Him and His Apostles and now, when she most needed Him, He turned away. But perhaps she had not tried hard enough to connect with Him these past few days?

She began to whisper a prayer she had first learnt as a child, and that Father Joshua used each day to end the blessing. "*Father, I abandon myself into your hands; do with me what you will . . . I wish no more than this, oh Lord—*" But the words stuck in her throat. How could she not have seen that this prayer handed Father Joshua the power to do whatever he desired? That all the talk of service referred not to the Lord who was their Father but to this man?

Joseph's frail figure, meanwhile, took shape against the pale backdrop of the ship. He was taller than her by three hand spans and Maryam could see, in the breadth of his shoulders and the muscles in his legs, the ghost of the fit young man he must have been. She wondered how long he had known Te Matee Iai stalked him. But pity did not stop her from feeling angry that his interference now held up her plan.

Stepping onto the shore he called to her, scanning the dark foliage. "Sister Maryam, are you here?"

She was tempted not to answer. But he had followed her intent on helping, and she could not turn away without first exchanging a few words. She stepped out from the shadow of the palm.

"I am here."

His head lowered like that of a dog that knew it had done wrong. "I couldn't let you go alone."

"Why not?" She did not mean to sound quite so impatient, but she really just wanted to go.

"What will happen to my supply of blood if you are gone?"

Her jaw dropped in horror and she was ready to flay him with her outrage, when she saw the grin that lit his face.

"Got you!" he laughed, and began to walk along the palm line toward the south. "Are you coming," he asked, "or will you just stand there catching moths?"

"Pig," she retorted, pushing past him to take the lead.

But she couldn't help grinning back. It seemed a long time since she'd shared a joke and it pleased her, even if it was at her expense.

They skirted the sleeping village in silence, keeping a wary eye out for the mangy dogs and chickens they might well disturb. In the distance she could hear the village goats snort and bleat, and the snuffling of the ever-hungry native pigs. As they passed the last occupied hut, Joseph suddenly veered off toward a cooking fire and drew a smouldering stick from it.

"For light," he mouthed.

Maryam nodded, mentally kicking herself for not having thought of this. Only once they'd passed the last signs of occupation did she relax, and she slowed a little now, thankful for rest. Joseph kept steadfastly striding forward, and she watched the determined way he took each step—as though he had to will each one.

"You should not be doing this," she quietly called out to him. "You really do not have the strength."

He shrugged, continuing forward. "Nor you," he replied. "But if you think I'm going to stay there, now I know what's happening, then you're very wrong." His voice shook with passion.

Maryam caught him up, and together they entered the lush coastal jungle, rather than risk the maze of mangroves along the coastal route. Around them, night creatures registered their passing in subtle undertones of chirps and squeaks. They slowed again to allow their eyes to adjust to the gloom, the night's ambient light now muted by the thick canopy of leaves.

"How is it that you never knew what was really going on?" she asked, as Joseph handed her the glowing stick. "Surely it is plain?"

He snapped a sturdy branch off a tree and tightly bound dry

bracken around one end. "That's true enough," he responded. "But I wasn't raised aboard the ship." He retrieved the lighting stick and nudged it up against the bracken wick, blowing softly until it flared.

His admission was news to Maryam. She knew that some Apostles spent time in outlying settlements to tend the villagers' spiritual needs, but she'd thought they returned frequently to the Holy City. Did distance, however, excuse turning one's back on wrong?

"Your father was still an Apostle." She could not prevent bitterness leaking into her voice.

"My father," Joseph bit back, "was a good man." He strode on ahead of her, his back blocking her path. But this extra exertion did not last: he stumbled over a trailing root and slowed, finally leaning on an upturned palm trunk to rest.

Maryam stopped beside him, first brushing the mossy trunk to clear it of the myriad tiny bugs that made their home there. "I'm sorry," she said. "I didn't mean to speak ill of your father. Tell me something of your life." Now that she had asked him she was keen to know. Her own life had been so simple, so happy, when she was young—but she had no real comprehension of how others lived.

Joseph took a ripe banana from his pocket and handed it to her. "Here, eat this." He rose again, barely concealing a groan. "Come on," he said. "It's important to reach Aneaba before light."

"Are you sure you're up to this?" Up close the torchlight accentuated just how pale he was. It frightened her. "You really should be resting."

"For what?" He shrugged and jerked his head toward the track. "Let's go." He took her hand, his fingers cold against her own.

At first she was taken aback. But no warning bells rang out inside her gut; instead, the two settled into a companionable silence as they walked. Above them fruit bats swooped and dived amid the canopy of palms, while below nocturnal frogs formed a moving carpet as they retreated from the light.

"So," she said, breaking the reverie, "where were you raised?"

"I was born on the ship," he admitted. "But my father had an argument with his older brother Joshua. He and Mother left the ship and moved to a small house near Motirawa, along the coast from Aneaba."

"What was it they fought about?"

He turned to her. "Can't you guess?" He dropped her hand to scratch his nose and Maryam felt the loss of contact as a small lurch inside her. "All he ever told me was that Uncle Joshua had lost sight of the Lord's basic laws." He laughed. "I told my cousin Laz that once—he beat me up."

"He's very like his father," Maryam said.

"He's not so bad, once you get him by himself." Maryam could not help herself. "I'd rather be dead."

Joseph's eyes widened. "What do you mean?"

"I have seen the way your cousin treats female servers first hand . . . let's just say it isn't nice." She found she was reluctant to reveal the extent of Lazarus's behaviour to Joseph. They were cousins, after all.

But Joseph didn't miss a thing. "He didn't—hurt—you, did he?" He kicked a fallen coconut from their path, swiping at it as if it were Lazarus's head.

"No." She felt herself blushing, wondering whether Joseph conjured in his head the same sinful pictures as she did in hers. "But I have seen a cruel and ruthless streak in him that scares me."

Joseph nodded. "You know, when we were young—before we understood the workings of the world—you could not have found a nicer friend. But when Uncle Joshua insisted that he train his only son to take over as the Holy Father, Lazarus got all screwed up. It's like there's this ball of anger building up inside him."

Maryam could find no pity for Lazarus. "What has he got to be angry about? He is free to do whatever he wants." *And to hurt whoever he likes*, she thought, but did not add.

"To tell you the truth I'm not too sure. Since my father fell ill I've had little time to dwell on much else."

The sadness in his voice flew like a wraith between them. Maryam reached out her hand and brushed it lightly across his arm. "How is your mother?" she asked, thinking of the distraught woman who had thrown herself upon her husband's shrouded corpse.

"Very bad."

She could not see Joseph's face—he had turned away—but she could tell he was crying from the watery waver in his voice.

"She and my uncle had a terrible argument just before my father died. He wanted Father to return to the Holy City with him but Father refused. My uncle thought Mother should have forced him—now he blames her for Father's death."

"Did he—" Maryam stopped for a moment, trying to think how to frame her words. The Apostles never died from Te Matee Iai because they stole the Sisters' blood. So had Joseph's father never taken it?

"No," Joseph answered, guessing where her mind had gone. "If he knew of the blood-letting then he'd never have allowed it in his name—of that I'm sure." He looked directly at her now, his wet eyes glistening in the torchlight. "He taught me we are all equal in the Lord's eyes. He'd never take the life of another to save his own."

"And yet . . ." Again Maryam dared not finish her thought aloud.

"I swear to you I didn't know," Joseph said. "My mother went so crazy after Father's death she made me promise to let Aunt Lilith heal me. They never told me what that meant— just pumped me full of toddy till I knew no more."

Ahead of them, the path began its winding ascent through the rocky hills they had to cross to reach the island's southern shore. It was a much less frequented path and more difficult to negotiate than the coastal route, but more direct and safer than crossing through the mangroves, which were tidal and really only safe to traverse during the day. Besides, the two were far less likely to be spotted here than on the track between the villages that hemmed the coast.

The jungle plants seemed to close ranks around them, the air hanging humid and moist as Maryam and Joseph passed. Now they struggled to find their footing through the crumbling volcanic rock, Joseph hampered by the need to hold the torch. Maryam cursed her choice of footwear—she had thought no further than the causeway, where her slippered steps would fall more quietly. Here, though, the shards of rock stabbed at her feet.

Before long she and Joseph were panting, and the pockets of dizziness Maryam had experienced after the blood-letting returned. The path narrowed to a natural staircase, formed by rifts between the rocks. Joseph clambered over each new obstacle before offering his hand to Maryam to help haul her up. Her legs were not as long as his: she felt the muscles in her thighs stretch and complain, until they quivered uncontrollably every time she called on them to support her weight.

The hiss of running water pulled them forward as they neared the top. One more bend and a small, furious waterfall took shape before them, its jet of aerated water luminous white against the rock. Joseph leaned in toward its spray, letting it cool him, and Maryam soon joined him, desperate for respite from the cloying sweat that drenched her. She stuck out her tongue, startling at the force of the droplets, like a horde of tiny stinging barbs. But they quenched her thirst.

Below the waterfall the stream ran down through mossy rocks. Maryam edged her way to one particularly large flat rock and lowered herself onto it, releasing her hot bruised feet into the cool water with a thankful sigh. Joseph joined her, planting the torch into the ground before tearing off his sandals and plunging his feet in as well. He groaned, collapsing backward to lie on the rock, his chest heaving.

"It's getting light," he wheezed, pointing at the hint of light in the sky.

Maryam followed the direction of his gaze. "Only another hour till dawn, I'd guess." She listened to Joseph's laboured breathing, worried at this exertion. Te Matee Iai fed insatiably upon weakness. The thought of him succumbing to its grasp pained her more than she'd have guessed. There was something in his openness—his decent spirit—that she'd warmed to.

She removed the small remaining bag of te kabubu powder from around her waist, scooping out a handful and cupping it in the palm of her right hand as, with her left, she reached down into the stream and scooped a little water up. This she trickled into the powder, mixing it into a thick ball of paste with her index finger before offering it to Joseph. "Here. Eat some te kabubu to give you strength."

He raised himself on one elbow, taking the food without a word and cautiously tasting it. "Not bad," he mumbled through a second mouthful, as Maryam formed another ball of paste.

"I mixed in a little tioka pollen with the powder to make it sweet." She bit into her own paste ball, surprised herself by how the mellow sweetness made the chalky powder palatable.

For a moment she closed her eyes, imagining the instant when she would finally make contact with her birth family— the surprise and joy in her mother's eyes; the warmth of her father's embrace.

Behind them, from the track, the sound of movement jolted both of them from their private thoughts. Maryam's heart beat so fast she could feel it in her throat. Had they been followed? Her panicked eyes met those of Joseph, who uprooted the fire-torch and plunged it into the stream to extinguish it. He pressed a finger to his lips and soundlessly stood, offering his hand to pull her upright. Searching for a place to hide, Maryam saw it, a narrow cave behind the waterfall's fast flow, cut into the rock from centuries of water passing by at force. She pointed, already scoping rocks and stones to guide them through the torrent. Joseph nodded and they fled across as, below them, the snap-ping of twigs and scrape of foot on rock drew closer to the spot where they had stood.

The spray of water soaked their clothes and streamed into their eyes and ears. The cave was barely wide enough for both of them to squeeze inside and they had to press against each other to fit into the rocky cleft. Maryam could feel the rise and fall of Joseph's back as he breathed, his body hot against her skin where they touched. All they could do now was wait.

Then, through the spray, she saw a squat shape break from the trees and head straight for the waterfall. Crouched low, whoever it was stopped exactly where only moments ago she and Joseph had lain. Then, to her utter confusion, Joseph started to laugh, his body shaking against her and his breath hot on her face as he twisted around to her. "It's only a wild boar!"

It was true. The boar was huge, at least as heavy as a grown man and twice as broad. Its curved tusks glowed against the coarse hair that framed its mammoth head and, although Maryam was relieved that their pursuer was not human, she was glad not to have come face to face with this monster all the same. Relief bubbled up inside her and she laughed, too, forgetting their cramped conditions until she swung her head and her ear slammed into jagged rock. She cried out, instantly feeling the pain and the ooze of blood.

"What happened?" Joseph yelled, unable to turn any further.

"I hit the rock," she whimpered, her ear burning and head buzzing. For a moment she thought she would be sick.

Beyond the cave, the boar drank from the stream then ambled back down the track. Immediately it was gone and Joseph extricated himself from the rock and guided Maryam to the bank, helped by the lightening sky. She clutched her ear, blood pooling in her hand. Joseph struggled out of his wet shirt, dipping it into the stream before gently dabbing the wound.

"Curse dousing the torch," he muttered, peering at the side of her head.

"How's it looking?" Maryam asked, her voice seeming to come from far away.

"Not too good," he admitted in a shaky voice. "I think it's nearly sliced right through the top half of your ear." Already, the blood welled up again and he pressed the shirt against her head and held it tight.

Maryam took a few deep breaths to calm herself. They were still a good two hours from Aneaba and soon their absence would be noted on the ship. But they'd come this far, and she was not about to give up now. "If we rip your shirt into strips and bind it tight," she ventured, "I think I can survive for now." She fought back tears, determined to get going again.

"Good plan." Joseph tore wildly at his shirt, until it lay about them in tattered strips.

Meanwhile, through the gloom Maryam scoured the banks for mossy clumps and was relieved to spot one a little further down the stream. "Praise be," she muttered, thankful to Mother Evodia for her lessons on herbal healing. She pointed to the spongy plant. "Could you pick some of that tabunea moss?" she asked. "It will help clot the blood and should ward off infection, with any luck." She felt a little better now, having found something to focus on beyond the pain. "Squeeze out any water and then pack it tight under the strips."

Joseph nodded, quickly collecting the moss and applying it. He knotted the strips of shirt together with shaking hands, winding them tightly around her head and apologising every time she winced. By the time he'd finished, both of them were in need of rest. But the day was marching forward now: the broad fingers of dawn had reached up above the treeline to light the entire sky.

Joseph pulled Maryam gently to her feet. "Are you able to go on?"

She looked at him, registering now his lack of shirt. Wisps of golden hair dusted his chest and she felt an overwhelming desire to place her hand there and smooth them down. "I'll be fine," she promised.

As he bent down to wash his hands she found herself studying the way his spine delicately stepped in a steady line up his long thin back. She forced herself to turn away. These thoughts, they grew like poison in her mind. She knew they were wrong, had been told this many times before, but now they kept ambushing her, popping uninvited into her head.

*   *   *

The hardest part of the trek was far from over. The downhill track was slippery and overgrown, and she and Joseph skidded on the loose flaked rock. Every time she jolted, Maryam's ear and head throbbed anew, and blood turned sticky as it seeped through the strips of cloth and met the air. All thought of reaching Aneaba was overshadowed by the hardship and exhaustion that now kept pace with them.

As the changing light brought the day more sharply into focus Joseph slowed, his eyes dull and his breathing coming in painful grunts. Even more worrying to Maryam, the skin around his neck was starting to mottle with the first new signs of Te Matee Iai she had seen on him since the blood-letting had swept them clear.

Finally, as morning light streamed through the leaves of mature pandanus trees, the terrain flattened out and eased. Beneath their feet, the rock was slowly swallowed by light soil and the rich decaying smell of the jungle was replaced by the lighter scent of sand and sea.

"That's it!" Maryam said, so relieved she nearly wept. "The worst is over."

She turned to Joseph, who lagged behind her now. But instead of returning her smile, he crumpled right in front of her. She bent over him, terrified. But although he looked like death, he did still breathe—shallow panting like that of a poisoned puppy she'd once found. She helped him to lie more comfortably on his side, murmuring words of reassurance she knew were trite.

"I can't go on," he mumbled, when his breath finally slowed. His voice was changed, as though his tongue had thickened and swollen. "Leave me here."

CHAPTER TWELVE

"Of course I won't leave you!" Maryam almost shouted the words.

"Just go!" Joseph told her, more able to speak now. "Seek out Sarah's family and say your piece. I will rest a little here."

"You think I'd just go off and desert you when you're ill?" she said, her ear throbbing mercilessly. What must he think of her?

In the silence before he answered, Maryam realised she could hear the distant whisper of the surf. They were so close to Aneaba now—it seemed as if yet again the Lord had dangled her desire in her face, only to sweep it away again the moment that she neared her goal, like a fisherman teasing fish onto a hook. What was it the Lamb had said to his Apostles? *Follow me, and I will make you fishers of men.* She sighed, shaking her head. Why, oh why, did everything she'd once held true now seem so sinister?

"Please," Joseph whispered, his eyes drooping shut. "I just need to rest. Send someone to help me if you must, but please just go." He coughed and began retching, each convulsion coiling up through his body like a whirlwind spinning the sea. Finally the retching ceased and he lay back.

Maryam scanned the coastal plain, hoping for some sudden aid. But besides the keening seabirds and the buzzing insects that rose to embrace the sun, no other life but hers was here to help. "All right," she said. "I'll go to Aneaba as quickly as possible and return with help."

He nodded, albeit slightly. "Take it easy," he said. "You, too, are weak."

"Don't die on me," she whispered. She brushed her lips across his sweat-drenched brow to lightly kiss him there, as a mother would a child. But he tipped his head and caught the pressure of her lips with his. Only a few seconds, but when she pulled away, embarrassed and confused, it was as if a thousand bright-winged butterflies had hatched inside her stomach and were flying there.

She started to jabber, to bury the moment. "I will find someone who can—" But no words could disguise her blush. Better now merely to leave. "I will be quick."

With that, she summoned up the last of her own strength and started running through the undergrowth toward the beach. Each pounding footstep reverberated up through her body to her ear and soon she felt the warm trickle of blood again, seeping through the bandages and down her neck. Above her, the sun rose hotter in the sky, promising a sparkling day.

As she broke through a glade of straggly breadfruit trees the air around her erupted in a mass of scolding sooty terns, their black beaks and eyes flashing dark and menacing against their stark white plumes. They were nesting: birds and more birds shot from their roosts amid the rocks, puffing up their feathers as they shrilled at her to stay away.

One painful step after another, she fought through the tangled vegetation, her lungs burning with each gasping breath and her muscles screaming out for rest. Then, at last, she reached the sea. And there, at the far end of a curving bay, the pandanus-thatched roofs of Aneaba peered out from their cloak of palms. The sight halted her in her tracks; it tickled at her memory and tugged her heart. She knew this place! It sat within her like a secret, buried deep. Now, as she stumbled along the hard-packed silver sand above the high tide line, it truly felt as if she were returning home.

Closer to the village she could make out figures moving between the palms while, down at the water's waveless edge, a gaggle of small children paddled in the shallows, playing with a barking dog. It was the stuff of dreams; the moment she had conjured up each time she sought comfort or calm. But now was not the time for happy homecomings—first she must seek help for Joseph and then find Sarah's parents, to break to them her tragic news.

The dog was first to sense her and it ran toward her, its lips curled back to bare its teeth. But, despite the threatening grimace, its tail wagged. Maryam offered it her hand and waited for the animal to sniff her thoroughly before she made another move. The dogs back on the atoll, too, had feigned aggression when first approached, but she knew if she did not react then soon the dog would realise she was friend not foe. She crouched down to meet it nose to nose, sprawling backward as the dog lunged forward and licked the blood that smeared her face. She pushed it away, blotting up the dog's sticky saliva with her sleeve just as the first of the paddling children spotted her. A cry went up, and now they raced along the beach, water spraying out around them as they scuffed the tide.

Maryam hauled herself back to her feet, jogging on toward the village with the dog bounding at her heels. The first of the children, a painfully thin boy of six or seven, caught her up and ran along beside her, questioning her incessantly. "Ko na mauri ! Ko nako maiia?" Maryam struggled to switch her thinking into the native tongue. Old Zakariya and some of the older servers had refused to speak only in English, and she was thankful now, as the words started to unravel and make more sense. "Where have you come from? What is your name? Why is your head bleeding?"

But it was impossible to answer him, however; the effort required just to keep moving sucked every scrap of energy. She smiled at him, trying to convey her good intentions, and as the other children joined the procession she felt as a mother hen would with her brood of noisy chicks.

Ahead, the first of the adult villagers broke from the cover of the trees to greet her. A man in his late middle years, he did not soften his wary posture even when she neared him and he registered her desperate state. The tattoos of his village ringed his neck, stylised frigate birds above a line of wavy sea. Maryam skidded to a stop in front of him, doubling over to ease the stitch that cramped her and allow a few seconds to collect her breath and plan her words.

The villager, meanwhile, took in her sweaty, soiled server's garb, and the blood-soaked bandage around her head. "What brings you to Aneaba, Sister?"

"Please," she puffed out, "my companion is very sick back there and needs your help." She pointed back along the beach, trying to pinpoint the exact place where she'd broken through the vegetation and found the sea. It all looked the same now, and panic stirred her as she thought of Joseph lying back there on his own.

The villager followed the line of her finger then flicked his gaze back to her. "What are two Sisters doing travelling across the Baluuka Track alone?"

The suspicion in his voice, and his unwillingness to act, infuriated Maryam. If someone had turned up at the atoll, the Sisters would have leapt to assist them, no questions asked. Perhaps he'd react more favourably to her pulling rank? "He is an Apostle's son—the nephew of Father Joshua himself!"

Immediately the man's countenance changed. He seemed to shrink. He turned, calling to the children who milled around. "Fetch Moreese and Katane now."

The children scuttled off like coconut crabs, their legs propelling them in the direction of their mission, while their eyes remained locked on Maryam as though she might vanish or they'd miss some fun.

Now he faced Maryam again. "How far along the beach?" he asked. "Take us there."

She wanted to weep at this. Did she look like she could walk further? But if it was the only way to help Joseph, she had no choice. "Of course." She was a server, after all. So much for thinking she was Blessed.

Two younger men ran up with the children still in tow. And, behind them, a group of curious villagers now watched from the shadows of the trees. Maryam swayed, as exhaustion swept her. The pain of her shredded ear was still so bad it burrowed like a stinging renga termite into her brain, and her legs felt like they'd turned to stone. The three men quietly conversed, then turned to her expectantly. She had no choice but to start making her way back down the beach.

She was hobbling now, both knees so sore from the downhill trek through the jungle that she half expected to hear them creak like branches in a wild gale. She bit her bottom lip to stop the wobble in her chin that warned of tears.

"Let the poor girl rest," a woman's voice rang out behind them, full of scorn. The men stopped. A big-boned woman stood there, hands spread on her ample hips. She spoke directly to the oldest. "Natau, what were you thinking? Track the girl's footsteps instead. Can't you see she's had enough?"

She did not wait for the leader to respond, just closed the distance between them and wrapped a strong brown arm about Maryam's shoulders, claiming her. Natau grunted and motioned for the other two to carry on. "It is Father Joseph's nephew we aid," he snapped at her. "Prepare a resting place for him on our return." He turned on his heel, stalking off after the others as the woman laughed.

"That one claims he is the boss," she chuckled, her arm slipping down around Maryam's waist to support her as they walked toward the village. "But all men are made small in bed!" The woman's tawny eyes swept over her, inspecting the blood-soaked strips of shirt.

As they reached the line of trees that framed the village, others came. Soon, Maryam found herself at the centre of a bustling group, the women chattering among themselves while casting shy glances at her.

She was led into a low cool hut. "I am Vanesse," her rescuer told her, sweeping a pile of sleeping mats down from the rafters and stacking them for more comfort, on the neatly swept dirt floor. "Rest yourself here while I go and find the things I need to clean you up."

Maryam fell gratefully onto the mats, closing her eyes and listening to the excited murmur of the other women gathered outside. She let her tears fall freely now, washing away the worst of her tiredness and worry over Joseph with their warm release. Something hard pressed into her hip, and she reached down to brush it away—realising then that it lay in the pocket of her skirt. She reached inside and drew out Ruth's precious blue stone. The thought of Ruth brought Maryam's rebellious actions back to her in stark relief. By now Rebekah would have found her gone, and the unknown consequences would be set in motion.

But now Vanesse returned to the hut with an elderly woman close behind. They laid out the many things they carried next to where Maryam lay, and immediately set to work. "This is Umatu," Vanesse said, nodding in deference to the stooped and densely wrinkled woman who'd already started to unravel the bloody mess on Maryam's head. "She's lost the power to speak, but her hands can heal."

The words rebounded in Maryam's mind. How excited she'd been when Mother Michal told her she was blessed to heal. What a fool.

Vanesse soaked a sea sponge in water and gently dabbed away the blood. As Umatu removed the last of the bandage and carefully worked the blood-soaked moss free, she clucked her tongue.

"How did this happen, child?" Vanesse asked. Her eyes seemed to transform from brown to black as she studied Maryam's ear.

"I hit it on a sharp rock," Maryam said, digging her fingernails into her palms to fight the pain when Umatu rinsed the sponge and started to clean out the wound.

"It was quick thinking to use the tabunea moss. Without it you'd have lost more blood than this, I think."

Maryam could not resist a sardonic smile. "I have lost more blood already than I care to think."

Vanesse looked up at her sharply, her brows knit in puzzle-ment. "What are you doing here, Sister? The children said—"

"Maryam," she interrupted. "My Blessed name is Maryam." She drew in a deep breath, her heart abruptly beating fast. "My birth name was Nanona. I think that I once came from here."

Umatu's hands froze mid-stroke. She peered into Maryam's face, those ancient eyes seeming to delve into her very soul. Without warning the older woman tugged up Maryam's blouse and leaned in closer to her skin. Then suddenly, she chuckled and poked her finger into a small dimple beneath Maryam's left breast. Their eyes met—Umatu knew!

Vanesse glanced between the two, sensing something secret and significant had taken place. But she did not press Maryam to explain, just took a handful of succulent matutu leaves and split them so the thick clear sap released. She collected it on another clean sea sponge, using this to paste the sap gently on the wound. "This will numb the pain," she said. "Once it's worked its magic we can close the tear and, so long as it does not infect, the sap should set the wound in place and hold it there until it heals."

The two women worked in silence now, concentration tense upon their faces as they pieced her fragile skin back together. Maryam could hardly hold herself still: if Umatu knew about her dimple, surely she must be a member of her family, or know them well. If only Umatu could speak. . . . But she must try to contain herself—must first deliver Sarah's message and make sure that Joseph had been helped. By then she hoped the vil-lagers would trust her, and be prepared to shelter her from the Apostles if they tracked her down.

Now, after one final close inspection, Vanesse and Umatu

packed more fresh tabunea moss around her ear and wrapped it all in a clean cover of pliable leaves. Vanesse patted Maryam's hand. "You should only need to wear this overnight. By tomorrow the matutu should set."

Maryam released a shaky sigh. The sap had dulled the ache almost instantly, and for the first time since the dawn had come she noticed she was hungry—and thirsty, too. Vanesse must have sensed as much, for she now handed Maryam a bowl of lime-drenched fish. "Eat this, to help regain your strength," she said. "And tell us why you have come. It seems our wise old one holds you dear." She nodded toward Umatu, who now gazed at Maryam's face with loving eyes.

Through mouthfuls of succulent fish Maryam started to explain. "I have come from the Holy City to seek the family of Blessed Sister Sarah—known to you as Tekeaa."

Vanesse gasped. "The Lamb be praised! My cousin Lesuna's daughter Tekeaa was Chosen many years ago." She was silent for a moment, obviously counting off the number of years inside her head. "By now she'd be nearly fourteen."

Reality hit Maryam full force. What had she been thinking? These were real people who had loved Sarah and now would grieve. And what was she to tell them? The truth of how Sarah had died? Would they even believe her if she did, or would they accuse her of heresy and pack her back to the Holy City to face punishment there? Suddenly the fish grew rancid in her mouth, and she spat it back into the bowl.

"I'm sorry," she apologised. "I find myself suddenly full." She pushed the bowl away, conscious of Vanesse and Umatu's expectant gaze. "Does Lesuna live here still?"

"Indeed she does," Vanesse answered. She shook her head

sadly. "Her husband fell to Te Matee Iai years ago, and two other of her children as well, but she struggles on and looks to the Lord. That's why I left my own village five years ago, to ease her loneliness and pain. To hear news of Tekeaa will greatly soothe her heart."

There was no point delaying it. Besides, to forewarn Vanesse might help with the ordeal of telling Lesuna another precious child had died. Maryam slipped her hand into her pocket, rubbing Ruth's touchstone for comfort as she drew a nervous breath. "I'm afraid I come with tragic news."

She watched the light extinguish from Vaneese's eyes and felt her throat constrict as though it did not want to say the next cruel words. "Sister Sarah—Tekeaa—has died."

Vanesse's hand flew to her mouth. "This cannot be: she was Blessed by the Lamb!"

Maryam sighed. "I'm sorry, but it's really true. She died yesterday morning, with the dawn." Was it really only yesterday? Everything had stretched and warped, so much happening in so little time. "She was a true Sister—strong and good. And she died with thoughts of her family uppermost in her loving heart."

"My cousin . . . my poor, poor cousin," Vanesse wailed. "This will be the end of her." She dropped her head into her hands, huge sobs shuddering through her body. Utamu shuffled over to Vanesse, wailing, too, and rocked her gently in her arms.

To hear such anguish tipped Maryam back into her own outraged grief. It was anger, real anger, which stoked the fire inside her now. There was no need for Sarah to have died this way. The thought cemented in her heart—she was no longer concerned that maybe she'd offend the Lord. He either condoned these evil acts—in which case He was evil, too, for how else could he kill so many innocents solely to test her fragile faith?—or else He was merely a myth, like the story of Nareau the Wise, for others to corrupt and own.

Even as she thought this, it scared her. Everything she'd believed since she was small was swept away with this sudden understanding, leaving only anger and a gaping void.

But now, above the wailing, other voices filled the air outside the hut, and the two young men who'd been sent for Joseph struggled through the doorway with him strung limply between them.

Maryam rolled off the sleeping mats, scouring Joseph's face for signs of his condition as they laid him down there to rest. Feverish sweat glossed his forehead and upper lip, while the marks of Te Matee Iai stood out like ugly bruises against the pallor of his skin.

His eyes met Maryam's and, despite his obvious discomfort, he sent her a wan smile. "I'm sorry."

Behind him, Natau eased into the hut and knelt before Joseph, blending humility and pomp. "I have sent a runner to your sacred mother Deborah in Motirawa. Meanwhile we are here to serve you, nephew of Father Joshua, at your will." He glanced at the two tearful women, before turning to Maryam: "I see they've tended to your wounds."

She nodded but chose not to reply. The hut was full to bursting now, the air growing hot and stale. She reached over for a clean sea sponge and wiped the sweat from Joseph's upper lip. "How do you feel?"

Another wispy smile lifted his face. "As if I fought that wild boar." He sipped a little of the water Utamu now offered him, then sank back with a groan. "I'm sorry," he whispered to Maryam. "I've let you down."

Before she had a chance to reply, Utamu lunged between them and tore open Maryam's stained shirt to reveal her breasts. As Maryam fought to cover herself, the old woman grabbed Natau's hand and thrust his finger straight into the dimple that confirmed her birth.

"What are you—" The question died on his lips and he drew his hand away, his gaze travelling from the dimpled skin up to Maryam's face. He reached over and grasped her chin, turning her head first one way and then the other to examine her. "Nanona?"

To hear her birth name spoken like this, with such longing, moved Maryam profoundly. It seemed the world shrank to this moment of connection between her and him. "You know me?"

Natau clasped her face between his hands, tears springing to his eyes. "Know you, child? I am your father." He pulled her to him, embracing her so tightly she could hardly breathe. "Praise the Lord. Oh, praise the Lord," he murmured over and over, his sinewy arms refusing to relinquish what he now had found. When, finally, he released her and drew back, he ran a finger down her cheek. "How could I not have known you? You are so like your mother, may she rest in peace."

The words flew like a spike into her heart. "She is—dead?" Burning tears rolled down her face as Natau took her hand. "She did not last a year after you were Chosen, little one. The Lord took you to serve the great Apostles, and then took her to Heaven to serve in His house."

"Amen," the other villagers chorused around him. Their response brought Maryam back into the present, as she refocused on the others in the hut. She glanced from face to face, trying to gauge each person's mood. Nothing but warmth and welcome transmitted back to her, and she felt the horrors of the last few weeks lift off her as a parting cloud.

She turned back to her father—her father! Even thinking the word made her smile—squeezing the hand that still so lovingly held her own. "I have come home, Father. I want to stay."

Natau blinked, his hand dropping hers. "The Apostles have sent you home?"

She swallowed. "Not exactly . . . I chose to come."

There was a murmur in the room, as if a chilling breeze had slipped in through the open door. "Chose to come?" Her father shook his head, confused, the smile slipping from his mouth.

"I couldn't stay there, Father. If I go back they will kill me as they killed my dear friend Sarah. . . ." She swung around in time to catch the stinging impact of her words on Vanesse's shocked face.

Now her father straightened, his back rigid with scorn. "How dare you speak so ill of them? Has Lucifer seized your soul?"

She threw herself before Natau, hoping he would take her back into the comfort of his arms. "Father—please. You do not understand the evil that is taking place within that ship."

"Enough!" he shouted, shoving her away from him as if she were a poisoned snake. "You turn your back upon the Holy Fathers and you think that I will take you in?" He spat at her, his phlegm hitting her full force between the eyes. "I see you are no child of mine. *If any man come to me, and hate not his children, and brethren, and Sisters . . .*" he recited, "*he cannot be my disciple*"—the damning words straight from the Holy Book.

He turned: "Moreese, Katane—take her and bind her to a tree where everyone can see her shame."

As the two young men moved toward her, their expressions teetering between disgust and awe, Joseph rose from his resting place. "You mustn't do this to her," he said.

Natau hit back. "You, of all people, should not protect this heathen tia tabunea te aine." He closed his eyes, obviously fighting hard to gain control.

Maryam stared at him open-mouthed. A witch? He thought his daughter was a witch?

When his eyes reopened they were cold as the fierce winter gales that sometimes swept in from the south. He turned to Utamu and Vanesse now. "Tend to our Holy Father's nephew until his people come for him." He would not look at Maryam, instead gesturing impatiently toward her as he straightened up to his full height. "Now take this faithless whore and cast her out." He stormed from the hut.

Maryam stared after him, momentarily frozen in anguish. Flanking her, Moreese and Katane hoisted her up, taking an arm apiece. They dragged her outside, kicking and crying.

CHAPTER THIRTEEN

The crowd stood in silence. Maryam's hands were bound behind her back with harsh flax rope and then secured to a coconut palm outside the entrance to the village maneaba. She searched each face, hoping for an ally as she begged Moreese and Katane for her release, but no one dared to meet her gaze. The children who had followed her in from the beach were herded off, and Natau darted beneath the eaves of the maneaba to oversee her public disgrace.

"We are all true believers here," he declared, his irises two angry dots inside the toddy-stained whites of his eyes. "You have brought our village shame."

"I do not mean to shame you," Maryam sobbed. "But if you send me back to the Holy City, I will die."

Her father was enraged by this, rushing out at her like a fighting cock and slamming her across the face. The pain exploded in her brain as her head was jolted and her damaged ear connected with the dense palm trunk.

"You know the Rules," he screamed at her. He pointed now to one strapping youth amid the crowd. "Savaese, find your father and your uncle and tell them to hurry here now. They can escort this sinner back to the Holy Fathers for them to punish as they see fit. Meanwhile, journey to the Holy City yourself to warn them she is coming back."

The young man nodded and ran off, leaving the villagers shuffling and whispering uncomfortably behind their hands. Natau puffed out his chest. "This piece of nothing, this blot upon my family's name, would slander our great leaders and bring their wrath down on us all." He strutted before them, his voice growing ever more menacing and cold. "Remember, brothers and sisters, the words of the Holy Book: *In the land of your origin, I will judge you. I will pour out my indignation upon you . . . You shall be fuel for the fire, your blood shall flow throughout the land. You shall not be remembered, for I, the Lord, have spoken.*"

There was a swell of restless muttering from the crowd. Natau now marched from villager to villager, eyeballing each to regain silence. "We must work to redeem ourselves in the eyes of the Apostles, or the Lord will send another Tribulation to punish us for this one's sins. We must heed the Lamb's lesson: *If your right eye offends you, pluck it out and cast it from you; for it is better for you that one of your members should perish, and not that your whole body should be cast into Hell.*"

"Enough!" Joseph limped from the healing hut, shadowed by Vanesse. Fury scorched his cheeks as he gathered himself up to counter Natau's wrath. He drew himself to full height, turning his back on Natau to address the villagers. "I am Brother Joseph, son of Father Jonah from Motirawa. My uncle is Joshua, Father to us all." He swayed a little and Vanesse stepped forward, clasping his elbow to help balance him. "This heathen girl is mine to take. I will escort her back to Motirawa and then on to the Holy City where, I promise you, justice will be done." He gestured feebly to Katane. "Cut her down."

Katane looked from Joseph to Natau, confused. Natau, servility just masking his rage, jerked his head toward Maryam to signal Katane to proceed. Raising his machete, the young villager sliced right through the rope of flax that trussed Maryam to the tree. He seized her by her bound hands and held her, waiting for his next command.

Joseph approached Maryam, bearing over her so threateningly she dared not look into his face. "Sister Maryam, pray now for forgiveness from your ancestors. You have forsaken the Lord, and only Father Joshua now has the right to judge your actions and to find a fitting punishment." He pressed her down on her knees. As she knelt, she heard him whisper softly, "Play along."

Her heart skipped a beat. She bowed her head, forcing herself to put aside her fear and to recall a prayer convincing enough to pacify her father. The Lord's Prayer didn't seem contrite enough, and if she made her own prayer up she might somehow offend Natau still further and bring down more rage. Then it came to her—one of Mother Elizabeth's favourites, a psalm. *"Have mercy upon me, Oh Lord, according to thy loving kindness . . . blot out my transgressions. Wash me thoroughly from mine iniquity, and cleanse me from my sin. . . ."* She chanted on, the rhythm and familiarity of the words helping to calm the chaos in her head a little and to slow her pulse.

Beyond Joseph the villagers stirred now, sensing perhaps that the show was over and that if they wanted to escape the toxic fallout of Natau's anger it was best to leave. They peeled away in silent groups, eyes set on the ground. Natau himself paced up and down behind Joseph, glaring at their retreating backs.

As Maryam ended her prayer, she realised that a fragile kind of peace now reigned. She dared not lift her eyes, trying instead to remain small and insignificant as the two men Natau had summoned ran into the clearing between the huts. Once again, Joseph transformed from ally to imposing Apostle. "Plans have changed. Wait here for further instructions."

Natau approached Joseph and Vanesse, who continued to hover beside Joseph with worry written clear across her face. She was right to be concerned, for although he now stood without support his colour was still frighteningly pale and deep indigo circles ringed his eyes.

"As head man of the village I will be happy to accompany you to Motirawa," Natau told Joseph, his voice clipped. "You are in no state to manage this heathen yourself."

"You are right, Natau, and I thank you for your concern." Joseph paused and drew in a shaky breath. "The village is indeed lucky to have such a strong and faithful leader as you, and I will be sure to tell my uncle this." Natau seemed to relax and preen a little at his words. "However, I think it is important for you to remain here and lead your people."

Joseph glanced over at Maryam and she dared flick her gaze up at him, incredulous that he could play this game so well. It scared her. Was he really still on her side? But in that fraction of a second, she was sure he winked.

There was nothing Natau could do but agree to Joseph's request, with the same air of self-importance he had demonstrated with the crowd. "May I suggest you allow our two men," he simpered, pointing to the two who waited by the maneaba, "to carry you upon a litter, and a third to supervise the girl?"

"Thank you," said Joseph. "That would be much appreciated." He turned directly to Maryam now. "Rise to your feet now girl, and go with Sister Vanesse to prepare for our journey. If you do not obey her every word, you will not be dealt with so leniently a second time."

Maryam rose stiffly to her feet, her muscles screaming out in memory of their trying trek across the hills, and Vanesse led her back into the healing hut. Once inside, the brutality of her father's rejection sank in, and Maryam started shaking uncontrol-

lably. Her mother was dead, and now her father hated her. Even
Mother Elizabeth, whom she had loved so dearly, had forsaken
her. Was there any point continuing to fight for her survival now?

Vanesse gently wrapped her arms around Maryam and
rocked her as the storm of grief swept through her. "Hush,
child. You are safe for now." She led Maryam to the pile of
sleeping mats and pulled one free, seating herself upon it and
pulling Maryam down beside her.

"You are lucky to have such a faithful friend in Brother
Joseph. He has told me all." She offered Maryam a cup of
coconut milk and didn't speak again until she was sure Maryam
had drunk every drop. "Now you must listen to me."

Her gaze drifted off toward the doorway. "You must understand that your father's status as village leader gives him power
and influence, and he will fight to retain this. The fact that his
daughter was Blessed helped him gain this exalted position—
he has used this as a means to show his dedication and loyalty
to the Apostles. To take a stand against them would destroy
everything he has built up."

"But he didn't even listen—"

"And he never will. Accept this, child. There is a hunger in
men's minds that feeds on power, no matter how small in reality
that power is. The Apostles dictate all our lives—they can aid
us or destroy us and we have no choice."

"But why? If everyone stood up to them—"

Vanesse placed a finger to her lips and shook her head.
"Never even *think* these words again," she hissed. "What looks
peaceful on the surface is a deadly whirlpool underneath." She
closed her eyes for a moment, sighing deeply. "Right now you
have more pressing problems to concern you. Your flight has

greatly weakened Brother Joseph and his performance just now
has drained him further than he shows. My fear is this: that if he
dies, your own life will be sacrificed to atone for the loss of his."

"What must I do?" Maryam begged Vanesse, some small
part of her brain wondering how the villagers could reconcile
the evidence of Te Matee Iai with Joseph's status as an Apostle's
son. "I cannot let Joseph die."

For a long moment Vanesse said nothing, instead staring
into Maryam's eyes as if weighing up the mind inside. Finally
she spoke, her own voice shaking. "I do not understand the
blood-letting he spoke of—cannot believe that the Apostles
would do such wrong. But if, as you both say, they have used
this, this—wickedness—to save their lives from Te Matee Iai,
then this is Brother Joseph's only chance. There really is no
other cure." She took Maryam's hand and squeezed it tight.

Maryam's mind spun, scared to dwell on the consequences
of Vanesse's words. "You mean I should give him more blood?"

Vanesse shrugged. "You must ask yourself what the Lamb
would do, little Sister. More than that I cannot say." She rose
then, patting Maryam's shoulder reassuringly as she made her
way toward the door. "I will send Utamu with more food to
build your strength before you leave." She forced a smile, before
wiping a hand across her face as though averting some unseen
evil. "Right now I must find my poor cousin Lesuna, and tell
her our precious Tekeaa has gone to the Lord."

*   *   *

There was no chance to talk with Joseph for the first hour of
their journey to his home at Motirawa, along the coast. He lay,

restlessly dozing, in the litter carried by the two men Natau had chosen. Maryam was escorted by Moreese, who insisted that she trail behind and did not speak. Her predicament churned with such force inside her head it started to ache, but it seemed there was nothing she could do now except walk steadfastly toward her fate. Joseph had tried his hardest to protect her, but by now the young man Savaese would be well on his way to the Holy City. Even if they had not noticed her absence before now, his presence would alert them, and she knew her punishment would be harsh.

The route around the coast was flat, nothing more difficult than the odd crossing of a stream that wound its way toward the sea. The jungle crouched at the edges of the sandy beach, alive with tuneful birdsong that competed loudly with the raucous black noddies and sooty terns swooping around the small procession as it passed.

As the midday heat grew too oppressive and intense, they fled the coastline for the shade, stopping to rest beneath the wide spreading branches of an old fig tree, its roots reaching out across the dry leaf litter like the sinewy tendons of a hand. Moreese laid out a picnic of freshly baked flat bread and soft goat's cheese, along with fresh coconuts he had gathered as they walked. He untied Maryam's hands and she fell upon the food thankfully, first quenching her thirst with coconut milk sipped straight from its machete-split shell.

When the meal was over, Joseph asked the three villagers to step away so he could speak to Maryam alone. They looked uneasy, but dared not defy the order of an Apostle, especially one who carried Father Joshua's blood. "Call us if you need our help," Moreese urged, eyeing Maryam suspiciously before they left.

Now Joseph turned to Maryam, his smile stretched and tired. "I'm sorry for your father's acts."

"Why should you be sorry?" Maryam asked. "I brought this down upon myself." She shuffled closer to where he lay, unconsciously batting away a fly that buzzed around Joseph's fair hair. "It is I who am grateful to you—and sorry for causing you such ill." She studied the delicate sweeping lines of his lips, self-conscious as she remembered their tender kiss. "I have been thinking . . . and I want you to accept more blood."

Joseph lifted himself onto one elbow. "Are you mad?"

Maryam laughed at the shock upon his face. "Not mad, just worried that my—friend—is ill." Her smile died and she grew less sure. "We are friends now, are we not?"

Now Joseph grinned. "So close it's like your blood runs through my veins!"

He reached over and took her hand, pressing it into the hollow of his neck. Beneath her fingers she could feel his pulse, running far too weak and fast. The contact, so intimate, set her own heart racing to catch up with his. She drew her fingers away, turning her face from him so he could not see the blush that heated her face.

"I will give myself up at Motirawa," she declared, resolved to cause him no more harm. "From now on I'll accept my fate."

Joseph sat up fully now and shifted so she had to meet his eye. "How can you give up when you've come this far?"

"Because there's nowhere else to run." She shrugged. "If my family—my father—had been prepared to shelter me, it might have worked. But we live on one small island and there is no real place to hide."

Joseph reached over and took her hand, weaving his fingers

in through hers. She did not pull away. After everything that had happened in the last few hours, the sense of comfort that this human contact gave her was too great to deny. "Have you ever thought of leaving Onewēre altogether?"

"Now who's mad? There is nothing out there but certain death. The Tribulation destroyed all." She'd known this fact her whole life, yet what was it that Hushai had said to her? *Where there is one deception there may well be others.* Was this what he referred to, or was he offering her some scrap of hope just to buoy her up?

Joseph stared at their two linked hands, his as pale as coral sand against the nut brown of her skin. Her wrists were marked from where the bindings had chafed, and he turned her hand over, caressing the tender reddened underside of her wrist with his thumb. He was about to speak when, from the direction of the beach, they heard Moreese clear his throat. Maryam tugged her hand away, springing up and backing off as far from Joseph as was possible before the villager approached.

"We should continue on, Brother Joseph," Moreese called, "or we will miss the tide and be forced to walk further inland."

"Then let's be off," Joseph replied. He waited for Moreese to fetch the other two men before whispering urgently to Maryam: "Do not give up. There is something I must show you when we reach my home."

She had no chance to delve further, as the men arrived and bound her hands again, even more tightly than before. Then they raised the litter from the ground and set off, right into the face of the searing midday sun.

* * *

At the river crossing they were met by two of Mother Deborah's men, who relieved the litter bearers: the runner from Aneaba had brought news of Joseph's state. As the group made their way up through the dunes toward his village home, Mother Deborah herself hovered at the edge of the trees.

She ran toward them, eyes only for her son. "My darling boy. What were you thinking?"

The bearers lowered Joseph to the ground and Mother Deborah flung herself upon him, showering him with kisses as his colour bloomed from pink to red. Around him, the men averted their eyes, but their suppressed smiles spoke of indulgence for this woman's obvious signs of love. It gladdened Maryam's heart to see such warmth between the two and yet it pained her. *This* was what she had so longed for with her own mother, and her father, too.

Joseph brushed Mother Deborah off, rising unsteadily to his feet as she turned to those who had borne him there. "Thank you for your efforts," she said, smiling. "Go with our men. They will find you food and drink, and somewhere cool to rest before you make the return trip."

Only Moreese now remained. "What of the girl?" he asked Joseph.

"I will guarantee she does not escape the village—untie her now and leave her with me."

Moreese frowned, but bowed his head. "As you wish." He released the bindings from her hands then followed the other men, but the defensive rounding of his back told Maryam he did not approve.

She turned from watching him depart to find Mother Deborah's gaze fixed upon her, taking in her soiled clothes and the bloody bandage on her ear. "You have caused much trouble, Sister," she declared. "If I find that you have hurt my son—"

"Mother. Please." Joseph slipped a weary arm around his mother's shoulders and clasped her close. He grinned reassuringly at Maryam. "Sister Maryam, rather than hurting me, has saved my life."

"Indeed?" she mused. "I guess we'd better get you both inside and hear this tale from start to end."

She wrapped her arm around Joseph's waist and, together, they made their way over to a large thatched hut, Maryam following close behind. Inside the central room, three walls were strung with brightly coloured tapa hangings and the other was lined with shelves stacked high with ancient books, more than Maryam had seen before all in one place. Other doorways led off this room, and it was through one of these that Mother Deborah now led Joseph and gently lowered him onto a bed. It was lavish by village standards, not the usual thin sleeping mat, but more like the beds back on the ship. He sank onto it gratefully, unable to hold back a groan.

Mother Deborah perched beside him, stroking back his sweat-drenched hair. "Fetch me some water and a washing cloth from the main room," she ordered Maryam, not even bothering to look around.

Maryam hurriedly did as she was told, returning with the washcloth and bowl of water from the table in the room next door. From the doorway she watched as Mother Deborah prepared to sponge Joseph down, unbuttoning the new shirt Vanesse had found for him and freeing its sticky fabric from his chest. Maryam bit back a gasp when she saw how the ugly purple marks of Te Matee Iai were spreading over his shoulders and now down his arms. Their rapid advance frightened her and made her more determined to help. It was her blood after all and, as Vanesse had suggested, she could gift it to him if she chose. There was nothing more to live for now. At least her death would have some meaning if she managed to regain his health.

As Mother Deborah wiped the cool cloth down Joseph's sweat-slicked chest and belly Maryam tried to look away. But the pale smoothness of his skin held her eyes, and she wished that she, not Mother Deborah, was beside him there to ease him so. She glanced up to find Joseph watching her. Mother Deborah caught the focus of his stare and spun around.

"You are dismissed for now," she barked. "Go and bathe yourself down at the beach. My men will keep close watch on you, so do not even *think* to escape."

Joseph began to speak to his mother in urgent tones as Maryam left the hut. Whatever was said between the two, it was clearly for their ears alone. She strolled out through the village, trying to avoid the curious and disapproving stares, and found herself standing beside the sea.

The village sat at one end of the sweeping bay, tucked into the crook of a rocky tree-clad arm that stretched out into the sea and no doubt sheltered the buildings from the worst of the prevailing winds. Maryam dared not strip off her sweaty clothes; instead she waded right into the tepid surf and stood there as the waves washed up around her and her feet dug down into the sucking sand. It was so refreshing, so deeply satisfying, to rest here in the sea's warm grasp—how she'd missed its smell, its taste, its life that kept rolling on regardless of the wickedness or indifference of human beings.

She knelt, careful to keep the water from her wound, then slowly swam out through the gentle waves and floated on the crystal surface, with the sun shining golden pink through her closed eyelids and her thoughts stilled and silenced by the steady whisper of the sea. If she were to die right in this instant, Heaven could not be more peaceful, more glorious and deeply calm.

CHAPTER FOURTEEN

Maryam trudged back up the stony beach. Further down the shoreline she could see a group of village women and their children collecting seaweed from the rocks, and four men wading slowly out just past the wave-line to drag in a net.

She wrung the water from her clothes as best she could, rogue tendrils of her hair escaping from the thick knotted plait upon her head to spring into ringlets around her face. The calmness that had seeped into her tired body and relaxed her while in the sea dropped away: she saw the upright figure of Mother Deborah breaking through the palms and making straight for her. Maryam stood her ground, waiting for the woman to approach.

"Sister," Mother Deborah began, holding out a drying cloth and wrapping it around the younger woman's shoulders in a surprising motherly display. "It seems I may have judged you wrongly."

Maryam said nothing, drying herself as best she could. Every time she spoke she ended up in more trouble than before and it had struck her, as she floated out there in the bay, that sometimes the best defence was silence.

She studied Mother Deborah from the corner of her eye, noticing the deep lines of sadness that carved through the delicate ivory of her skin, and the sleepless circles under her astonishing blue eyes—eyes that possessed the same beguiling intensity as Joseph's. But she seemed frail, despite her stature and demeanour, as though she fought to hold herself together beneath a mask of calm. And that was hardly surprising, given how recently she'd watched her husband die and now faced death again with her treasured son.

"I am sorry for your loss," Maryam said. "From what Joseph has told me Father Jonah was a good, kind man."

Mother Deborah startled, tears flooding into her eyes. She pressed her lips together tightly, holding back her sadness as she looked out to the horizon line beyond the reef. Finally she sighed and sat down on the springy grass that marked the border between sand and soil. She patted the ground next to her. "Please. Come and sit here."

Maryam joined her, glad for the sun that so quickly dried her clothes to salty stiffness. The numbing effect of the tabunea moss was wearing off now and the covering over her ear had grown heavy and uncomfortable with her collected sweat. Carefully, she removed the makeshift bandage and offered the wound up to the healing powers of the sun.

Mother Deborah leaned across and studied Maryam's ear. "Whoever treated you did a good job. If you are careful it should heal well."

In the silence that followed, Maryam's heart beat strangely fast. She felt as though the whole world held its breath and strained toward them, waiting for some sign she was yet to see. How much had Joseph told his mother—and how much, if any, was she likely to believe?

"My son thinks much of you."

"And I of him."

Again the silence stretched between them, punctuated only by the distant tinkle of the children's laughter further down the shimmering beach. The men had dragged their nets in now, tossing the array of fish on the sand. A small haul, this, but not bad for the time of day. No doubt they'd lure more fish into their nets when the day slipped into night. Somewhere far behind her, Maryam heard a woman's voice fly free in song, a joyous hymn to the Lord. She knew the words, but found she could not even form them in her head, her anger at His betrayal still so wild and raw.

She felt, suddenly, that it was better to know the ugly conse-quences of her defiance than to sit here passively waiting for the axe to fall. So much for yielding, obeying, and sacrificing her life with willingness and joy. She, who had been raised to comply so completely with the Rules, had somehow managed to question or break every one. Maryam took a deep breath, hoping Joseph had told his mother everything that he now knew.

"I will give him more blood," she said, turning to face Mother Deborah and gauge her reaction.

The woman's eyes widened, but there was no bewilderment or shock. So, indeed, it seemed she knew. She looked steadily back at Maryam, who was struck by how much the mother was like the son. There was the same unassailable goodness there; the same aura of honesty and truth.

"He will not ask it of you," Mother Deborah said.

Maryam smiled wryly. "That I know!" She glanced away, trying to still her see-sawing emotions. "But even if I hadn't run away, my fate is sealed." She met those blue eyes again and shrugged. "It seems pointless that we both should die when I can save him."

Mother Deborah nodded, clearly too honest to deny the logic of Maryam's words. She leaned forward and scooped up a small pebble from the beach, turning it over and over in her thin weathered hands. "I owe you an apology. I knew the rumours of blood transfusions, but I was so desperate to get help for Joseph that I never really questioned how it might be done. I feel deeply ashamed."

A lump welled up in Maryam's throat: to finally hear someone apologise was immense. Mother Deborah looked so unhappy it took the sting out of her confession and warmed Maryam's heart to her. She cleared her throat. "There is no need to be ashamed. If Joseph was my child I'd probably do the same."

Mother Deborah turned to her and cupped Maryam's face in her free hand, leaning forward and kissing her lightly on the cheek. "I see now why my boy thinks so much of you." Her hand dropped away, she nodded to herself decisively and tossed the pebble as far away as possible. It scuddered across the beach, coming to rest at the high tide line. Then she rose to her feet, offering Maryam her hand. "Come. Joseph has asked me to show you something."

She led Maryam along the rim of the beach in silence, toward the rocky outcrop at the crook of the bay. Where the village compound stopped the ground quickly grew rugged and unkempt, apart from one barely trod track that wove between the trees. It took them down to the huge layered rocks which spilled out from the surrounding cliffs into the sea. Here the track dwindled to almost nothing, coming to a halt before two massive pillars of rock that leaned in toward each other, forming a low-slung doorway to the cliffs beyond. In a cleft at the junction of the pillars an ancient wooden mask stood guard, not unlike the ancestral masks in the rafters of the maneaba where Maryam had been raised. But these blank eyes stared down upon them balefully, warning them to stay away.

The small hairs on the back of Maryam's neck and arms bristled and she hung back as Mother Deborah stood framed by the layered limestone. "This is the entrance to one of your ancestors' most secret burial grounds," she said. "It was once known only to the highest ranking shamans and village chiefs." She pointed to the threatening mask. "Te Ikawai, the old one, prohibits any but the Lord's chosen few to enter through. It is the place where dead men rise again and stalk the shadows of the night—and it is said that any who dare enter through this gateway uninvited will be cursed, along with all their family throughout time."

Maryam took a step backward, amazed by Mother Deborah's calm indifference to this threat. "Why, then, are we here?" she asked, her disquiet building as the ancient eyes continued to stare her down.

Mother Deborah smiled. "Where better to hide something precious than in the sacred belly of the Lord?" She dipped down and passed beneath the stones, gesturing for Maryam to follow. "How can I be more cursed than to lose my husband and, shortly, my only son? And you more cursed than to lose all hope of rejoicing in a loving family and a long fulfilling life?"

That the wife of a high-ranking Apostle—Father Joshua's sister by marriage—could share Maryam's own bitter disillusionment was astounding indeed. She felt her chin rise to match Mother Deborah's defiance, and stepped on through this ancient portal toward the place where dead men reigned. If the mother of Joseph was not afraid, neither was she.

Now they had to clamber over jagged rocks between myriad pools that wheezed and whispered with each respiration of the tide. They worked their way around the headland until the bay was far behind them, hidden from view. Mother Deborah changed her tack now, bearing, it seemed, slightly inland. Then suddenly they left the rubble of rock behind to be confronted instead by a loose barricade of straggly trees, knitted together in tangled defence. Mother Deborah pushed through the web of brittle branches, only now waiting for Maryam to catch her up.

Before them, the gaping mouth of a cave sucked the sea in to its murky depths. The gilded sunlight of the lengthening after- noon fractured on the water, throwing phantom-like reflections up on the ceiling of rough rock inside the cave. Around them, crickets rubbed their wings together, setting up an orchestra of chirps and clicks while, further off, the constant boil of sea on reef seemed to fill all other air with its noise.

Mother Deborah turned to Maryam, smiling at her obvious surprise. "We're too early for the tide today. Are you prepared to swim, my dear?"

Maryam peered into the cave, shuddering despite herself. But she swallowed down her nerves and nodded, touched by the woman's growing warmth. "Of course."

She followed Mother Deborah down the bank, slipping into the surprisingly deep channel to breaststroke after her from day- light into gloom. Inside, refracted light bounced off the mineral- streaked walls, dancing and skittering around them. The cave's fruit bats, disturbed by the presence of interlopers, flapped and scolded as the two swam by. Further in, stalactites rained down from the ceiling in a petrified storm, some so huge they married with the soft muddy bank at the edges of the seawater to form living columns from roof to earth. The gentle swish of water, as the women swam on, echoed around them as the high tide nursed them in its warm embrace. Then, up ahead, it was as if a handful of tiny suns beamed down their rays, onto one of the most astonishing sights Maryam had ever seen.

Beneath a series of tiny sinkholes streaming light, some kind of boat sat marooned on a glistening rock-strewn internal beach. Two sturdy hulls, linked together by a shelter on a wooden deck, and two long smooth tree trunks—lying along the length of the hulls, as though they waited to be raised.

Ahead of Maryam, Mother Deborah stood now, wading through the water up onto the rocky ledge that housed the boat. Maryam lowered her feet, feeling her toes sink into the soft cluggy mud as she, too, was drawn toward this miracle. Without a word from Mother Deborah, she circled the craft.

It was longer by three lengths than any village boat she'd seen: its hulls almost as wide as the length of Onewēre's six-seater longboats—the only seagoing vessels allowed by the Apostles for generations past. If what old Hushai had told her was correct, the existence of this craft contravened their will.

"Is it not a thing of beauty?" Mother Deborah ran her hand along the timbers forming the central deck, coming to rest on the bindings that secured the thatched shelter between the hulls. "You can see now why its presence here begs utmost secrecy and stealth."

"I don't understand," Maryam answered. "How did it come to be here? And how could you, an Apostle, know of this and hide it still?" Her eyes travelled every inch of the craft, taking in its form and shape. Between its two bows, spiralling waves of wood reached out, bearing the delicately carved image of a warrior crouched low in battle, his lustrous abalone eyes fixed firmly ahead toward some great unknown shore.

Mother Deborah settled on a rocky outcrop, summoning

Maryam to join her there. From their perch, the boat seemed to stretch out like a vision from a dream. "Let me start from the beginning. If you decide to go along with what I am about to propose to you, it's better that you know it all."

"Propose?"

Mother Deborah laughed. "Wait, Maryam! A story must unfold from the beginning of its journey, in order that its destination satisfy the human heart." She patted Maryam's knee then leaned back against the slimy rock.

"After the Tribulation, chaos reigned. Man and beast, sea and air, were poisoned by the sun's deadly rays and battered by relentless storms. Later, those who crewed *Star of the Sea* deduced the Tribulation was not sent by the Lord at all, but resulted from something they recorded as huge solar flares—the outcome of the sun gone wild."

"Not sent by the Lord?" To say this in the belly of Onewēre's ancient god was undoubtedly foolish. Maryam genuflected to ward off ill, in case Te Ikawai could somehow hear. "How do you know?"

"Each ship's captain writes a log, and in this he records everything from weather, position, to the workings of the crew."

"You've seen this log? It still exists?"

"Indeed I have, and yes it does. But it is not in the Apostles' interest to make such knowledge known to all. They locked it in a hidden place and only those holding the power have access to the key.

"But this is of no consequence," Mother Deborah went on, raising her hands in a gesture of impatience. "The thing that you must know is this: the Apostles of the Lamb were formed from a desire for power, based on greed. And, because the *Star of the Sea* had been such an abundant refuge at the time of loss, no one thought to question them—indeed, their presence gave the poor surviving villagers comfort in a world gone mad."

"But what about the countries in the paintings on the ship?" asked Maryam. "The far-off places where the first holy passengers were born? Did they not return to seek their loved ones once the dangers of the Tribulation had passed?"

"From my reading of the log, it seems all countries in the world were struck as we were here. Everywhere human life was plunged back as though to ancient times—small roving tribes that fought over the little food and water not destroyed by the solar storms. Their old technology, which they in their arrogance thought could outstrip the natural processes of the world, blew up or failed, and spewed their poisons out into the newly devastated lands—and without access to technology they were lost; had forgotten how to live more simply within nature's laws."

Maryam shook her head, trying to make sense of what she heard. "But why, if this technology once made them great, did the Apostles ban all sailing craft? Surely there was someone who'd have come to help?"

Mother Deborah sighed. "By then the lies were set in place and the first Apostles—my forefathers—were already in control. The Rules. Server and master. And news back from the outside told of dangerous shifts within the power structures—of a world where man was reduced to desperate beast. Those first leaders of the Apostles, begun by great-great grandfather Saul, decided that the best way to maintain control was to remain cut off, ensuring that the villagers would never know the possibility of other ways."

"But why didn't the villagers ask more questions, refuse to be enslaved like this?" Maryam demanded to know. If she could see the evil in the Apostles' actions, why did others look away or remain blind?

"Why indeed?" Mother Deborah shrugged her shoulders. "Hunger. Hardship. Illness and death. But, mostly, fear. Fear of punishment, fear of retribution from a judging Lord." A wave of antipathy splashed across her face and she shuddered. "Think of all the fear-provoking stories in the Holy Book, where those who did not faithfully obey the Lord's many commandments were killed or maimed. You must know yourself the power such stories hold. All of us are raised to love the Lord, to place Him at the centre of our every thought. And we want to love Him, and to believe He loves us back. When the world is at its most threatening and bleak, He's the one person we feel really cares for us and heeds our prayers. He fills the void in people's hearts."

"Is that so wrong?" Maryam asked. Her own heart was filled now with nothing but a desolate loneliness and constant pain.

"No, child . . . not wrong. But understand that faith and religion are two entirely different things. The Apostles of the Lamb created a new kind of religion to seize control—as with many in the past, their declared love of the Lord was just a means of holding power and keeping those who revered them in ignorance of bigger truths."

Maryam stared at Mother Deborah, shocked that she would say such things so plainly, right out loud. Surely this was sacrilege? Blasphemy? Evil lies? And yet . . . deep down, hadn't she come to this very conclusion all on her own?

There was a subtle shift in the water lapping at the cave's secret beach, and Maryam realised that the tide had turned. The sleeping bats, hanging from the ceiling like pods from some strange creeping plant, shifted and stirred. They were attuned to the ebb and flow of nature within these walls.

She took a deep breath, shoring herself up against any possible anger arising from her next question. "If this is true, then why did you and Father Jonah remain Apostles?" She felt heat flame up her face, burning and pulsing the wound on her ear.

Mother Deborah smiled, her face creasing in tired lines. "Ah. Here we reach the crux of it." She stood up, pacing the short distance to the boat and once more caressing its smooth carved sides. When she spoke again, the measured storyteller was gone, replaced now by a feverish fighter. "You know yourself how you were raised—never questioning the rights or wrongs of what you were taught. We were the same. But there came a point, about the time I first fell for my sweet Jonah, when I looked around at what was happening and it made me sick. Jonah felt the same way. But, believe me, there's no room for dissenters in our world—neither server nor Apostle is safe to voice disquiet—and once Jonah's brother took over as High Father things grew much worse."

She rubbed her hand across her face, and the hand shook when she lowered it to support herself against the boat. "They fought, but Jonah had no power to win against the circle of bullies Joshua had built around himself—and we did not want to risk Joseph's future, so we left. Oh, it was covered up all right; the villagers were told we'd come to live among them to spread the Lord's word. But we knew we'd angered Joshua beyond repair, and that if we tried to undermine him, we risked losing Joseph or being killed."

Maryam gasped. "You'd be killed? But Apostles are Chosen—"

"Stop!" Mother Deborah threw up her hands in anger. "If you are to survive this, girl, you need to toss away such brainwashing and think for yourself! Power is maintained by control—and control by fear and threat. It has always been so. Those in power always win out." She paced the beach, the scrunching of stones beneath her feet amplified within the cave. Then she drew in a deep steadying breath. "Here's the point. The ship contained a library—a place where many books are stored—and Jonah made good use of this. He found books of maps—charts of all the islands in the sea—and more. Pictures of sailing craft like this. Stories of those who used the stars to guide their way."

"You mean to say that Father Jonah built this craft?" Maryam asked.

"Indeed he did." A longing came into the older woman's eyes and she stared up toward the roof of the cave, as though silently communing with his soul. Finally, she sighed again and carried on. "He worked on it for many years: his plan was for the three of us to sail away." Then, surprisingly, she laughed. "I suppose we took advantage of our Apostle status even then, first secretly building a smaller craft to learn to sail. When distant glimpses of the boat led to rumours, we said it was a warning sign sent straight from the Lord—that evil lay beyond our shores and only by complying with the Apostles' commandments were we all safe from harm."

Her smile twisted into a grimace. "In this, we helped to feed the fear and trample any glimmers of hope." She slowly shook her head. "I see now this was wrong. But we were desperate to keep the secret safe—not even Joseph knew until just before dear Jonah died. We did not want to place him at risk, until we were completely ready to take our leave." She turned to Maryam now, her eyes ablaze. "Now, finally, to my proposal. We want you to take this sailing craft and to escape. Joseph is not strong enough, and I will not leave him behind. All that I have loved is here."

"Me?"

"Why not?" She returned to Maryam's side, taking up her hands between her own and squeezing them tight. "You are the first I've seen who has shown the necessary will to fight. And, besides, if you stay here there is no doubt they will see you dead. . . ."

Now it was Maryam who could not remain motionless. Her head started shaking "no" before she even formed the reasons in her head. She shook off Mother Deborah's hands and stumbled to the far edge of the stony ledge, peering up at the sinkholes as the filtered sun bathed her with light. Take this boat, and set forth into an unknown sea? Was Mother Deborah totally mad?

She spun around, angered at having been offered something so seemingly lifesaving, yet impossible to have. "I cannot sail this craft. I cannot read the stars. I do not know the first thing about heading away from land." She kicked a stone across the space, listening as the sound reverberated down the cave to stir the bats. "I am a girl. Fifteen years old. A brown-skinned server whose only use, it now appears, is as a temporary vessel for my blood."

Mother Deborah charged at her, gripping her roughly by the shoulders. "How dare you throw this chance away? I would draw a machete across my throat right now if it somehow gave me the power to offer this same chance to my son, but he has grown too weak. This is not even about you—your whole race has been devoured by us, abused and manipulated and intimidated into losing hope. You have the chance to seek out help. Somewhere out there in the world, there must be others who will fight to set your people free again. . . . Others who might have a cure to save my son."

The force of her anger served to move Maryam from her state of shock. How could it be that the freedom of her people fell to her, she wondered, peering into the shifting water in the channel. She was nothing, no one, a beast for sacrifice, a womb to fill. But then she thought of Sarah and how, even in dying, her fury lit a flame of resistance that refused to dim. *We're nothing more than slaves to them . . . but you, Maryam, should flee.* At the time she could truthfully have answered that fleeing was pointless and impossible, the stuff of dreams. Yet now . . . it was being offered up to her and she was too scared to heed the call. How disappointed Sarah would be if she knew.

The tide was dropping quickly now, revealing a narrow walking track that must have been etched into the rock to follow the channel out to sea. Suddenly Maryam was overwhelmed by the need to be free of this suffocating place, where the walls and ceiling closed in around her like the ugly corridors in *Star of the Sea.* She craved the warmth of sunlight and expanse of sky.

"Can I have time to think on this?" She spun back to Mother Deborah, anxious to see her response.

The older woman nodded, sadness clinging to her like a mist. "Of course. It is right that we return now. Joseph will be desperate to know your choice."

CHAPTER FIFTEEN

Maryam crouched in the fresh water of the women's private bathing pool, scrubbing away the sticky layer of salt still clinging to her after the swim. Checking she was unobserved, she slipped out of her clothes and frothed them up with coconut soap to try to remove the stubborn stains. Once she'd rinsed them out as best she could and wrung them free of water, she spread them out to dry on the surrounding rocks, which were still hot despite the afternoon nearing its end. She uncoiled her hair to wash it, too, careful to protect her ear, and rested her head back so the long black tresses floated up around her like lush strings of kelp. In the dappled late afternoon sun her silky skin so closely matched the golden undertones of rock and earth it seemed as if she and the water were one. It was strange how quickly the sensation of being gently held by water calmed her mind when the very thought of setting forth on the ocean in a boat appalled her right down to her bones.

She'd felt so ungrateful, so terribly feeble, when she and Mother Deborah had returned to Joseph and he'd scoured her face for her reaction to this crazy scheme. And she had disappointed him; she had seen hope die in his eyes. It hurt, that disappointment: it dug down deep. If only there was some way she could take him with her. Seek, as his mother dreamed, some way to save his fragile life—and that of Ruth, and poor terrified Rebekah. And dear old Hushai and Brother Mark. What if she took them all with her, in search of some new peaceful land?

Holy Heaven—that was it! She dug her feet into the smooth

pebbles lining the bottom of the pool and pushed herself upright in one determined movement, water spilling off her as her hair plastered her naked breasts and back. There was no reason to go alone . . . she could take them all! Could give Joseph another gift of blood so he was strong enough to make the journey and then—

"Strike me down, but you're a fine-looking little upstart."

She scrabbled for her clothes, clutching them to her as Lazarus leered at her from the bank. He looked travel-worn and weary, blooming circles of sweat beneath each arm. As she stood there too embarrassed and stunned to move, he slowly began to unbutton his shirt, first revealing his chest and then, holding her eye with his arrogant gaze, unbuckling his belt and brazenly slipping off his pants. "When they sent me to arrest you . . ." he started, slowly making his way down to the water, the belt still trailing in his hand, "I didn't think I'd have the pleasure of washing away your sins as well."

He waded within arm's length of her, and finally she felt the power to move again. She splashed through the water, desperate to get away, but he caught her tightly around the wrist.

"No need to rush. It's time we were acquainted properly, just you and me." He tugged her toward him, twisting her arm further and further up her back until she could endure the pain no longer and ceased her struggle. Then he grabbed her other arm, dragging it, too, behind her. Her clothes fell in the pool.

"Leave me alone!" Maryam tried to fend him off with her glare alone but Lazarus merely chuckled, looking instead to her nipples which, to her shame and great dismay, tensed and hardened into rosy buds.

He whistled admiringly between his teeth and bent down, brushing his tongue ever so delicately across one bud. Despite herself, fire shot down to her abdomen and detonated deep inside. He lifted his face to her again, a lazy smile rippling his lips. "There. That wasn't so bad, now was it?"

There was such smugness in his voice, full with the knowledge he could violate her and no one would dare raise a hand against him. It was just as Mother Deborah had said: *Those in power always win out.* And now they'd sent this beast to humiliate her and drag her back. What chance did she have of resisting him? What chance at all?

He drew her even closer, until her betraying nipples brushed against his skin. So quickly she did not see it coming, he wound his belt around her wrists, binding them together to free up his hands. He ran his fingers down her back, cupping her buttocks in his palms.

"There, you see?" he whispered up against her ear, breathing his hot moist lust right into her. "Humility, little Sister. You're not so special after all."

She could hear the distant mew of hungry children and the sounds of those preparing food, but she knew if she cried out for help no one would dare disturb his game. Power and control. Yet what else had Mother Deborah said? That she, alone, had shown the necessary will to fight. And Hushai, too: *You have a task that none but you can carry out. . . .* She gritted her teeth, her hands clenching behind her back. Mother Deborah was absolutely right. If she did not fight this wickedness head on, no one else would step in to take up the cause.

He was nuzzling her neck now, pressing the live evil part of himself against her stomach in an odorous gyrating dance. Enough! She jerked her knee upward, driving it into the centre of that threatening manhood with all the strength she had left.

He grunted pain, releasing her as he doubled over to clutch the site of her attack. "No one owns me," she shouted, her voice shaking with fury and fear. Lord in Heaven, of all the risks she'd run to date, this was the most dangerous by far. She stumbled toward the bank of the pool, frantically trying to work her hands free from the belt. But the bank was slimy and without her hands to balance her, she slipped and splashed back down again, muddy ledges crumbling under her and spewing a dirty cloud out into the water. By now Lazarus was recovering; he threw himself toward her as she tried, again, to scale the bank. This time she dug her toes in hard and made it up, finally freeing her hands as she ran, naked and terrified, along the path that led back to the village huts.

Memories of her humiliation at Aneaba flooded back, and it struck her that her naked arrival in this village might cause further disruption and outrage. She could not bear the thought of this and veered off the track, crashing through the under-growth in desperate hope that somehow there would be, ahead, a place to hide. But she heard Lazarus close behind her, and realised now the dreadful error in her logic. Panicked, she spied a fallen tree branch on the ground ahead and scooped it up, rounding on him and holding it as threateningly as possible above her head.

"If you come any closer I *will* attack." She braced herself, knowing in her heart this act was futile but determined to go down fighting.

He stopped, throwing up his arms to ward her off. "Whoa there, wild woman," he jeered. "I think I'll just rest here a while to enjoy the view."

Embarrassment radiated from her cheeks and neck but she

dared not lower the branch to cover herself and hide her shame. Then the strangest change came over her, as if some lost spirit had seen her there and slipped itself into her skin. She straightened, feeling the power of her presence—her glistening skin, her streaming hair, the fire she knew was in her eyes—and found herself weighing the branch in her hands as if she were a warrior woman from days long past. And she could see this strange possession affect him, too: he crossed his hands defensively across his own nakedness and something indefinable about his manner seemed to change.

"Look all you like," she challenged him, finding in her mind a place of searing clarity she hadn't known existed. "If you take me by force then all you will have proved is that you're bigger and faster. I'll still know that the thing you most covet—my awe and respect—you'll never have."

Her words struck true, his face flushing a blazing pink, and she drove the message home ruthlessly, curling her top lip a little as she looked down at his fast reducing manhood with a mocking smile. And he was disconcerted, right enough, one of his hands unconsciously sweeping back his dishevelled fringe while the other still struggled to cover himself from her scornful gaze.

But his fluster did not last long; she had to give him that. He laughed, more naturally now, and very purposefully folded his arms across his chest, standing with his legs apart so she could see him in all his naked glory, and it took her all her willpower not to blush again or look away.

"What would you know of respect?" he said. "Have you not sacrificed yourself—your very soul—to the Lord? To us?" He shifted, taking half a step closer, his eyes locked in a war with hers. "Why should I respect your kind? You let us steal away your lives."

She felt his accusation as a blistering slap, for what he said was all too true. She had to try to reason with him, in the few precarious minutes before he grew bored with this game and struck again. "Does our powerlessness give you the right to treat us like animals?"

"Yes," he shrugged, "why not?" He shifted a little, one hand straying to his hip as he watched her recoil at his words. "I know we've all been raised to worship a judicious Lord and Father—someone who is kind and fair. But where's the evidence, dear Sister? Show me where?" Something close to sadness swept his face before he transformed it to a sneer. "One day I looked around and saw my father and his cohorts do exactly as they please, while all you ignorant servers continue to slug back toddy like it's sacred water and kiss the ground beneath their feet. And they're not struck down by the Lord, my little lovely—oh, no. The Apostles are rewarded for their sins. Revered."

His cynicism sickened her. "You call it sin yet still condone it?"

"Again, why not? You'd rather I shunned my birthright? I'm not about to join the ranks of drugged-up weaklings such as you. Grow up."

All that Mother Deborah had spoken of inside the cave came sharply into focus now in Maryam's mind. "Do not mistake submission for weakness, Brother Lazarus, when its underlying cause is fear."

"Bravo!" Mother Deborah stepped out from behind a tree and clapped her hands, their discarded clothes now lying dripping across her arm. She looked to Lazarus, one eyebrow raised.

"It seems, nephew, if we put aside her astounding disobedience, you may finally have met your match!"

Lazarus blushed scarlet as his aunt surveyed his naked form. She plucked his trousers from the pile of sopping clothes and handed them to him, winking at Maryam as they watched him struggle into the wet clothing as fast as he could. For the first time since Maryam had seen him, he appeared more boy than man, hopping unbalanced from foot to foot as the fabric tangled and clung to itself, refusing to cooperate.

With Lazarus distracted, Mother Deborah placed herself as a barrier between him and Maryam, who struggled back into her own wet clothes.

"Thank you," she whispered gratefully. Her whole body began to shake, only now revealing the extent of her terror and shame.

"Come." Mother Deborah took Maryam briskly by the elbow and escorted her back to the track. "Oh, nephew," she called over her shoulder, "when you have pulled yourself together, kindly join me in my hut. Joseph is there."

They left him struggling in the undergrowth, while they hurried back along the pathway to the village. "It's lucky that I came in search of you. Lazarus has yet to learn much self-control."

Maryam shuddered, thinking how close she'd come to discovering this first hand. "Of all the people they could have sent to take me back, I truly wish it wasn't him." She swallowed hard. "He frightens me. And he said I'm under arrest. What does that mean?"

They reached the entrance to Mother Deborah's hut and paused outside. "I'm really not sure, my dear. But I understand my brother-in-law well enough to know he will use this as a lesson to subdue any further unrest."

As Mother Deborah made to go inside, Maryam held her

back. "I have reconsidered," she admitted, and excitement dawned in the older woman's eyes.

"But we need to talk. I think I may have figured out a way to work your crazy plan."

* * *

From her lowly position at the rear of the room, Maryam watched Joseph, his mother, and Lazarus complete their meal. Joseph hardly ate a thing; indeed, he seemed to grow more pale and weak with every passing hour now. A harsh dry cough wracked his thin frame, and the ugly purple marks of Te Matee Iai continued to creep across his skin with the same voraciousness as the kona roroana vine showed in suffocating tall trees.

She picked away at her own meal of steamed fish and taro with her fingers, playing up her servility to throw Lazarus off the scent of their newly formed scheme. She had not needed to work hard to convince Mother Deborah of its merits: the two of them had hurriedly conspired together as they prepared the meal. Mother Deborah would return with them to *Star of the Sea*, where she could contrive the means to postpone Joseph's death and set in motion their eventual escape. All it now took was Lazarus's unintentional co-operation and the hook was baited—so long as Joseph lived that long and he, among all others, did not suspect the purpose of their plan.

Mother Deborah now pushed her empty plate away and leaned in toward Lazarus, touching his arm. "Nephew, I would seek your help. I need someone with stealth and strength."

He looked at her, surprised and pleased. "Of course, Aunt Deborah. I'm glad if I can be of help." He straightened himself, preening with such an air of self-importance Maryam hurriedly hid a smile behind her hand.

"I know you must make all haste to get the girl back to the Holy City, but Joseph and I need to travel there as well." Her gaze turned to Joseph, who had slumped back against the wall and closed his eyes, and worry creased her brow. "He is in need of your mother's expert care, and I am worried that the trek will further weaken him—especially since his strength was sapped by trying to recapture this stupid girl."

Joseph's eyes flickered open and he looked confused. It seemed he was about to speak—perhaps to chastise his mother for her change of tack over Maryam's position—when Maryam saw a subtle look pass between them. He nodded almost imperceptibly and sealed his lips.

"You want me to arrange a litter?" Lazarus asked. In his self-absorbed state he'd clearly missed their silent exchange.

Mother Deborah shook her head. "I fear the trip is still too slow." Now she shimmied closer to him and murmured conspiratorially: "I have a much, much faster way."

"Indeed?" Lazarus's face lit up with curiosity.

"I first must ask you for your word not to reveal this to a soul." She gestured dismissively at Maryam. "The girl I can keep silent on the threat of death, but from you I expect loyalty not to say a word." She paused, playing on the drama of the moment. "Not to your friends. Not to your pretty server playthings. And, most especially, not to your mother or father. On the memory of my darling Jonah you must swear this."

How he is lapping this up, Maryam thought, watching as his eyes widened and he licked his lips. His greed for power was playing right into Mother Deborah's hands.

"For you, Aunt, and in the memory of my uncle, Jonah, I solemnly swear."

Mother Deborah reached over to him now, cupping his face between her hands to kiss each cheek. "I will not forget this, my sweet nephew. I will be indebted to you till my dying day."

Again Maryam struggled to contain her mirth: the vain boy had puffed up like a frigate bird luring its mate. Joseph's eyes were on him also, equally amused, although still clearly puzzled by his mother's intent. He looked over at Maryam for one long searing moment before he was consumed by another cruel bout of coughing. It hurt her to see him struggle so, and took all her willpower not to rush to him and offer help. How could she feel so deeply for him when so little time had passed since first they met? The emotion, strange and raw, was heightened by his failing state.

"So," prompted Lazarus, "what is your great secret plan?"

"I have a sailing craft—a small longboat converted to use the wind to push it forward." She held up her hand to ward off his response. "I know it is against the Rules of the Apostles but . . ." Here she lowered her voice and smiled in a perfect replica of his own cynical smirk. "We all know there's one set of rules for the servers and the villagers, and a completely different set for us."

Lazarus nodded, not appearing to find this at all out of the ordinary. "And you can sail this craft?"

"Indeed I can. And I intend to show you, too. Now that Jonah has died and Joseph is . . . weakened—" her casual tone cracked at this, and she had to swallow hard before she continued "—I'd like to give the boat to you. But first, I want to use it to transport Joseph quickly back to *Star of the Sea*."

Lazarus sprang to his feet in his eagerness. "Count me in! When do we leave?"

Mother Deborah laughed. "I fear we'll have to wait the night. But if you help me to prepare everything, we'll leave at dawn. It's easier to learn to sail when you can see!" She, too, rose and then turned to Maryam. "Stay and clear this mess up, girl. Brother Lazarus and I will go now and prepare the boat." She towered over Maryam, weighting her words for Lazarus's benefit. "Do not attempt to leave this hut. I will have villagers posted outside to stop you should you try—and I will not be responsible for how they choose to carry this order out."

"Yes, Mother," Maryam replied, in her most submissive voice. She watched them leave the hut, Lazarus romping around Mother Deborah like an excited puppy let loose from its cage.

"What is my mother playing at?" Joseph now asked.

Maryam started to collect up the discarded remnants of the meal. She shrugged. "Concern for you. She wants to get you back there without more strain."

"But why, when I would rather stay where I was raised? Besides, I don't want those blood suckers anywhere near me now. Mother knows that."

Maryam could not contain her frustration. She squatted down next to him and pressed her cool hand on his feverish forehead. "You are lucky," she quietly chastised him, "to have a mother who loves you so. She will not rest until she can relieve you of this awful plague. If you love her in return then you must do everything in your power to help save yourself." She let out a sigh of yearning. "Cherish your time with her. What I'd give for just one more day with mine."

A tear slid from the corner of her eye and Joseph reached

up to wipe it away, brushing one finger gently across her cheek. "How can I argue with that?" he asked wryly, pressing her teardrop to his lips.

He looked so sad, so totally exhausted by the need to fight, now, for his life, Maryam leaned over and kissed the place her tear now sat. She intended just a peck, to offer him some slight comfort, but his hands reached up and dug themselves into her thick curtain of hair to draw her in—and this time, comfort was clearly not the driving force behind their brief, yet tender, kiss.

*   *   *

Dawn was still just a vague promise on the horizon when four figures made their furtive way through the sleeping village, heading for the private cove where Mother Deborah hid her small training boat. She and Lazarus had prepared the craft the night before, freeing it from its camouflage of low-growing plants to erect the mast and fit the sails.

Now, in the silence before the birds broke into song, they dragged the boat down the sandy slip of beach and floated it out into the surf. One by one they climbed aboard, Maryam helping Joseph to settle in a corner where he would be protected from the wind and surf. Lazarus guided it until the water reached his thighs, then leapt aboard himself just as the first faint breath of wind caught in the sails.

Mother Deborah threw the tiller around and pushed the boom out wide to catch the breeze. She steered the boat out through the reef, pointing out the way the waves broke differently between the deadly coral shelves. Maryam listened intently, knowing she must take in every lesson of the trip in preparation for her own. And

Mother Deborah was a good teacher, explaining each maneuver and technique with detailed care. When they reached the safety of the open sea, Lazarus took the tiller under her guidance and showed, although Maryam hated to admit it, he was a natural sailor, able to read the subtle shifts of wind and tide with ease.

"Sister Maryam, I may as well put you to work here at the ropes," Mother Deborah said casually.

Maryam's heart raced as she edged down the boat to take her place, all the while waiting for Lazarus to protest this plan. But he was in his element, really relaxed and happy for the first time since Maryam had known him, an unambiguous smile lighting his face.

They tacked along the coast, zigzagging forward and back to practise each new maneuver. Lazarus laughed aloud as the spray washed over the bow, something that happened each time they cut too sharply across the swell. It was exhilarating, there was no denying it, even Joseph cracking a smile. And soon, despite themselves, Lazarus and Maryam worked as a single unit without the need for Mother Deborah's aid.

With the dawn finally breaking salmon-pink across the sky, the little boat dipped and dived its way through the gentle ocean swells, the breeze scuffing over them as screeching sea-birds reeled above and silver flying fish leapt from the ocean out in front of them, seemingly to guide their way. Maryam tried to imagine how it would feel to sail the big boat Father Jonah had built back in the cave. With its two tall masts and much bigger sails, would it handle anywhere near as easily as this? What a speed it must reach out in the open sea, flying across it with all the ease of their small silver-scaled guides.

Then Mother Deborah insisted Maryam and Lazarus swap

places, Maryam taking the tiller and learning how to monitor the feather flying from the tip of the mast to gauge each slight shift in the wind. Once, distracted by one of Joseph's coughing bouts, she allowed the sails to slacken: they flapped loudly until she finally managed to swing the boat back to its course. There was so much to think about—wind, tide, swell, reef—and she found herself so absorbed in the process that it seemed no time at all before her much-loved atoll home came into view just off the coast.

Now Mother Deborah took the tiller again, Lazarus on ropes, the little boat skimming over the reef and hugging the coast. With Maryam's help they lowered the sails, rowing in through the mangrove maze until the boat was nestled into a small wharf formed from one enormous rotting log. They tied it off there, clambering up onto dry land.

All that exhilaration, that sense of freedom on the sea, disappeared as quickly as a speck of dust borne on the breeze. On the far side of the mangrove swamp the local village would be stirring now and there, across the causeway, the Apostles lay in wait to receive their errant server back into the fold.

Try as she might, Maryam could not prevent her legs from trembling as they approached the causeway and took the first tentative steps along its snaking bamboo deck. Her head started pounding and her stomach twisted into knots. The plan had seemed so easy when they'd plotted it last evening, but now all her fears gathered back around her.

Lazarus, too, must have sensed the change: he grabbed her by the arm and marched her forward like that first struggling sacrificial goat. So this was how it was to be. All power stripped away from her, she had no choice but to be led back into Father Joshua's brutal, unforgiving world.

CHAPTER SIXTEEN

The platform began its laborious journey up the side of *Star of the Sea*, each of the four aboard pensive and silent and every scrape and groan from their advance up the rusting hull shocking through them. Even Lazarus lost his air of supreme confidence as they were hoisted ever closer to the top. He dropped his grip on Maryam, his arms hanging like dead weights as he closed his eyes and drew a curtain of indifference across his face.

Maryam's knees weakened and continued trembling despite her resolve to stay calm. If she knew what lay ahead of her it might have been a little easier, but this not knowing—this gnawing sense of real doom—ate away at her defences, even though Joseph and Mother Deborah had both privately assured her they would do everything within their power to help diffuse Father Joshua's wrath.

She peered upward into the faces of the four strong servers who manned the ropes, hoping to find Brother Mark among them. But Maryam did not recognise the men and his absence ratcheted her anxiety up a further notch. What if his part in her escape had been discovered and had caused him harm?

This guilt continued to build as they followed the unidentified servers through the corridors—to the theatre, no doubt, where Father Joshua would lie in wait. Here she was, headstrong and stupid, risking the wellbeing of the very people who had shown her care. It was blatantly clear now that no life under Father Joshua's iron rule was free from fear, not even those within his fold. If Mother Deborah and Joseph backtracked now and offered her up for punishment, she would not blame them. Indeed, perhaps it would be better if they did—this way she, alone, could take the blame.

As they stepped in through the theatre doors and made their way toward the stage, Maryam could see Father Joshua sitting up there on his throne. Mother Lilith stood to his right, Mother Michal to the left, like an unholy trinity, while what seemed like light from the Lord streamed down upon them from its power source up in the ceiling, accentuating the pale marble of their skin. Maryam felt her stomach contract and twist as the great man's eyes lazily traversed the group, narrowing when they locked on her. There was such hate in those eyes, such a cold consuming fury, that before she even reached the stage her legs froze mid-stride. All bone seemed to dissolve and she staggered, slumping forward onto the patterned floor to prostrate herself before the group. Humiliating and cowardly as it was, at least this way she did not have to meet his eyes.

"Leave the sinner and come forward, my dear family," Father Joshua called, his voice surprisingly warm and inviting.

Maryam felt the stir of feet overtaking her, as the other three made their way up to the stage. She dared not watch, focusing, instead, on catching every passing word.

"You have done well, my son, bringing this foolish sinner back so quickly." Father Joshua's voice sounded relaxed, as though he was smiling, and the image of his bared teeth flared in Maryam's frightened mind. He smiled like a shark, without soul or conscience.

"I had the help of my aunt and cousin, Father. In fact, Joseph here deserves the praise. He saw the girl escape and followed her all through the night." Lazarus must have accepted the story

Mother Deborah fed him as they'd rigged the boat. Even if he was not entirely convinced by this, the promised prize of the small boat was obviously enough to win his silence—at least for now.

"Indeed? Well, Joseph, my boy, then it is you who I must thank." Although his words were pleasant enough, his tone grew tense. "Why don't you go and rest from your journey now, nephew. You look done in."

Maryam peeped up through her hair, just able to see the way Joseph swayed precariously from fatigue. Lazarus came to his aid, hooking his arm through Joseph's and propping him up. She recalled him at Joseph's side the first time she had seen them at Jonah's funeral. His thoughtful concern, both then and now, seemed so contradictory, so unlike the Lazarus she loathed and feared.

"If you'll excuse us, Father," he said, "I'll take him to my room to rest."

"Of course." Father Joshua waved them away, worry knitting his brow. He flicked his gaze back to Maryam, who quickly lowered her head again to avoid his eyes. When he continued, the concern in his voice astonished her. There was a real family bond there, after all. "He looks terrible, Deborah. You should have sent for Lilith to come to you and let him rest."

"Perhaps. But we are here now, and that's what matters." Mother Deborah paused. *Now, it starts.* "Dismiss the other servers, Joshua. What I wish to tell you about my plans for this foolish girl must be for our ears alone."

Father Joshua clapped his hands. "Leave us now. Go out and blow the conch. Gather everyone together outside the doors and treat them all to extra toddy. Let them enter here only at my command."

Behind her, Maryam heard the servers' footsteps recede and disappear—the door clanging shut behind them as they complied without a word. In the silence that followed, Maryam heard the low reverberating thrum of the conch shell. This was not good. Whatever her punishment was to be, he had decided to make it public—a sacrifice to stamp his mark of power on the group. *Dear Lord,* she desperately prayed, *if you are here and still listening, aid me now.*

Meanwhile, Mother Deborah laid the foundation for their plan. "You are right, dear brother-in-law, that Joseph is almost spent. I realised when I saw him that I never should have tried to stop Lilith from curing him." Her voice dropped, as though divulging precious secrets to a friend, and Maryam had to strain to hear. "When I saw how he was struggling to please you by capturing the girl, it cleared my head. *You're* the sole head of our little family now—and if it pleases you to cure Joseph then there's nothing I would rather see. I cannot bear another death."

Mother Lilith spoke up now. "Well, praise the Lord! If we continue with the process we can maintain his strength."

"Indeed, it's time we joined together as one family again," Father Joshua said. "Too long we've been at loggerheads. It's time we all started anew."

"Thank you, Joshua. You're truly as kind and forgiving as our sweet Lamb." Maryam strained for any hint of irony in Mother Deborah's voice, but none leaked through. She sneaked another look, not surprised to see pompous satisfaction on Father Joshua's face—the same overt vein of conceit in the father as the son.

Mother Deborah was certainly good at baiting the hook, and now she expertly cast her line. "With this in mind I have a suggestion that may suit us both. I now recognise my Joseph needs special blood to save his life, and it occurs to me that this wayward girl needs a life-changing lesson to curb her pride."

Father Joshua leaned forward, rubbing his hands together like a hungry man. "Go on."

"Give my boy her blood at once. If it breaks dear Jonah's moral code then so be it—I want my son to have a life."

"You know he has undergone this procedure once already?" Mother Lilith broke in. "And that to really make a difference now and save his life, we'll almost have to bleed her dry?"

Mother Deborah nodded. "Yes, I gather you've already tried to help him—and I thank you—but I understand he needs more blood." She squatted down at Joshua's feet, clasping his hand as humbly as a disciple would the Lord's. "Look, I know it sounds sinful but, quite honestly, I really don't care about the girl. Please—Joshua, Lilith—just save my boy." She broke down now, crying as if her heart would break, and Maryam knew that in this show of emotion, at least, she did not lie. Joseph meant everything to her. To lose him really would destroy her, too.

Mother Lilith bent down and patted Mother Deborah's heaving back. "Hush now, dearest sister-inlaw. Of course we'll do everything in our powers to make him well."

"It's an excellent suggestion, Deborah, and will solve two pressing problems in one." Father Joshua sounded pleased with himself. He looked to Mother Lilith: "Now you and Michal can take Deborah to rest, and further discuss these plans. I have another fish to fry."

In the moments it took for the women to make their way from the room it seemed to Maryam the temperature dropped, sending shivers up her spine. She was alone with Father Joshua, and neither Joseph nor Mother Deborah could protect her now.

The doors clicked open and the sound of others gathered outside filled the void. "You may enter now and take a seat," Father Joshua called out to them. Almost instantly, Maryam felt the surge of people around her.

Somewhere in the crowd would be Ruth. And Rebekah, Hushai, and Brother Mark. Yet this did not comfort her. Whatever happened to her now, they would be powerless to help.

It seemed an eternity before the last of the servers found a seat and the crowd grew quiet, and in this eternity Maryam felt her mind go strangely still. What could he do to her that hurt more than the enraged rejection of her father? Kill her now? This, she was fairly certain, he would not do—not now Mother Deborah had planted her seditious seed. Her blood was too important to them to spill for punishment's sake alone. No, he would defile and humiliate her, no doubt, but she could survive this—knowing that, so long as he did not suspect their secret plan, she still might have a chance to beat him at his cruel game.

Now Father Joshua clapped his hands and his voice grew loud and dangerously commanding. "You are here to witness the Lord's punishment on one who has deceived us all. This girl, who we all so generously welcomed to our Holy City only weeks ago, has spurned His word and spread Lucifer's lies."

An outraged murmur rippled through the crowd and Maryam felt as though hundreds of eyes branded her. When Father Joshua spoke again, his voice filled even the far recesses of the theatre with its tolling strength. "Remember the Holy Book, good Children: *Anyone arrogant enough to reject the verdict of the judge or of the priest who represents the Lord your God must be put to death. Such evil must be purged.*"

Throughout the crowd, voices rose to back his words. "Hallelujah!" "Praise the Lord!" "Stone her!"

"Purge Lucifer's spawn!"

He laughed then, a great full-bellied guffaw that collected the crowd up in their excitement and egged them on. "I know, I know, it's hard to comprehend why one who has behaved so sinfully should not be slain but, Children, we are greater than our basest instincts—we are Blessed. We do not need to stone this foolish heathen here to mete out punishment, when we can bring her back to the Lord. Besides, He is bigger and kinder and more forgiving than all this. *There is nothing that keeps wicked men at any one moment out of Hell, but the mere pleasure of the Lord.* And He has spoken to me on this matter and shown His will— that we, sweet disciples, teach this poor sinner lying here before us a lesson in humility she'll not forget. As the Holy Book says: *Obey your earthly masters with deep respect and fear.*" He wound his voice up in a dramatic crescendo as he demanded: "Speak out now and remind our fallen Sister of Rule Three."

All around Maryam the crowd chanted, *"Through the mandate of His Blood, the Lamb speaks to His Apostles and gives them dominion over His entire congregation on the earth."*

"That's right, my Chosen. Heed the Rules. *By the power of the Lamb's Blood, Lucifer and all his heathen followers shall be overcome.*"

All around the theatre, frenzied voices shouted "Hail the Lamb!" as though possessed. Father Joshua, meanwhile, strutted the stage, clapping along in time to their chanting until it built into a thundering roar—baying for blood. Then, at the chanting's peak, he held his hands aloft and all fell quiet, with such an air of expectation Maryam felt all vestiges of calm and confidence flee.

"Stand up now before me, girl, to learn respect."

She rose, her face burning with embarrassment and shame, and staggered up onto the stage. She dared not look to right or left, scared by the unbridled hostility she could feel emanating from the crowd. When she finally stood before the puffed-up Father Joshua, she prostrated herself again at his white-slippered feet. "Forgive me, Father: I have sinned. I did not mean to—"

"Silence!" Her pulse thundered in her ears as he edged up so close the sour smell of his slippers caught in her nose. "How dare you throw the Lord's generosity up in His face? From the moment you were Chosen we have nurtured you as one of our own. Yet how do you reward such gifts? Betrayal! Slander! Casting your poisoned lies out upon the land."

He reached down and grabbed her by the hair, jerking her upright as her nerves screamed pain from each strained follicle. The crowd clapped and jeered as he pulled Maryam toward him, yanking her head back so she could do nothing but stare at him, horrified, full in the face. Then he spat into each of her eyes— two great sticky globules of saliva blinding her and sending the contents of her stomach heaving up toward her throat.

"Because you have sinned against the Lord, I will make you as helpless as a blind man searching for a path. Your blood will be poured out into the dust, and your body will lie rotting on the ground. . . ." Father Joshua recited.

He followed this with such a swipe across her cheek that her neck cracked backward and her world dissolved into one violent explosion of fiery red. Sharp pain retrieved her just in time to have him grind her face into his musty trousered crotch. She could not breathe, pressed so roughly up against his clothing, and her ears rang with a shrill buzzing.

Then, just as unexpectedly, he flung her from him, sending her sprawling out across the floor. *"Woe unto them! for they have fled from me: destruction unto them! because they have transgressed against me: though I have redeemed them, yet they have spoken lies against me,"* he bellowed.

Maryam tried to focus, but her world was blurred and ringed with pain—and she a writhing, hated insect left trampled on the filthy floor. But even this was not enough to stem his wrath. He kicked her in the soft part of her belly, driving all the air from her and, as she curled defensively into a ball, he drew back his foot to strike again.

Above the braying of the crowd one solitary voice rang out. "No! Stop!" Maryam coiled toward the sound. There, alone in a far aisle, Ruth stood her ground. So shocked were those around her their voices died away, and all that was heard in the great expanse was Ruth's small tremulous voice. "In the Holy Book the Lamb tells us: *Be ye therefore merciful, as your Father also is merciful. Judge not, and ye shall not be judged: condemn not, and ye shall not be condemned: forgive, and ye shall be forgiven.*"

Father Joshua looked at Ruth intently while the hush grew in the room like one collectively held breath. Then a smile twisted his lips. "Out of the mouths of babes . . ." He nodded to himself, tapping his foot upon the stage as though keeping time with his passing thoughts. "You're right, little angel. Our rage is spent and our Lord is merciful." He crossed to Maryam, who shied away and tucked her knees up to her chin to protect her vulnerable stomach from another blow. But now he reached a hand down, offering to help her up. "Come, sinner, back into our fold."

She refused his hand, scrabbling unattended back to her feet. It was almost as if Father Joshua was tired now, his bluff had been called. He gestured to the servers who had brought her in. "Take her to her room for now. Lock her in and let her make her peace with the Lord."

The servers filed straight-backed down the aisle and flanked her, escorting her back off the stage. Behind her Father Joshua didn't miss a beat, rallying the congregation in song. *"When the Bridegroom cometh will your robes be white? Are you washed in the blood of the Lamb? . . ."*

Maryam dared not glance around her as she walked the long aisle; could not bear to read the faces of these scavengers who'd wished her dead. But as for Ruth . . . dear Ruth, who'd stood up for her so bravely in her time of need, she'd not forget.

*   *   *

Curled up on her bed, nursing her bruised and aching belly, Maryam heard the key turn in the lock. She roused herself, ready for another fight, but it was Hushai's kindly face that appeared in the gap as the door was pushed open.

He padded into the room, a laden tray in his hands.

"So you return, little one. You've caused quite a stir."

Maryam relieved him of the tray, laying it down on the bedside table. "So much has happened in so little time," she told him, taking his hand and leading him over to the bed to sit. "I found my father, but he rejected me."

"So I have heard, child, from Mother Deborah. I am so sorry for your pain."

"You've spoken with Mother Deborah?"

"Indeed. I have known her since she was small. A good woman and one you can trust."

"Did she disclose our plan?" Maryam peered at his wrinkled old face, alert for any shift or gesture that might contradict his answer.

"That's why I'm here." He turned to her, as though he could see her through his milky eyes. "Joseph has been primed with toddy by Lazarus, to counter any resistance. It seems they are wasting no time—you are to come with me directly once you've had this meal."

Despite her eagerness to save Joseph, the news still hit her like a second kick in her guts. "Mother Deborah will be there? I need someone to monitor how much they take."

Hushai reached out, finding her hand without effort and patting it to soothe her nerves. "She and I, little Sister. It seems she has convinced them I'm so elderly my knowledge of the process is no longer a threat." He paused, shaking his head. "Sadly, things are not so good for Brother Mark."

"Oh no!" Her heart raced, powered by her guilt. "Tell me, quickly, what they've done."

Hushai sighed. "When your disappearance was discovered there were some rumblings, but nothing bad. But when news came that you'd approached your father in Aneaba and it was recounted what you said, all hell broke loose. Meanwhile, Brother Mark faithfully kept his word to watch for you, but he was discovered and questioned under—difficult—circumstances, and his guilt laid bare. He was tied up to the handrails on the upper deck and publicly lashed."

Maryam's hand shot to her mouth. "No!" *She* had done this dreadful thing to him. It was her fault. "Does he still live?"

The old man's face rippled with emotion. "His spirit is not broken but his body suffers cruelly—the wounds are deep."

She could not hold back the bitter tears. "Take me to see him, Hushai? Please. I must ask forgiveness for inflicting this pain."

"He will see you when he's ready, child, and meanwhile I must prepare you for the taking of blood. Eat and drink your fill now while I wait outside. There is another who would speak with you, and I will watch to see you're undisturbed."

"Another? Who?"

But already he was rising and making for the door. "Ten minutes only, then we really must go." He slipped outside, Maryam struggling to pull herself together. Poor Brother Mark. How could she have asked him to run such a risk?

She had no chance to dwell upon this further: her dearest Sister slipped through the door.

"Ruth!" Maryam threw herself at her friend, forgetful of her aches and pains, and embraced her with such ferocity neither could breathe.

"Enough!" Ruth protested, pushing her off. She held Maryam at arm's length, studying her. "I knew no good would come of this."

"You've not been punished for speaking out?" This fear had pressed on Maryam since Ruth's selfless act.

Ruth shrugged. "Mother Elizabeth stood up for me—said I was one of the most loyal Sisters she'd ever known. Father Joshua seemed quite impressed—in fact, he's invited me to dine with him at the Captain's table tonight."

Maryam could not keep from shuddering. What Ruth read as kindness and approval, she saw in a much more sinister light. What if Father Joshua planned to breed with Ruth himself? After the last few weeks of unfolding this unholy city's secrets, nothing would surprise her. The very thought of Father Joshua's old-man hands on her friend, his mouth, his ugly probing *thing*, disgusted her. She had to convince Ruth to come away—somehow break down her brainwashed trust.

She wrapped her arm around Ruth's waist, and sat them down upon the bed. *First things first.* "I found my father, Ruthie. My mother is dead."

Ruth hugged her again, her smile as pure as tide-washed sand. "Maybe now that you know this you will find some peace."

"Never!" Maryam burst out, images of the shrieking, strutting Father Joshua—and then her own betraying father—inside her head. "I *will* escape." She lowered her voice, staring intently into Ruth's eyes as the words tumbled from her. "It is not the Lord who calls the shots here, Ruthie, it is Father Joshua and all his kind. They do not care for us—they long only to have power to keep us all enslaved." Ruth's eyes widened uneasily as Maryam continued. "I have the means to get away. You, me, Brother Joseph, Hushai, Mark. Mother Deborah and Rebekah, too, if she is brave enough to take the chance. There is another world out there, a world where—"

Ruth pressed her hand over Maryam's mouth. "Are you mad? The Lord sent the Tribulation to destroy the world. Only we were saved, by His great grace. Outside you will find only death and destruction—Hell on earth. Here we are safe."

Maryam peeled away Ruth's hand. "Safe? To live our lives like animals, primed for the kill? As worthless slaves? This is no life. I want more."

"I want, I want. Can't you hear yourself? This is Lucifer speaking through your mouth."

"Not you, too? Please, please don't listen to what they say.

I'm going to leave this place and take you with me, even if I have to tie you up and drag you off."

"But we are Chosen—"

"Chosen for what? Our blood, that's all they care about. Think about it, Ruthie, use your head. If we're so special, why did Father Joshua beat me and humiliate me, when all I did was leave the ship? And why lash Brother Mark for this? They've killed dear Sister Sarah and many others of our kind. Rebekah and our older sisters here are bred to death. That'll be your lot, Ruthie. I'll not stay to see you dead."

Ruth reared up, pacing the room in her agitation. She shook her head side to side, as if arguing inside herself and losing ground. Such confusion and distress filled her face that Maryam truly wanted to weep. If she lost Ruthie, her dearest Sister for so long, was there even any point in trying to leave?

She rose now, too, grasping Ruth's hand to press the small blue stone into her palm. "In a moment they'll be fetching me to take my blood. There's every chance I won't make it through— the balance between life and death is very fine. Swear to me, please Ruthie, on our special stone, that should I survive you'll come away with me so we can live. The Lord would not want to waste our lives like this, He'd want us to be safe and free. To spread His *real* message—about mercy and forgiveness."

The stone lay cupped in Ruth's hand like the bright blue iris of a living eye. It glowed up at them, urging, seeking some magical response. Ruth did not speak; she just stood there staring down at it, silent tears descending her flushed cheeks. It was much to ask of her, Maryam knew. Like the faithful Ruth of the Holy Book, her Ruthie's heart was one with the Lord.

Ruth closed her fingers over the stone then opened them,

blinking the eye. When she finally responded, her voice trembled. "If it really *is* the Lord's will that I accompany you to keep you safe . . . then I will come."

She looked up through her tears into Maryam's eyes and a smile wobbled on her lips. And as she spoke again, it was the Ruth of the Holy Book whose words she used. *"Whither thou goest, I will go; and where thou lodgest, I will lodge . . . Where thou diest, will I die, and there will I be buried too."*

CHAPTER SEVENTEEN

The anga kerea toddy burned all the way to her stomach. Maryam did not resist taking it this time; she wanted its mind-numbing qualities to help block her terrible apprehension and to thin her blood so as to speed its flow. Time was of the essence now. Joseph lay in a drugged-out sleep below her and Mother Lilith prepared the hypodermic needles for the exchange.

Mother Deborah stroked Joseph's pale sweaty forehead as she watched Mother Lilith sterilise the equipment. She glanced up at Maryam, her tired eyes full of concern, and murmured softly so Mother Lilith would not hear. "I promise I won't leave you, child, until you wake."

"How is Joseph?" Maryam whispered back, her tongue already thickening and her brain starting to fog.

"If the transfusion is big enough, it should have some positive effect. That's as much as Lilith will say for now."

"Sorry?" Mother Lilith said, looking up from her task. "What was that?"

Mother Deborah smiled. "It was nothing. I was merely praying for my son."

Mother Lilith seemed to accept this, nodding as she laid the last of her equipment on the trolley and wheeled it over to the bed where Joseph lay. Maryam tried to watch the process going on below her but as his blood started slowly filling up the bowl beside him on the bed and Mother Lilith began to attach the second tube to his other arm, her brain started swimming around inside her head, losing focus and drawing her down into the deep, confusing toddy-induced sleep.

She fought it hard, fearful these would be her last few thoughts upon this earth. Should she pray for forgiveness now? Repent her sins? Every cell of her childhood conditioning screamed at her to make her peace and yet . . . and yet . . . her rage with the Lord, her disbelief that such atrocities were meted out in His name, took the words and spun them around. *Father, I forgive you for your sins.* . . . She almost laughed aloud at this absurdity, just as the needle pierced her skin and burrowed in along her fragile vein. *By the sacred power of His Blood* . . . what was it now? Her blood. Her power. Her life pouring away in this thin streaming flow of red. . . .

"Mother!" she cried out. Both Mothers turned, but it was neither of these two white women she so frantically searched for in her drifting state. Instead, she was rewarded by the image of the gentle brown face of one who once loved her, loved the little Nanona, there amidst a miraculous aura of white light, holding wide her arms to welcome her. And in this peaceful, surreal world Maryam ran to her, her heart beating ever faster in a race with time, collapsing into her mother's reassuring soft embrace . . .

*   *   *

Something roused her, wrenching her reluctantly from her mother's arms. Who would do this cruel thing, when she was so happy here and so content? It infuriated her. *No! Leave me here! There is no better life for me back in the world. Just let me die.* But the hand shaking her so insistently would not cease.

"Maryam, you must wake now. Answer me. Give me some kind of sign." The voice was frantic, drilling into her like a sand-hopper into the sand. "Come back to us, child. You must not die."

The urgency pressed on her and she tried to free herself of the need to respond. Her body was a slab of stone, cemented to the very bedrock of the earth, and would not move.

"Open your eyes, girl—do not give up on us now." It was a woman's voice, a voice she knew she should recognise, but the effort to put a name to it was just too great. There was nothing left in her—no blood, no substance. Better to go back to that happy place, the place of light . . .

Cold water splashed her face and she startled, her eyes jolting open. Mother Deborah's pale face hovered over her, tears freely running down her cheeks.

"Oh, thank the Lord." She leaned down over Maryam, gently kissing her. "I thought that we had lost you, too."

Too? The word took flight inside her mind, stirring up an agitation she could not decode. Someone else had died? But who? Then the answer struck her with the force of a mud-slide and she pushed up through her lethargy to say his name. "Joseph?" Could it be possible that she'd bled her life away and still he'd died?

"No my child. He sleeps still but has not been lost." Mother Deborah placed a warm soothing cloth on Maryam's forehead and wiped her brow. "You have given me quite a fright, though, I must admit. I've been trying to rouse you for the last hour."

Maryam closed her eyes again, no longer able to resist the summoning back to sleep. "Thank you for caring," she managed to murmur to Mother Deborah, before nothingness shrouded her mind.

*   *   *

"You must drink something, little one. Wake up!" Hushai's crackly old voice broke through the shroud and she felt herself being gently lifted and a cup placed to her lips. She swallowed automatically, the water a soothing balm to her desperately dry mouth. "We must get as much fluid back into you as possible now, otherwise you'll not survive."

Again he offered her the cup and again she drank. The leaden weight of her body had not abated, but now her mind began to clear.

"You saw the blood-letting?" she asked, then realised the stupidity of her question. Of course he could not have seen it: he was blind. "Sorry, I mean—"

Hushai chuckled. "I sensed the blood-letting, and it was frightening to experience, believe me." His voice lost its joking edge. "She took so much from you I feared you'd die. And then you started going into shock."

"Shock?"

"I've nursed enough injured people who then bleed to death to know the signs of deadly blood loss. Believe me, child. The Lord was on your side today." Once more, he raised her head and offered her water to drink.

"Not the Lord," she spouted carelessly, her bitterness clear in her voice. "He has deserted me. And I Him."

"Child, child, do not say such things, even in jest. Now is not the place or time." He placed the cup beside her bed and quickly strode across the room. She watched him crack the door open and tilt his head, listening. When he returned he leaned in close to her ear, whispering urgently. "They have posted a guard outside the door, and I will only be able to attend you when he takes a break or I can find some way to distract him from his post. It seems that, though you are so seriously weakened, they worry still." He drew up a chair and sat beside her, his voice so low she strained to hear. "Do you realise no one in living memory has ever broken free before? It has rattled those in power—caused great unease. If one can think this way, they fear others will follow suit." Maryam found this difficult to comprehend. "No one else?"

Although Hushai smiled, his milky eyes somehow still managed to convey great sadness. "Once, long ago when I was young, my friends and I started to scheme. But we were discovered before we could execute our plan and severely punished for our crime. My friends they crippled and kept as slaves, down in the basement of the ship, and me . . ."

Despite her dreadful tiredness, Maryam rose up and took his hand. Somehow she guessed the horror he'd endured. "*They* blinded you?" Even to say it shook her to the core.

He nodded, his fingers warm in her bloodless hand. "I was barely older than you are now. At the time I thought my life was at an end. But, eventually, I came to see their actions as a gift. From great suffering can come new gains—I realised I did not require my eyes to see the truth of human folly nor to ease the suffering of those in need. I have waited all my life to find another with the spark to take a stand. I thought once it might be young Lazarus." He shook his head. "But his rebellion has soured into an angry rage." For a moment he said nothing, blindly staring off into a distance Maryam could not even guess at. Then he sighed. "In my youth there was no one who dared to aid us, so I vowed that if I ever found another willing to take up the fight, I'd be there to lend a hand. I've waited far too many years for you to come along. I will not let them beat me twice."

"But how can you swallow down such cruelty and serve them, knowing what they've done to you all this long time?"

"Faith, my child."

How could he be saying this? "You still have faith?"

"There are many different kinds of faith. Mine, I take not from the Rules that fetter us. I look to the mountains and the sea, the sun and moon, the distant stars. We are all bonded together with this hallowed earth on which we stand—our old ones understood this well. My faith is in the part of every living thing that fosters life and acts from love."

His words moved her in a way she hadn't known before, but still the crushing tiredness refused to release its hold. She dropped his hand, exhausted by the effort required to think and speak. Would she ever rise above this lethargy? Find the energy to run? She closed her eyes, ready to sleep, when Mother Deborah's words rang again inside her head.

"One thing more, Hushai, before I rest. Has someone else I know died?"

Hushai startled. "How could you have known this, child?"

She wanted to answer him, to explain Mother Deborah's words. But now a shrug was all that she could muster.

He sighed. "I was hoping not to tell you this until you had regained more strength. Not one, but three, have died during this fateful day. Your Sister Rebekah's unborn child came far too soon and did not live. Her grief was just too much for her. She took her life."

The news struck Maryam like a lightning bolt. *Rebekah dead by her own hand?* Anger flared inside her, exploding with such force she groaned. "And the third?"

"I'm afraid to say it's Brother Mark."

No! Not Brother Mark! "But how?"

"His wounds infected so quickly there was nothing I could do to help. I failed him and it pains me more than I can say." The old man's voice crumbled away, his chin quavering as he struggled to regain control. "They say that before the Tribulation such infections were treated with ease, but now . . ." He shook his head.

Maryam started trembling, her body too weak to counter the assault of her distress. "Then I have killed him. I'm the one who caused his strife." How it hurt to say the words aloud, forcing them past a throat swollen with guilt and grief.

She curled into a tiny ball, her arms wrapped round herself, trying to hold together as her plan for freedom fell apart. She could not go through with it now—too many people's lives would be held hostage by her selfish desire to escape.

"Do not blame yourself, little one. Mark knew the risks and took them willingly to see you free. Those of us who once dreamed of slaying our Father to seek the light, like our ancestor Nareau the Wise, gladly walk back into the Emptiness so long as we have lived to see someone younger and stronger take up the torch. I, too, will die a happy man now, knowing you will bear that torch across the sea—and one day use it to ignite freedom in the hearts of all our people here."

Maryam gasped. So he knew about the planned escape?

Hushai had sensed her unease. "You forget that Mother Deborah and I are friends," he reassured her. "Your secret is safe. But can you not see how much this means? You light the way."

How could he be saying this? Did he not realise how weak she was? How full of guilt? Of doubt? Of fear? "If I go now," she said aloud, "those of you who helped me will be punished even more cruelly than Brother Mark. Don't you see that I can't let this happen—that your life lies in my hands?"

"Remember the teachings of the Holy Book? *Greater love hath no man than this, that he lay down his life for his friends.* If those of us who wish to help then perish . . ." He shrugged. "So, we perish. But far better that than never to have tried. Even the Lamb had grave doubts about his capacity to carry out the Lord's will."

"But how can I go forward with the blood of good people on my hands?"

Hushai's face screwed up in anger and he clasped Maryam's shoulders and held her tight. "Not *your* hands, Maryam. The stain is theirs alone to bear. Never forget this. Darkness cannot drive out darkness; only light can lead the way. You *are* that light—that torch—and this is your destiny, just as it is ours to follow the light."

Maryam stared up at him, her own fearful face reflected in Hushai's opaque eyes. What he said was true, no doubt of that. She had no other choice but to proceed. For how could she bear living if she gave up the chance to flee when others had suffered far too cruelly for this goal?

* * *

The clattering of feet and hum of distant voices echoed through the corridors and leaked into the cell-like room through cracks beneath the guarded door. She could hear the guard outside, pacing up and down at times, obviously bored. It was tempting to call him in, to explain that even if he wasn't there, she had no strength at all to flee.

She presumed the day was drawing to a close by now, yet here she had no feel for either night or day. The air was thick with the sour smell of rising damp, which ate into the floor coverings and traced the paint-cracked edges of the room in grimy blossomings of lurid green moss. She lay exhausted, as insubstantial as a fallen leaf, struggling even to raise her head to drink. Hushai, bless him, helped her when he could distract the guard, and ensured she always had fresh jugs of water to appease her raging thirst. But she knew he did this at his peril—that Mother Lilith had made no provision for her welfare since Joseph had received her blood. It seemed this was to be her punishment—no grand execution or public flogging, merely death by omission and a lack of care. How little they must think of her.

She didn't even have the strength or moisture left to cry. Instead, she drifted in and out of restless dreams that shrieked at her of thirst and death. So much for all of her grand escape plans. She had no chance of making it if someone did not help her build her strength.

She was just slipping back into a dream where none of those who she loved survived, when she heard some one speaking in the corridor then the departing foot steps of the guard. Seconds later Mother Deborah slipped in through the door. She rushed to Maryam's side, the rustle of her clothing loud in the room.

"I'm sorry it has taken me so long to come to you again," Mother Deborah said. "I have been with Joseph, who is starting to revive."

Maryam smiled weakly. At least her blood loss was not entirely in vain. Mother Deborah propped her up with two more musty pillows to help her drink. Then she took a ripe banana from her pocket and peeled it, holding it so Maryam could take small bites. Even the effort to chew exhausted her, but the soft sweet flesh of the fruit settled in her belly and the juices rumbled out their gratitude for this simple yet much needed feast.

"I cannot stay long—I've sent the guard off on a message but our time is brief." Mother Deborah reached into her pocket again and revealed a small ragged book. "I'm afraid they plan to leave you unattended, taking more blood every few days until you either live or die here all alone," she told Maryam, confirming her fear. "But Hushai and I will make sure you have food and water enough to survive and build your strength. Meanwhile, please study this book." She thrust it into Maryam's limp hand and smiled. "It belonged to my husband, Jonah, who found it years ago here on the ship. It tells how the stars may guide your way. You will need this knowledge on the boat."

"But why? Are you not coming too?"

"I've given this much thought, but no. If I leave Onewēre now, I leave behind the only tangible reminders of my Jonah's life."

"What of his boat? He built it specially for you! Isn't that enough reason for you to come?"

"But he's not here to journey with."

"You have a son—"

"Enough!" Mother Deborah cried out, crushing her face into her hands. Her breath strained out between her fingers as she fought to regain self-control. The eyes that finally met Maryam's were ringed with grief. "Without him I have grown . . . afraid." She sighed. "There's the truth. When Jonah died it felt as though the world I'd known was ripped away. To sail off now, into some new unknown land . . ." She shook her head. "I don't expect a girl like you to understand. But, trust me, I have not the strength or courage now to make this journey."

"But Joseph—"

Mother Deborah pressed Maryam's hands around the book. "Please do not tell Joseph this. I doubt he will agree to leave if he knows . . . Believe me, I have thought this through. Besides, this voyage marks a new generation's fight for freedom—that alone is all I need to comfort me when you are gone."

Maryam fingered the rough black cover, any remaining strength sapped further by this revelation.

"Just study it as best you can," Mother Deborah urged her.

As Maryam opened the old book at a random page, the sharp stench of mould wafted up. She glanced at the tiny print. Although she had been taught to read the Holy Book when she was young, her reading skills would be hugely challenged by this complex text. "I'll try," she muttered unconvincingly, not wishing to disappoint.

Mother Deborah perched on the bed. "I have set in place our plan. Tomorrow, the Lord willing, Joseph will be well enough to make the trip back to our home. He is stronger already and the mottling on his skin is fading fast—a promising sign. I do not know how much time your blood will give him, but I gather that the more he receives, the longer the gaps between his relapses. We can only pray it will have been enough to travel to a new country where medicine can cure his plague." She closed her eyes and placed her hand across her heart. Finally, she shook herself and carried on. "I will stock the boat with everything that you might need. Water, food, a means to fish. And, on the night the moon is at its fullest, three days from now, we'll sail around to meet you at the mangroves where we moored today. You understand?"

Maryam forced her head to nod. "Three days from now. At the full moon."

"Indeed. It's vital this timing works. They plan to take your blood again on the fourth day if you live, and I fear greatly that if this happens you will not survive." She let the horrifying implications of her words sink in. "All that you can do now is to concentrate on getting well—and studying the stars, of course."

"I'll do my best," Maryam promised, hoping her brain would clear itself of this fog.

Mother Deborah leaned down and pecked her quickly on the cheek. "There are no words to thank you enough for what you have done for my son. I only pray that this one extra treatment is enough to keep him well." She sighed, so full of motherly concern Maryam felt almost guilty she had not given Joseph more of her blood.

The older woman made to leave, but Maryam reached out for her and drew her back. "Please. I need to speak to you of Sister Ruth. She dines tonight at Father Joshua's table and I fear for her. She'll not dare resist him if he—" She choked, unable to voice the content of her fears. Ruth was so innocent, so ripe for plucking by this man.

An angry shadow darkened Mother Deborah's face. "I understand. I will eat at the top table and watch her well." With this, she carefully checked the corridor, then slipped outside.

Maryam listlessly flicked over pages of the book on her bed. At first the drawings there made little sense. But slowly the meaning started to detach and seat itself inside her brain. These marks were stars! Masses of tiny dots of different sizes linked by lines defining different patterns and shapes. Then she recognised the Maiaki Cross that pointed straight toward the south, and the wondrous Ingabong star that heralded dawn—all the constellations she'd gazed up at with such awe when first she realised that the sparkling orbs up in the night sky were the lights of distant suns and other worlds.

She studied the pictures as best she could, trying to memorise the intricate patterns each page revealed, but found she could not concentrate. The weariness refused to shift and, finally, she hid the book beneath her covers and rolled over to seek solace in sleep.

*   *   *

When next she woke, the room had grown so dark the markings on the pages were no more than a blur. Outside a wind must have arisen, for she could hear the pounding of the sea against the reef. It reassured her; connecting her spirit back to the outside world in a way that was not physically possible locked in this tiny claustrophobic room. Somewhere out there in the night her father roamed, so caught up in his status and his fear he could reject her like a poisonous stonefish cast from the net. And out there, too, in the star-studded night, must roam the grieving soul of Rebekah, clutching her lifeless, half-formed baby in her arms. Perhaps she would be comforted by Brother Mark, the two of them free at last. *Forgive me,* Maryam sent out to them, *I planned to save you from such harm.*

Hushai must have been in while she slept, for on the bedside table stood a bowl of soup. She wrapped her hand around the bowl to test its warmth. Only tepid, but her hunger was not fussy and she guzzled it. The chunks of snapper were overcooked and dissolved into bland mush inside her mouth, but nothing could take away from the relief of filling her belly with a nourishing meal. Once replete, she lay back exhausted—and increasingly concerned. If eating a meal could tire her so greatly, how on earth was she to sail a boat just three days hence?

The low rumble of the guard's snores drifted into her consciousness, followed by the tiny scratchings of the key being turned ever so gently in the lock. The next thing she knew, Ruth's glossy black-haired head popped around the doorway and she snuck inside. Light on her bare toes, she raced across the room and threw herself into Maryam's waiting arms.

"Praise the Lord that you still live!" Ruth released her, climbing up onto the bed beside her and burrowing under the blankets, too. Her toes were cold as mountain spring water and Maryam feebly kicked them away.

"Keep your frozen feet to yourself !"

"If they feel frozen to you then that is good! A corpse would not complain of cold!"

They grinned at each other, for a moment forgetting all else but the pleasure of lying side by side, as they had done since they were small. But then Maryam remembered her concerns for Ruth's safety and her smile died.

"Tell me of your evening meal."

Now Ruth's smile fled as well. "They were all so nice to me, asking me about growing up on the atoll. About Mother Elizabeth—and you. I told them you were a true believer and that you had long pined for your mother and that's probably why you ran." She turned her smooth broad face to Maryam, staring intently into her eyes. "This is the line that you must take. Mother Elizabeth made me promise that I'd pass this on."

"Mother Elizabeth?" Maryam snorted. "She must be trying to protect her back."

"What do you mean?"

"Come on. My running will look bad for her. She doesn't care for me at all—she's already made this clear. But if the Apostles thought she was somehow on my side . . ."

Ruth shook her head. "I can't believe she'd say that to you. She loves us, Maryam. She brought us up."

"It was her job, Ruthie. Can't you see?" She wanted to explain it further, but the weariness left her panting after every sentence. She waited until her breath had slowed, then tried again. "And Father Joshua?"

Ruth plucked at a stray thread. "He made me sit right next to him and underneath the table he—handled—my legs."

It was just as awful as she'd feared. "Anything else?"

Even in the gloom of night, Maryam could sense that Ruth was blushing as she spoke. "When I was about to go he asked, right out in front of everyone, when my bloods would be finished and I could wed with the Lord." Ruth was ambushed by a shiver she could not control. "He looked at me so—so— hungrily, Maryam. Like te bakoa eyes its prey out on the reef." Her voice wavered. "Mother Lilith looked at him sharply. Maybe you are right about him, after all."

Outside the door, the snoring stopped so suddenly both girls held their breaths. Then a long loud explosion of wind erupted and the guard, again, began to snore. The friends giggled, the tension and fear forgotten in this one moment of childish mirth. But the seriousness of their situation soon re-emerged.

"Listen to me now, Ruthie. This is what you must do. Lie to him and anyone who asks again. The Lord will forgive you this once—just say your bloods are still there even if they stop. We only have to last three days. I will work at regaining my strength and learning how to read the stars, and you must secretly pack for our voyage. We'll need our clothes and personal things—pack my feather and the blue stone you gave to me—and try to get down to the storeroom and take as much te kabubu powder as you can hide. I do not know what else we'll need—but Mother Deborah tells me she will sort this out."

Ruth's eyes had widened, their whites shining like mother-of-pearl. "How will we get off the ship?"

"I still don't know," Maryam said. "But I have plenty of time to plan, so leave that problem up to me. All you need to do is come to me three nights from now, at the full moon. Say that you are sick and go straight to your room without dinner. While they are eating we will run."

Ruth slowly nodded her head. "But what will happen if we're caught?"

"We'll *not* get caught," Maryam hissed. "I have only one shot at this or I am dead."

CHAPTER EIGHTEEN

Joseph came to see Maryam the next morning, barging in despite the protests of the guard. She greeted him with her warmest smile, happy to see him looking so much better.

"How dare you?" he started straight in. "You and my conniving mother planned this behind my back, knowing full well I'd never agree to it. How dare you?" he repeated, standing there in the middle of the room with his hands on his hips and his legs apart as though he were about to leap at her in his fury.

Maryam felt as though he'd slapped her down and her cheeks turned crimson as his angry eyes bored into hers. All the strength she'd regained after a deep night's sleep deserted her, and she found she could hardly lift her tongue to respond. "You look better," was all she said, and she could see how her words unnerved him: obviously he expected her to wade right in to defend her role.

He dropped his pose, baring his thin white arms to her to reveal the puncture wounds the needles had made. "You could have died!" There was such pain in his voice, such remorse, it touched her heart.

Again she lit him with her smile. "But I did not. And now you have a better chance of living, too."

"But why would you risk this for me? I'm an Apostle, nephew of the man who'd see you left to die." He jerked, as a new thought occurred to him. "Did my mother put you up to this? Did you have no choice?"

Maryam wearily pushed herself up the bed to prop herself

against the wall. It was so good to see him standing there, such a relief. Tears spouted in her eyes and she bit down on her bottom lip for a moment to halt their flow. "The choice was mine." One lone tear escaped, gliding down her cheek before it dripped on her chest, landing in one small damp circle right over her heart.

Two steps and he was at her side, collecting her up in his arms and pressing his lips against hers in a kiss that left her dizzy, and her heart beating very, very fast.

Joseph drew back, brushing a springy ringlet from her eyes. "I don't want to lose you now. Promise me there are no other plans I do not know." His sky-blue eyes fixed on hers, demanding that she tell the truth.

"I promise," she whispered, her voice still struggling to regain some kind of calm. That kiss . . . that kiss! It was enough to fight for, all on its own. She reached up and traced her index finger around his curvy pink mouth, their eyes still locked as he took her hand and pressed that finger to the centre of his lips, kissing its tip.

"Tell me, really, how you feel," she said to him now his rage was spent.

"I hate to admit it, but as soon as I woke from the toddy I could feel the energy returning to my body, and the fevers went." He squeezed her hand. "Though knowing that it came from you makes me feel so selfish and ashamed."

"Don't," she pleaded with him. "My motives were selfish, too."

He scoured her face, trying to understand. "How so?"

"Your father and mother built the means for my escape— to take this gift without you would be wrong." She smiled, squeezing his hand in return. "Besides, I do not want to leave without you, simple as that."

For the first time since he had entered the room Joseph now smiled. He pulled her to him again, embracing her as he sank his face into her fragrant hair.

"Then we must plan quickly," he mumbled, his hot breath tickling inside her ear. "I leave for home this afternoon."

*   *   *

Maryam counted down the days, each moment trapped inside the small damp room adding to her discontent. Each time Mother Lilith or Michal came to check on her she just had time to feign exhausted sleep. Once, they came together, their obvious glee at her apparently declining state was hard to digest. Their callousness preyed on her mind in the long hours she was left alone to brood and scheme. How could they stand by so happily and watch her die, while speaking of the Lord's will?

It was beyond her comprehension. But it hardened her resolve to leave this place and flee as far from it as wind and sea allowed.

When she was sure no one would come to check, she crept out of bed and worked at rebuilding her strength. It was hard, at first, even to walk across the room: it left her shaky and short of breath. But slowly, as the hours blurred past, the weakness eased—thanks, in most part, to dear Hushai, who fed her well and brought her special herbal remedies to boost her blood.

Occasionally he'd sit a while and speak of the cherished long-lost days when their ancestors had ruled the lands and travelled vast distances across the sea. At times like this she'd question him on details in the star book that she found hard to grasp, or quiz him on his knowledge of currents and tides. If he did not have an answer, he would go away and search it out, ever adding to her store of facts. When the enormity of what she was about to do overwhelmed her, it helped to feel she'd have these scraps of knowledge to aid her once they made their break. She tried to think of the great unknown ocean as her friend, but late at night, when the old ship creaked and groaned upon its ragged bed of reef, new fears arose and swamped her mind. Even if they managed to escape the clutches of the Apostles and sail away, what guarantee was there they'd not be drowned, fodder for sharks?

She fretted, too, for Joseph and for precious Ruth. Joseph, she could only trust, was restored enough to make the voyage. As for Ruth . . . she worried her friend could not further resist Father Joshua's carnal clutches and would be debased. In this Hushai tried to comfort her, checking in with Ruth and passing messages between the two. Yet in her late night musings, Maryam was not convinced that Ruth could muster up the nerve to come. She had such faith in the Apostles, despite everything she'd learned. Would she really have courage enough to spurn the Rules?

Then the morning of the great day dawned, pallid light spilling in through the filthy window as Maryam rose to wash herself in the bucket of warm water Hushai had kindly smuggled in moments before. She stripped away her stale clothes, standing naked to lather soap all over herself and shift the grime. As her hands rubbed over her breasts, she paused mid-sweep and closed her eyes. Her breasts had grown larger, no longer the small buddings of a child. How would it feel, she wondered, if the fingers that so tenderly caressed them were not her own but Joseph's? A deep shooting current gathered force inside her stomach and fired down into the secret place from which life sprang. She dropped her hands as if poisoned, her eyes springing open to dispel the thought, and hurriedly rinsed off the soap. Those thoughts were foolish. Dangerous. She must not let them cloud her mind.

How the day dragged on, as she paced the floor. Before her stood two possible futures—one, a voyage into the great unknown; the other, brutal seizure and death. Her head grew jumbled with such thoughts. Try as she might, she could not dampen down the tension that churned inside her like a storm-tossed sea. She pressed her nose so many times against the window, trying to decipher weather and winds, it formed a smear upon the glass. What if they couldn't escape the ship? If someone spied them as they left? Or if the sea rejected them and carelessly tossed them back to land? Or, worst of all, swallowed them whole?

For what she fervently hoped was the last time, she underwent the gruelling inspection of her health. Mother Lilith came alone, frowning as she picked up Maryam's arm and watched it drop, lead-weighted, back onto the bed. She leaned in close, listening to Maryam's heart. Again she frowned, as the pulse clattered out its fear at alarming rates.

"Tomorrow we will see an end to this," she murmured, more to herself than Maryam, who lay as passively as she could bear.

Maryam fluttered her eyes open, meeting the woman's gaze for what she prayed would be the final time. She licked her lips and swallowed hard, giving the impression that her mouth was dry. "May the Lord grant you all that you deserve," she muttered, smiling with a sweetness she did not feel as she recalled the words from the Holy Book. *They that plough iniquity, and sow wickedness, reap the same.*

The physician, meanwhile, smiled back, a shadow of regret now in her eyes. She placed her cool dry hand on Maryam's brow. "Such a waste. If only you had accepted the limitations of your birth." She brushed her finger tenderly down Maryam's cheek. "You never were the *real* Chosen, little one. That place is ours alone."

Such rage swept Maryam at Mother Lilith's arrogance that she closed her eyes again to hide this window to her soul. If she'd had doubts of what she was about to do, they now took flight. She would never again accept the lies, the treachery, from those who took the word of the Lord and twisted it to their own will. Better to be dead. The risk she was about to take seemed suddenly less terrifying.

Later, just before the evening call to dine, Hushai drugged the guard, filling him with such a potent brew of anga kerea toddy that the poor man didn't stand a chance. His drunken snores accompanied Ruth as she tiptoed into the room, laden with two bags filled with their few meagre belongings and as much te kabubu powder as she could lift.

The two girls hailed each other with a quick embrace, both so on edge they could not remain still for long. Ruth jumped at every little sound, haunted and apprehensive as she passed one of the bags to Maryam.

"I have begged off sick from dinner," she explained, helping adjust the straps that tied the loads on their backs. "Told them I am taking a toddy tonic and will sleep it off."

Maryam laughed. "You and that poor guard as well!" A strange sense of exhilaration swept her now, all fear retreating to one tiny corner of her brain. She longed to go, could not wait another moment to be free of this unholy place. But first she had one more private task to undertake. She took a deep breath, as though about to dive into the sea, and beckoned to Ruth. "Follow me."

"Where are we going?" Ruth whispered, as they headed back the way she'd come.

Maryam did not bother answering. Instead, she stopped outside the treatment room where Mother Lilith had stolen her blood. "I'll just be one minute," she whispered back. "You wait out here."

Despite Ruth's nervous state she nodded silently and did not question further. Maryam opened the door, already reassured by Hushai that no one lay inside.

The room reeked of the astringent Mother Lilith used to clean all her equipment, a sharp acidity that stuck in her throat and conjured up the terrors she'd experienced here. She didn't pause for reflection on this, however, instead heading straight for the benchtop where the implements of torture were displayed. She tried not to think too much about the implications of her actions as she gathered up all the transfusion instruments and carefully stashed them in her bag. She would not risk Joseph's life again; she would find a place to cure his ills, and if that meant shedding more blood along the journey she'd do it gladly for his sake.

Now she left this torture room behind, about to grab Ruth's arm to guide her back down the corridor toward the open deck, when Mother Elizabeth walked casually around the corner and found them there.

She stared open-mouthed at Maryam, struggling to contain her shock. "Te bebi! I can't believe you're standing there. I just came down to say goodbye."

Goodbye? Did this mean she somehow knew of their escape plan and approved? Maryam was so overwhelmed by this sudden show of love and understanding she dropped her guard, rushing to her surrogate mother and flinging her arms around the woman's neck. "Thank you, Mother. This means a lot."

"It is a miracle to see you so defiant in the face of death." Mother Elizabeth eyed Ruth over Maryam's shoulder, small lines of puzzlement forming on her brow. Her gaze lit on the bags both girls carried on their backs and the lines deepened to a frown. She stepped back. "You're going somewhere?"

Maryam's smile faltered. This was a strange question for someone who'd come to see them off. She turned to Ruth.

Ruth's normally friendly, open face was tense and closed. She sidled closer to Maryam, her voice shaking with anger. "She came because she thought you were going to die."

Maryam felt like she'd been flogged. Appalled, she lifted her eyes to Mother Elizabeth's exquisite face. "You knew that I was being bled to death and only came to see me to say goodbye?"

Mother Elizabeth, now defensive, crossed her arms. "Whatever my motivations, I see now it is fortunate I came. What game are you playing, Sister Maryam? Where do you go?"

Maryam could not answer her, still so caught up in Mother Elizabeth's collusion with the Apostles.

Instead it was Ruth, sweet mild-mannered Ruth, who stood her ground. "You will leave here and not say a word. If it felt right to you that Maryam would die, then think it so. You do not need to betray us over and over again—let us go."

At this, Mother Elizabeth seemed to rouse, now fully understanding their intent. She slowly shook her head. "You know I cannot just let you leave. Father Joshua would punish me as well."

"Then don't tell him," Ruth spluttered. She shook Maryam's arm, trying to bring her back into the moment they were facing now, but her face had leached of blood and her body hung listless under Ruth's strong grip.

"But it is my duty to uphold the Holy City's law."

"What law is this? The one that says the Sisters can be sacrificed like Maryam—or defiled like us?"

Defiled? Maryam emerged from her stupor and seized Ruth by the shoulders, holding her fast. "Oh, Ruthie. No! Tell me he didn't do that to you." But then the rest of Ruth's sentence resounded in her head. *Us?* She spun back to Mother Elizabeth, who had herself turned sickly pale. *Could that mean . . . ?*

Mother Elizabeth's arms fell to her sides. "How did you know?"

"He followed me to the storeroom and locked the door," Ruth said. "I had no choice. I could not run—and, anyway, no one was going to argue with Father Joshua. After he'd . . . done it . . . he said that I should learn to be as humble and compliant as you." She met Mother Elizabeth's eye and held it, disillusionment flattening her voice. "He laughed at you, you know. Said he hoped you had a daughter that you'd raise to be as yielding— that he looked forward to having her as well."

Mother Elizabeth's hands shot to her mouth, holding back a whimper as she slumped to the floor. Meanwhile, Maryam took Ruth up in her arms and embraced her as tightly as she could. Angry tears sprang to her eyes and she brushed them away roughly with her arm.

"Why didn't you say? I heard no word of this from Hushai."

Ruth shrugged. "What could you do? After it was over I told myself I only had to last here one more day."

Maryam crossed to Mother Elizabeth and crouched down at her side. "We are leaving, Mother who has raised us both. You can either call the servers, or let us go. The choice is yours. But think on this: if we were your daughters by birth, like the one you carry inside, would you want to see us suffer any further under this man? Or would you want us to escape?"

Mother Elizabeth did not speak, her mouth quivering as tears rolled down her beautiful tormented face.

"Come on." Maryam rose and grasped Ruth's hand. "It's time to leave." They did not glance back at Mother Elizabeth, had no idea what she would choose. But they had to risk carrying out their plan, and now that Ruth had revealed Father Joshua's abuse, Maryam would rather die in the process than see her dear friend violated again.

They ran along the corridor now, not pausing until they reached the door that led them to the outside deck—the one where Sarah had died. Hushai awaited them, beckoning them over to the two thick ropes he'd tied securely to the rusty bollards and then dangled down the side. There was no moving platform this time to descend the ship. No Brother Mark to ease them down. This time they must rely on the ropes alone.

Hushai took Maryam in his arms. "Thank you, little one, for bringing such hope to this old foolish heart." He kissed her forehead, his bristly chin prickling against her smooth face. "Go with the blessing of our ancestors—and don't look back."

"It's not too late. You still could come."

The old man smiled. "What use would an old blind man be? No, child. I will rejoice in the knowledge that you're far from here. That is enough."

Maryam took the rope between her hands and cautiously

eased herself out over the drop down to the causeway far below. "I'll never forget you, Hushai."

With that she pushed herself off, wrapping her legs around the rope to slow her as she saw, out of the corner of her eye, Ruth bravely do the same. It was a daunting drop, the wind buffeting them as they edged downward, the rough rope cutting into Maryam's hands and cruelly grazing and burning the soft unguarded skin around her inner thighs. Her arms shook with the effort of holding fast, the muscles spasming and screaming out their pain as, inch by inch, the formidable descent took its toll. The causeway was so far and unforgiving down below and capture only one potential glance away.

Dusk was settling around them, the full moon swept by fast-moving clouds as the two girls slowly scuffed their way down the flaking rusty hull. It was still light enough to be spotted if a villager cared to look, and the excruciating minutes seemed to stretch until Maryam's cramping arms felt they'd never hold her long enough to reach the ground. Blood started to ooze from the rope burns down between her legs. But then the causeway rose to greet them and Maryam let herself freefall until her feet, at last, slapped down onto the solid bamboo slats.

She dropped down to her haunches and crouched beside the massive hull, biting her lip to suppress sobs of self-pity as she waited for Ruth to join her there. Over on Onewēre the village appeared quiet: they were preparing for night and she could only hope no one would see them on this, the most exposing part of their escape. When Ruth finally dropped beside her with a grunt, Hushai immediately started reeling the heavy ropes back up to the ship.

Both girls overrode the pain messages that shrilled in their ears; they ran down the causeway as if Lucifer chased them. The causeway swayed beneath their feet, rocking in the swell, and Maryam turned her head toward the open sea, her heart skipping a beat as she saw the crests of waves break on the reef. It was no docile sea this night, and the thought of setting forth on it filled her with dread. But there was no time for regret now, and finally they jumped off the end of the causeway onto dry land.

Hand in hand, they sped along the sandy beach, trying to put as much distance as possible between themselves and the village before someone discovered them and called a halt. They skirted the compound, cutting in behind the vegetable patches and bent almost double to conceal themselves in the shadows of the scrubby vegetation. Just as they thought they were free of the worst, they came upon a village dog snuffling at the remains of a rat. It reeled around, baring its yellow teeth and barking savagely as they detoured and resumed running. Soon other village dogs answered this one and a pack of them came after the girls, snapping at their heels until Maryam scooped up a handful of rocks and threw them. But the barking had aroused interest and, somewhere behind them now, men's voices rang out.

"Into the jungle," Maryam panted, sure she could hear the sound of running feet behind them now. This was the stuff of her late night terrors, that they'd not even make it to the boat.

Somewhere off behind them seabirds screamed and reeled in the blustery air and, as the friends plunged into the lush coastal jungle, the evening filled with the calls of many tiny creatures marking the transformation from day to night. Already Maryam was exhausted, her breath ragged and painful as her legs cried out for some reprieve. But now Ruth's skill for running came into its own: she linked her arm to Maryam's and hauled her through the thick undergrowth toward their goal.

"You can do this, Maryam," Ruth puffed. "Remember how you nearly won our race back on the atoll?" She somehow managed to grin at the memory, using it as ammunition to spur Maryam on.

Only deep inside the jungle did they stop, Maryam doubling over and dropping her hands onto her knees to ease her cramps. Her rope-burnt thighs stung like fury and her pulse thundered in her ears. Each breath stabbed as if she drew in jagged coral from the air. "I don't know," she gasped, "if I can keep this up."

But already Ruth was restless, wanting to move as far away from habitation as they could. "Come on," she urged. "Someone could be following. Just one more burst and then we're there."

She was right, of course. There was no choice now but to carry on. Maryam drew in one last deep breath then straightened and began, again, to run. It was a nightmare world, the light fading fast around them and the hostile noises of the jungle sending prickles down her spine. As the two girls blundered past, birds burst from their roosts, screeching their annoyance to the underworld of tree and bush. Somewhere behind them, something crashed through undergrowth, fighting through the vegetation much as they did. *Please let it be an animal*, Maryam prayed, remembering the huge wild boar she and Joseph had encountered on her last gruelling attempt to flee. A boar they could contend with, perhaps, but a group of angry villagers they could not.

At last, the thickness of the undergrowth gave way to the trailing air-roots of the mangroves and they fought their way through them, Maryam anxious she might not recall the precise spot where Joseph was to moor the boat. Then an even greater fear assailed her. What if they had made their break, only to discover Joseph had not come? She dared not voice her doubts: the weight of responsibility for Ruth was so heavy it made her

want to retch. All this turmoil, this risk, and she relied upon
the word of white Apostles to aid their flight. Was she mad?

But now they stumbled on a faint pathway and she thought
she recognised the rough-formed track. She led now, clasping
Ruth's hand as they stumbled through brackish puddles in the
growing dark. If they were being pursued they would be safer
now; the mangroves were one huge tangled maze. Above, the
moon seemed to have deserted them, and only its pale aura lit
the edges of the streaky clouds.

Then there they were! The masts of Father Jonah's beautiful craft standing out against the sky. And Joseph ran to greet
them, wrapping his arms around them both as all three laughed
in sheer relief.

"You made it!" he cried, lifting the exhausted Maryam
and swinging her around. Then his jubilant mood collapsed.
"Mother has already left. She would not come."

His distress cut through her guilty knowledge of Mother
Deborah's desertion like a knife. Had she not lost a mother as
well? She took his hands between her own and tried to steady
him. "You have her love, and know it to be true and strong—
that will travel with you no matter what." She saw the words
take root and tried to think of something else to help ease his
loss. "She shows much faith in you to make the voyage without
her." She squeezed his hand and forced a cheeky smile. "Besides,
one day, so long as you can read the maps, we will return."

"You have a map?" Ruth asked, peering over her shoulder as
if she expected to see a horde of villagers break through the trees.

Joseph nodded, his wary eyes now also scanning the dark jungle
from which they'd come. "It's in the boat. Come take a look."

Maryam studied the craft, which suddenly appeared so

much smaller and more vulnerable under the vast expanse of sky. "How did it sail?" she asked, the enormity of what they were about to undertake suddenly hitting her full force.

"We only set a storm sail. The wind is quite shifty around the reef and Mother thought it better that we take our time and do not call upon the full power of the wind until we are well out to sea."

Maryam swallowed hard. She could do this. She could do this! She blew out a tensely held breath and took off her bag, swinging it over the side of the boat and gingerly climbing aboard. Her legs shook from the effort to move and, yet, she felt a surge of energy flow through her as she ran her hand down the closer of the tall timber masts. She studied Joseph's face, his neck. No signs of Te Matee Iai—for now. "How do you feel?" she asked him gently, brushing her hand across his arm.

He grinned and shrugged. "As if I am about to launch myself straight into Hell—so let's set off!"

She laughed, his humour soothing her, calming her down. He was right. There was no point delaying or debating now. If they were to do this crazy thing, they had to do it before they were discovered—and while her nerve still held. "Okay. Ruth, you climb aboard. We'll use the oars to get us out into the clear."

Joseph started untying the mooring ropes.

"I cannot go." Ruth's small frightened voice broke through the gloom.

"What?" Maryam spun back around to her, seeing how Ruth's eyes locked on the boat. She knew what Ruth was thinking, could see her utter terror at the sudden reality of their voyage clear in her eyes. "Come on, Ruthie. You've scaled the side of a huge ship. You've defied Father Joshua. You've been so brave. Of course you'll come."

"But you don't need me now. Just go. I only said I'd come so I could make sure that you got this far."

Maryam shook her head, not believing what she heard. "You never planned to come?"

Ruth shook her head and backed away from them, toward the trees.

Maryam stamped her foot, frustration and fear riding on her back as the mangroves seemed to fill with noise. "But I'm not going unless you come, too. I refuse to leave you here to be defiled or killed."

"I can't," Ruth squeaked, tears swilling in her eyes. "What if the stories of the Tribulation are true and we are sailing out into a poisoned void?"

"We must rely on faith, Sister Ruth," Joseph answered steadily. "I believe there's somewhere we can build a new and better life."

"Faith?" she echoed weakly. "What of the faith with which we're raised?"

"Quite right!" A dark shadow broke from the overhanging trees and pounced on Ruth, capturing her around her neck with an unrelenting arm. As he spoke again, Lazarus's voice was clearly recognisable. "Well, well. Look what we have here, then." He twisted his arm further, squeezing Ruth so tightly that her eyes bulged in their sockets and she fought to breathe. In his free hand he brandished a knife, collecting all the light spilled by the moon to sparkle menacingly before their eyes.

"Don't do this, cousin. Step away." Joseph edged across the boat, pushing Maryam aside. "We mean no harm to you: just let us go."

Lazarus laughed, the sound brutal and mocking in the night. "Go, dear cousin? But where?"

"Let her go!" Maryam railed, scrabbling through the ropes that cluttered and tangled at her feet.

"*Sister* Maryam. You think you are so clever yet I was in the village and I saw you pass with little goodie-two-shoes here." Again he jerked Ruth by her neck, pressing the knife blade to her chest.

Maryam froze, not daring to move and risk him ending poor Ruth's life.

"Whatever this is about, Laz," Joseph said, "hurting Ruth won't make it right. Come on now, be reasonable." All the while he untied the final rope, working as stealthily as a lizard stalked its prey. He pushed Maryam down beside the tiller, lowering his head so only she could hear. "Be ready to move when I say." Then he casually picked up an oar.

"Here's what I think," Lazarus mused, driving Ruth a little closer to the bow of the boat. "I think you're leaving Onewēre and I plan to come."

"You!" Maryam could not contain herself. "I'd rather journey with a shark."

Lazarus greeted this insult with a smile. "That, Bleeder, can be arranged."

Joseph lunged toward him with the oar. "How dare you speak to her like that?" he yelled, struggling to steady the boat as he tried to disembark.

But Lazarus was too quick for him, forcing Ruth's head back further and holding the tip of the knife blade up against her exposed throat. "Try that again, cousin, and you'll see this little Sister bleed as well."

Ruth moaned, her knees buckling. Lazarus manhandled her up onto the forward deck to tuck both of them up against the wall of its thatched shelter. All the while he kept the pressure tight around her neck and continued to brandish the knife. "Here's the deal. When we're far enough from land to stop you turning back for home, I'll set her free. Until that time, I suggest that you get paddling or someone else will happen along. I'm sure I'm not the only one who saw you run." He grinned again. "In fact, I think I might have accidentally told the chief."

Maryam sighed. So this was how it was to be. Escape, but only if they took Lucifer, too. She drew Joseph back to her side. "If he's telling the truth," she whispered urgently, "we can't risk being caught out here."

Joseph was furious. "But if we give in to this, we're stuck with him."

From the jungle came the rumble of voices. "Hurry!" Maryam said. "We really have no other choice."

She rose now, taking up the oar and pushing the boat, with one desperate heave, out into the waterway between the spindly fingers of the trees. If it was to be like this, then so be it. There would never be another chance.

Joseph, muttering angrily, scooped up the other oar and put his full weight in behind it so they glided out, free of the mangroves, and met the sea. Behind them, a mêlée of raised voices carried toward them on the wind. *No going back*. He hauled the storm jib up the forward mast, Maryam pointing the bow toward the foaming gap in the reef as the wind caught the sail and pushed them out into the rolling swell.

Beside the shelter, Lazarus still held firmly onto Ruth but lowered the knife to steady himself against the bucking of the boat. They sailed toward the passage at surprising speed, waves slapping and churning while Maryam fought to hold the tiller steady: it was so much bigger and heavier than the small training boat. Joseph shouted orders from the foredeck, where he eased the ropes and struggled to untie the lashings on the big mainsail.

Then the reef was before them, its one small opening sucking them through to spit them out the other side with such ferocity they had no time to panic or to quake with fear.

Maryam twisted to look back across her shoulder toward home, where the light of several torches now flickered through the distant trees. Even a few more minutes there and they'd have been caught. But there was no more time to ponder this. She struggled to follow Joseph's curt instructions as he set about lifting the mainsail.

The boat wallowed on the waves, Maryam striving to position the sail hard to the wind. She felt a sudden surge as Joseph started hauling up the main, but the wind caught the half-opened sail and swung the boat around, pushing them at speed back toward the lethal coral. Joseph fought it as best he could, the wind flapping the patchwork fabric his father had sewn and the thunder of surf on reef blasting their ears. Maryam battled to turn the boat again to face the open sea. But it refused to turn, despite their frantic tussle with wind and sail.

"If we're going to be stuck with you," Joseph barked at Lazarus, "then get up here and lend a hand."

For one long terrifying moment Lazarus did nothing and the boat floundered in the swell, out of control. Then to Maryam's great relief he met the challenge, releasing Ruth and putting his weight in behind Joseph until at last they succeeded in heaving the wind-buffeted sail up the mast. At once, Maryam found she had more steerage and pushed the tiller round as far as it would go so the boat swung back onto its proper course.

They caught the wind again, pitching forward with such

force Ruth screamed with fright and slowly crawled back down the wave-drenched deck to huddle at Maryam's feet.

Maryam gulped in salty air, realising she had been so scared she'd hardly breathed for the entire crossing of the reef. Beneath them, now, the boat settled to a frisky trot, cutting through the waves as phosphorescence trailed, glistening and magical, from its bow.

She studied each of her companions—faithful Ruth, who cowered at her feet and no doubt cursed her for this plan; sweet, gentle Joseph, intent on the ropes, but turning to her now, his teeth white in the moonlight as he smiled for her alone; and, there, standing apart from the rest of them, the violent and unpredictable Lazarus, his hand gripping the boom possessively as he grinned into the raw face of the wind. What would become of them all, from this point on?

She glanced up to the heavens, to the myriad clusters of tiny stars and planets that would help to guide their way. She thought to pray, to appease her apprehension at whatever the future held in store, but in her heart no words would form. She just could not be sure, now, if the Lord was really there at all.

Instead, she brushed her windswept hair out of her eyes and turned toward the restless infinity of sea. What lay ahead now was unknowable, little more than unfamiliar names etched on an ancient map. But she believed, deep in her heart, that there was something better out there for them all. In this, at least, she must keep faith.

THE RULES

as written by Saul, the founding father of the Apostles of the Lamb

RULE ONE   There is but one thing in the world that can cleanse us of our sins, and that is the power of the Blood of the Lamb.

RULE TWO   By the sacred power of His Blood, peace is forged between the Lord and all who heed the teachings of His Holy Book.

RULE THREE   Through the mandate of His Blood, the Lamb speaks to His Apostles and gives them dominion over His entire congregation on the earth.

RULE FOUR   By the power of the Lamb's Blood, Lucifer and all his heathen followers shall be overcome.

RULE FIVE   At the time of Judgement, the Lord anoints His Chosen and entrusts them to serve under the wise and loving rule of the Apostles of the Lamb.

RULE SIX   By the Blood's great power, the most humble of us may Cross to the Holy City into the Lamb's presence and live there Always.

RULE SEVEN   Like the Lamb who suffered for us, we, too, must suffer in silence and pledge our obedience to the Lord and His Apostles of the Lamb.

RULE EIGHT   As with the Lamb who went so willingly to slaughter, we, too, must sacrifice up our lives in readiness and joy.

RULE NINE   None may question the authority of the Lord's chosen representatives: the sacred Apostles of the Lamb.

RULE TEN   Let any who reject the word of the Apostles of the Lamb be cast from the flock and punished in the name of the Lord.

AUTHOR'S NOTE

The native language spoken on Onewēre is derived from Gilbertese, the traditional language of Kiribati. Bible quotations are taken from either the King James (Authorised) Version, or from the Revised Standard Version.

Blood transfusion has a long human history, with the first official person-to-person transfusion promoted by the German doctor and chemist, Andreas Libavius, in 1615. Over time, various approaches and instruments were tried, including the method and equipment described in this book. The "special" blood referred to is blood-type "O" and people with this blood type are known as "universal donors," because their blood will mix with all other blood types without clotting.

Upon completion of the first draft of this book, I discovered a strange coincidence between the Chosen in this story, and those of the Inca empire in the early thirteenth century, where The Chosen Women, also called acllyaconas or the Virgins of the Sun, were selected from throughout the empire for their beauty and taken from their homes at about ten years of age. The most beautiful were often sacrificed immediately, but the rest were forced to live apart in separate compounds and forbidden to leave for at least six or seven years (and then only a few lucky ones ever did). They were trained to serve, and learnt domestic skills such as cooking and weaving. Although described as virgins, they were available for the "pleasure" of the highest classes—but if they were discovered to be in a relationship of their own making, both the Chosen Woman and her lover were buried alive. When they completed their "training," aged about sixteen years, they were either forcibly married off (with no say as to who their spouse would be), forced to stay in the secluded compounds and continue to serve until they died, occasionally released, or chosen as sacrificial victims. Some became mamaconas, and stayed to teach the new generations of Chosen Women. It is said that some of The Chosen Women in the Cuzco temple of Coricancha were killed and their blood painted on the Inca nobles by the leading ruler. In the famous temple Machu Picchu, several corpses of young women have been found.[1]

1. Sources: Division of Religion and Philosophy, University of Cumbria; Nora Raggio: "Pre-Columbian Sacrifices," San Jose State University, http://gallery.sjsu.edu/sacrifice/precolumbian .html; Colin Forsyth: "Chosen Women of the Inca Empire," http:// inca-history.suite101.com; Lisa Louise Brailey, MD.

ACKNOWLEDGMENTS

Many thanks to Lou Anders and the team at Pyr for their support; to Joe Monti of the Barry Goldblatt Literary Agency, New York, for his ongoing support and belief in the triology; and many thanks and much love to my family and friends, especially my "best boy," Brian, and wonderful children, Thom and Rose.

ABOUT THE AUTHOR

MANDY HAGER is an award-winning writer and educator based in Wellington, New Zealand. She has a drive to tell stories that matter—direct, powerful stories with something to say. She won the 2010 New Zealand Post Children's Book Award for Young Adult Fiction for *The Crossing*. Visit her online at www.mandyhager.com, at www.facebook.com/BloodOfTheLambTrilogy, and on Twitter @MandyHager.